As we began to move, Bernardo caught up with me to speak into my ear. "Tomorrow, La Bencina, I will come for you and escort you to Maestro Verrocchio. Your husband allows me the honor of commissioning a portrait." He smiled and stood back and let the crowd swallow him from my sight.

A portrait of me. I still couldn't believe it. Me! From the legendary studio of Andrea del Verrocchio.

Of course, I already knew which artist in that studio I hoped would paint it.

Da Vinci's Tiger

Da Vinci's Tiger

L. M. ELLIOTT

KATHERINE TEGEN BOOKS
An Imprint of HarperCollins Publishers

Jon Thiem (editor and translator), "Song of the Village Lasses, lines 29-33," in *Lorenzo de' Medici: Selected Poems and Prose*, page 155, Copyright © 1991 by The Pennsylvania State University Press. Reprinted by permission of The Pennsylvania State University Press.

Katherine Tegen Books is an imprint of HarperCollins Publishers.

Library of Congress Cataloging-in-Publication Data
Elliott, Laura, date
   Da Vinci's tiger / L. M. Elliott. — First edition.
      pages   cm
   Summary: In fifteenth-century Florence, the dashing Venetian ambassador commissions young Leonardo da Vinci to paint a portrait of his Platonic love, Ginevra de' Benci, a well-educated, teenaged poet in a passionless marriage, propelling her into the world of art, politics, and romance, with all of its complications.
   ISBN 978-0-06-074426-7
   1. Benci, Ginevra de', 1457–1521—Fiction. [1. Benci, Ginevra de', 1457–1521—Fiction. 2. Courts and courtiers—Fiction. 3. Leonardo, da Vinci, 1452–1519—Fiction. 4. Bembo, Bernardo, 1433–1519—Fiction. 5. Medici, Lorenzo de', 1449–1492—Fiction. 6. Milan (Italy)—History—To 1535—Fiction. 7. Italy—History—1268–1492—Fiction.] I. Title.
PZ7.E453Dav 2015
[Fic]—dc23   2014047920

Typography by Carla Weise
17 18 19 20 21   CG/LSCC   10 9 8 7 6 5 4 3 2
❖

First paperback edition, 2017

For my muses:

Megan and Peter

Prologue

I beg your pardon, I am a mountain tiger.

THAT'S THE ONLY LINE OF MY POETRY LEFT. A SINGLE SCRAP to reveal what I thought of myself. Oh, there are a dozen sonnets written *about* me—praising my neck, my skin, my hands, my virtue. Two were penned by Lorenzo de' Medici himself—Lorenzo the Magnificent, the de facto prince of Florence, the city where a riotous blossoming of new thought and art pollinated a springlike rebirth across Europe. I was the chosen Platonic love of one of his greatest political allies.

I beg your pardon, I am a mountain tiger.

One line. And, of course, Leonardo's portrait. The portrait that now hangs in Washington, DC's National Gallery of Art—the only Leonardo da Vinci in all of the Americas.

Ever since that portrait was rescued from a palace cellar and recognized as a work by the young Leonardo, art historians have asked: Why is Ginevra de' Benci not smiling? As if I denigrate Leonardo's genius by not grinning with gratitude. She is ill, some say. She's shy, suggest others. She was heartbroken by the departure of that charming ambassador from Venice. She could not have been very nice, a few have even pronounced—poor Leonardo to deal with such a formidable-looking young woman for his very first portrait. Can the spiky juniper bush behind her be a symbol of her prickly personality that the ever-so-clever Leonardo put there as a sarcastic joke?

They should see how I smile at them now, at such speculations. Indeed, Leonardo did enjoy word games. The backdrop of juniper, *ginepro*, is a pun on my name. But perhaps my expression was suggested by Leonardo to be a protest of my circumstances. Perhaps I influenced him to create the image of a mysterious but strong female, which became his hallmark. Or perhaps my reserve was something as simple as knowing that had I *smiled* out at my viewer, people of my day would have denounced me as provocative, dangerous even.

The fact that Leonardo painted me facing forward, in a three-quarter pose, my gaze outward and steady, engaging the viewer, was daring enough. He and I shattered the Italian quattrocento tradition of portraying women in profile, looking away modestly at nothing, bejeweled and elaborately coiffed, advertisements of a family's wealth to be assessed as one might a piece of silver. Instead, Leonardo risked painting me as a real person, with individual thoughts and personality that peek out at you in my gaze—the eyes being the windows to our souls, after all. He believed a portrait should reveal the subject's "motions of the mind," even if that subject was a mere woman.

Such a revolutionary concept it was! We Florentine ladies were not supposed to stand for long at windows, for fear our thoughts might wander beyond our domestic duties and, God forbid, invite improper imaginings of men passing by. A rulebook at my convent school claimed that if we exchanged a long glance with a man, we could inflame his carnal appetites. The poor man might fall helplessly into sin and be cut adrift from God, like Adam cast out of the Garden of Eden because of Eve's foolishness.

This attitude was held dear at the very same time well-read men like Lorenzo de' Medici were convinced that a woman's graceful, physical beauty was actually evidence of her having deep inner virtues. As such a woman could be a muse of spirituality that *saved* a man's soul. Lorenzo and his followers proclaimed a man grew closer to God by gazing upon such a woman—even a married one—and devoting himself to her in a nonphysical love affair.

Yes, a time of marvelous contradictions!

Such paradoxes allowed a woman glory—if she could find and walk the silken-thread line that divided women into either saint or temptress in the minds of men. If she could recognize and survive the politics involved. And if she was strong enough to also create an inner, poetic world that no one could sully or destroy.

I beg your pardon, I am a mountain tiger.

You see? As if a tiger would beg anyone's pardon.

I had to learn to walk in such contradictions. At sixteen years of age, I emerged from Le Murate's convent school, where I had been sent "to learn the virtues," chaste, practiced in modest deportment, groomed to achieve an advantageous marriage for my family. But thanks to a rare intellectual abbess, my eyes had also been opened to the power of thought and art, philosophy and poetry. That was the element of me that would most attract the attention, the imaginings (Platonic and not) of powerful men and the beautiful Leonardo. And would bring me love.

I beg your pardon, I am a mountain tiger.

Come, look in my eyes. Under Leonardo's brush, a thinking, feeling soul glimmers there behind a carefully composed expression of quietude—like a tiger partially veiled by the forest. Can you see it, waiting silently, watching for a chance to spring forth with a roar?

Leonardo did.

But I get ahead of myself. Leonardo would have hated

that. He believed in a systematic study of a thing, layer by layer, to discover what lay below and created the surface we could see. And so, let us begin my story—the story of the great Leonardo da Vinci and his mountain tiger.

It all started with a joust.

I

Piazza di Santa Croce, Florence
January 1475

"Quick! Shield your eyes!" Simonetta Vespucci cried.

Gasping, I raised my hands against a blast of dagger-sharp splinters spewing from the jousting field.

Giuliano de' Medici and his opponent had just raced toward each other, to deafening cheers from the crowd, their lances aimed straight for each other, their horses thundering and snorting toward collision. With a horrifying crash, Giuliano's lance shattered on his opponent's shield, pelting the front row of the stands where I sat with wood fragments.

The rider was hurled off his horse. He lay sprawled on his back in the white sand that filled the Piazza di Santa Croce for the joust. Rushing in, his men-at-arms helped him stand and walked him off the lists. The rider's armor had saved him. His exquisite horse, however, writhed on the ground. A huge shard of the Medici-blue lance was embedded in his flank.

Whinnying in agony, the horse kicked out wildly. The crowd hushed as men circled the beautiful animal, trying to decide what to do. Giuliano retreated to a corner of the piazza to await his next round, his own horse prancing in fretful impatience and agitation.

"Poor thing," Simonetta said of the injured horse. "Do you think it will die?" She reached to clasp my hand as we watched.

"Ouch!" My red gloves were spiked with a few azure-colored needles thrown from the shattered lances.

"Oh, my dear!" Simonetta began plucking out the tiny spears. "Thanks be to Mother Mary, your hands saved you. Many knights have died from lance splinters piercing their eyes." She leaned toward me and whispered. "Even so, jousting is an exquisite sport, don't you think? So exhilarating to see these men ride at such a pace." She giggled like the girl she was, before shrouding herself again in womanly reserve. "But at such a price." She shook her head as she pulled the last shard from the soft velvet.

I tried not to wince as Simonetta gently peeled off the glove to inspect my hand. She pressed her handkerchief to my palm to stop the tiny ooze of blood from the pinpricks.

"You will ruin that lovely lace with bloodstains," I warned. Such intricate handiwork was imported from Venice and was expensive.

"Your beautiful hands are far more important," she replied. "I have heard them praised by Lorenzo the Magnifico for their delicacy, and for the needlework and poetry they create. We must make sure they do not become infected."

I was a bit vain about my hands, I have to admit. My fingers were long and slender, and I rubbed lemon juice into my skin to keep it fair. So I smiled to hear the compliment, especially since it came from the city's most important citizen-statesman.

Simonetta smiled back. The way her face lit up reminded me why all of Florence was totally besotted with her. With thick golden curls, a long neck, creamy skin, and huge amber eyes, Simonetta Cattaneo Vespucci was gorgeous. Officially, the Medici had organized this joust to celebrate Florence's new diplomatic alliance with Venice and Milan. But Simonetta was its crowned "Queen of Beauty" and its focal point in many ways. The honor was no surprise as Simonetta was also the publicly celebrated Platonic love of the younger Medici brother, the handsome Giuliano, Florence's favorite rider in the joust.

Her image had been the first thing seen that morning as Giuliano and twenty-one other combatants paraded through Florence's streets to Santa Croce. Leading the procession, Giuliano was accompanied by nine trumpeters and two men-at-arms, carrying pennants of fringed blue silk, decorated with the Medici coat of arms. All their tunic skirts were of matching blue silk brocade, their silver-threaded sleeves embroidered with olive branches and flames. As dazzling as his entourage's costuming was, though, spectators couldn't help but stare at the enormous banner Giuliano carried.

On it, Simonetta was depicted as Pallas, the Greek goddess of wisdom and war, over a motto in gold lettering: *La sans par*, "the unparalleled one." The great Botticelli had painted her holding a jousting lance and shield, in a golden tunic and breastplate, looking up to the sky. Beside her, ignored, Cupid was tied to an olive tree.

The banner's message was clear. As Pallas, Simonetta was not distracted or beguiled by Cupid's earthly romances. Follow her gaze and her example to make it to heaven. When Simonetta climbed the grand dais stairs to take her throne, she had received as many cheers as the city's beloved Giuliano would when he rode into the lists to the fanfare of herald-trumpets.

How marvelous to be considered so beautiful, so good and true, that an artist such as Sandro Botticelli would want to paint you, I thought. Jealous, I pulled my hand away and spoke sharply. "It's fine."

The slightest of frowns creased Simonetta's brow. "We must be friends, Ginevra de' Benci Niccolini. I have so few since moving here from Piombino to marry Marco. We are, after all, cousins by marriage. And"—she paused—"I think we will have much to talk about." She giggled again, this time pulling my gaze with hers toward a handsome, debonair stranger sitting next to the great Lorenzo. The man bowed his head in salutation to us as we did. "He has been appreciating you for the last hour."

I felt my face flush. "Who is he?"

"Bernardo Bembo, the new Venetian ambassador."

I was about to turn to look at the diplomat more carefully—something Le Murate's sisters would have chided me harshly for—when a man's voice from behind stopped me.

"Observe! Here comes the Six Hundred."

Men around him laughed.

Again I flushed, mortified. The man was talking about my oldest brother, Giovanni. And not in a flattering way.

Walking onto the field, Giovanni approached the thrashing horse. He circled it slowly, while the other men who'd tried fruitlessly to calm it stepped back. As usual, my brother was dressed to the hilt, wearing a lavish emerald-green-and-gold taffeta tunic, his soled hose scarlet, his fur-lined beret threaded with silver and gold.

"Do you think he has enough florins on his back?" The man behind me kept up his sarcasm.

My brother's love of expensive clothes and fine horses had become the city's gauge for all things ostentatious. Giovanni had purchased a magnificent horse from the Barbary Coast of North Africa for a staggering six hundred florins (an amount that equaled the annual income of ten skilled artisans combined). He raced it in the annual *palio* for St. John's Feast. He

11

also loved to parade about town on the horse. I could hardly blame him. The horse was an incredibly fluid mover and a joy to ride.

But "Here comes the Six Hundred" had become a Florentine slang term for a braggart. A republic city-state of merchants, guildsmen, artisans, and bankers, Florence did not approve of showy everyday displays of wealth, despite its citizens' love of pageantry and spectacles like this joust.

I fumed.

Simonetta put her hand atop mine and patted it to keep me from turning round to glare at my brother's attackers. I wondered if he would cease if he knew who I was. But Florentine men were used to speaking their mind no matter what.

"Well, he is a Benci," another voice said. "His grandfather was Cosimo's best friend and the Medici bank manager. The Benci family earned its wealth. You have to give them that."

It was a typical Florentine assessment of politics and connections, the stuff of many street-corner conversations in a city run by the merchant class. I still wanted to kiss whoever said it. A commoner who made himself a fortune, Cosimo had been much admired in Florence for his generous patronage of artists and for funding the completion of the cathedral's dome. The Duomo had become one of the wonders of Christendom. The respect afforded Cosimo spilled onto my grandfather.

But my brother's critic didn't skip a beat. "Certainly old Benci earned his keep by stuffing the election purse with

12

Medici supporters to ensure that Cosimo stayed in power—the same as any common whore making her way by bending the ethics of good men."

Simonetta's hand closed tightly on mine. She squeezed hard, warning me to remain rooted in ladylike silence.

Instead, I laughed out loud at the insult. I couldn't help it. I was plagued with an impetuous temper that had always landed me in terrible trouble with the nuns. But this time, I swear the influence of Pallas's mythical intellect saved me. For once, I knew the right thing to say at the right moment.

Leaning toward Simonetta, I said in a loud, staged voice, "Look, Simonetta. My dear, dear brother approaches that poor, suffering, valiant horse." I drew out the adjectives with feminine empathy. "If anyone can save that beauteous steed, it will be my brother. He is a great scholar of ancient texts. He owns the manuscript written by a legendary Calabrian physic to animals, *Liber de Medicina Veterinaria*." The Latin rolled easily off my tongue.

I glanced back at the snide man and his companions, knowing that Florence's obsession with rediscovered ancient Greek and Latin writings granted respect and status to those who possessed them. I recognized the man as a Pazzi—a member of the aristocratic banking family that was the chief rival and a bitter critic of the Medici. I nodded at him, politely, of course. "Through studying that rare, important text, my brother knows everything about tending horses. If the beast is curable, my brother will know how to do it," I said.

With that, all persons within earshot fell silent. If nothing else, they anticipated an interesting display of equestrian husbandry and the value of ancient education. Florentines did so love publicly enacted drama.

Settling back in my seat, I pulled my cloak closer about me against the January chill and buried my nose in the collar's ermine—mostly to hide a self-satisfied smile. I dared to peep over the soft fur at Simonetta to see her reaction.

Her amber eyes sparkled in amusement. "You will go far indeed in this city, Ginevra."

Luckily, my brother proved me right. He moved closer and closer to the convulsing horse, dodging its kicks to stand next to its head. Giovanni knelt. The horse stilled and let my brother touch its muzzle. The crowd was transfixed.

Cautiously, Giovanni lowered his face to breathe into the horse's nostrils, just as horses greet each other. Then he stroked the horse's neck, whispering into its ear. He took hold of the shard of wood with one hand, while the other stayed on the horse's neck. He looked up and nodded, signaling the grooms standing by that he was ready for their help. Quickly, they laid hands on the horse to keep him still. Giovanni yanked the spear out of its side before it realized what was happening.

The crowd cheered. The horse struggled to its feet and let a groom stanch the wound with clean linen. Then, limping, it peacefully followed Giovanni off the course.

"I'll be damned," muttered the Pazzi man behind me.

But it didn't take him long to continue his jabs at my brother. "Now I am sure the Six Hundred will exploit the situation and try to buy that horse away from the defeated rider."

"In truth, that will be a good negotiation for the rider," his companion said. He lowered his voice a bit, since his gossip could be interpreted to be anti-Medici. "He was strong-armed by Lorenzo to compete in today's joust. He told me he was forced into spending enormous sums to properly outfit himself to the Medici satisfaction. He purchased fifty-two pounds of pure gold and a hundred seventy pounds of silver for his armor, his horse's decorations, and livery for his followers."

The men around him whistled.

"So he will be glad for some reimbursement."

I imagined the nods of approval from the gaggle of merchants and money changers behind me.

"But it's not as if that horse will ever be able to joust or race again, not with that wound to its back leg," the Pazzi attacker said, changing tack. "Only a fool would want to buy it. A fool like the Six Hundred."

He would still mock my brother? Even after such a triumphant display of horsemanship and bravery? I turned round and blessed the Pazzi man with the most innocent, demure smile I could muster in my fury. "But good, my lord," I said in a purposely dulcet tone, "would not this horse father wondrous colts?" I paused to allow my listeners time to consider. "After all, his most important . . . mmm . . . . leg . . . was not pierced."

15

The man's mouth dropped open.

His friends guffawed in appreciation. But this time the laughter was with me. Even ladylike Simonetta shook with mirth, but she pressed her lips together to keep from laughing out loud.

I turned back to face the jousting field, having won that round for my family's honor, just as Giuliano charged back into the lists for his next go at glory.

2

TRUMPETS BLARING, GIULIANO DE' MEDICI SPURRED HIS
mount to the grandstand where Simonetta and other special
guests sat. He pulled up in a shower of white sand. Bracing
his ten-foot-long lance against his hip, Giuliano bowed to
Simonetta while his horse pranced and snorted in place, anxious to get back on course.

It had been a typical Tuscan January day, cloudy and
cold with a damp chill coming off the Arno River. But at
that moment—as if the Fates wished to add to the moment's
symbolic drama—the sun burst forth, spilling golden light
onto the Piazza di Santa Croce and making Giuliano's fantastical armor gleam. His silver-steel breastplate was draped

in white silk embroidered with pearls, the gold border of his red cape encrusted with diamonds, rubies, and sapphires. His shield was the snarling face of Medusa, her hair of snakes so lifelike one could almost hear them hiss. Orso, his black-and-white-spotted horse, was just as resplendent. A silvery helmet covered its forehead, and its back was draped with a blue-cloth caparison embroidered with the Medici coat of arms.

We all gaped at the image created by the warhorse and its twenty-one-year-old rider, whom Florence affectionately called "the Prince of Youth."

"My lady," Giuliano called out. "May I ask the honor of your favor again?" The scarf she'd given him earlier must have been lost on the field or bloodied during the last round. He carefully lowered his lance as Simonetta stood. From inside her angel-wing sleeve she pulled a long ribbon of blue and silver, dyed and embroidered to match Giuliano's attire, and tied it onto the blunted pole.

Giuliano raised the ribboned lance once again in salute to the stands. The crowd erupted as he and Orso cantered back to the 125-foot-long jousting lane.

Trumpets sounded to announce his opponent. "Signor Morelli has now entered the lists," called the tournament official. I couldn't help but feel sorry for anyone tilting against Florence's favorite son that day. The poor man received tepid applause.

Trying to garner some support, his herald shouted, "Signor Morelli challenges the honorable, the champion

Giuliano de' Medici *a plaisance!*" A friendly challenge for the pleasure of the assembled to watch—no real danger to Giuliano.

At this, the piazza echoed with cheers.

Giuliano and Morelli lowered the hinged visors of their helmets. As if cued by the snap of the eye shields, both horses reared and pawed the air. The two riders struggled to balance themselves, their lances, their shields, and their armors' weight against the horses' excited cavorting. The crowd hushed.

A page approached the rail that ran the course, separating the horses from colliding. He lowered a crimson-colored pennant to the ground. He looked left, then right, to make sure each rider was ready.

The horses snorted, nickered, kicked up sand.

And . . . and . . .

Even the passing clouds above seemed to stop and hover in anticipation.

The page snapped the flag up into the air.

"*Heeaaah!*" Giuliano shouted, and jabbed Orso with his long golden spurs. Whinnying his own battle cry, Orso lunged into a canter. So, too, did Morelli's chestnut charger.

Daaa-da-dummm, daaa-da-dummm, daaa-da-dummm. The rhythmic surge of the horses' hoofbeats mingled with the music of jingling armor. The two men lowered and braced their heavy wooden spears across their chests at an angle, straight at each other.

Da-da-dum, da-da-dum, da-da-dum. The horses' rhythm quickened.

I felt Simonetta stiffen and hold her breath.

The riders hugged their shields closer, leaning forward and in toward the barrier fence to maximize the force of impact. And to survive it.

Crrrr-aaack! Giuliano's lance struck Morelli's arm guard and split.

Morelli lurched dangerously to the side but stayed in his saddle.

"A hit! One point to Giuliano de' Medici!" the joust's scorekeeper sang out. "That is his thirty-first broken lance of the day!"

Striking an opposing rider on his armor between the waist and neck yielded a point. Unhorsing an opponent was an automatic win. Each match lasted "three lances," unless one of the riders was knocked to the ground. Breaking a lance did not add points, simply a heightened drama to the hit.

Giuliano was handed another brightly painted lance and the riders charged each other again.

This time Morelli managed to hit Giuliano's breastplate. Giuliano was knocked askew so that his lance missed Morelli entirely.

"A point to Morelli!" the scorekeeper shouted with a little less enthusiasm.

The third and last round no longer seemed friendly at all to me. Simonetta shifted uncomfortably, tense. The two riders charged faster this time, their horses heaving, their necks lathered in sweat.

With a bone-chilling crash, the men smashed together

with such force they both fell backward in their saddles, their heads sagging toward the horses' rumps, their arms splayed out wide like Christ on the crucifix. Their lances dropped to the sand. Pages rushed forward to stop the horses. It took several of them to push their masters—weighed down by fifty pounds of armor—upright.

Sitting again, Giuliano and Morelli pulled off their helmets, shaking their heads as if clearing their vision. They smiled weakly at each other, trying to catch their breath.

But who had won their match?

The crowd waited. Silence from the scorekeeper. It became obvious the longer he hesitated that the scorekeeper was trying to find a way to award the round to Giuliano. Rumor had it the Medici family spent sixty thousand florins of their own for the joust's decorations, prizes, and grandstands, not to mention purchasing Giuliano's armor, his entourage's livery, and banners. Since a single florin could buy thirty chickens, the monies spent to delight Florence with such a spectacle were staggering. It seemed a proper thank-you to let Giuliano win.

Even so, Florentines were devoted to fair odds. A favorite maxim held that someone not appropriately rewarded for his efforts was like a donkey who carried wine on his back but was given only water to drink—in other words, anyone allowing himself to be exploited in such a way was an ass. So our expectation was that hard work guaranteed a fair shot at success, a share in the goods. It was the underlying, pervasive philosophy that kept our little republic rotating citizens in

21

and out of important offices every two months, to theoretically give all citizens the chance to influence policy.

And yet somehow these beliefs were thrown out the window like the contents of a chamber pot when it came to the Medici. The family essentially ran Florence. The Medici had achieved this power subtly. They did not use violence, poisonings, or assassinations, as did some power-hungry families like the Sforza in Naples. Nor did they flaunt their privilege, culture, and education to intimidate others, as did the noble-born Pazzi.

Instead the Medici granted favors and loans when a person most needed them. They brokered advantageous marriages and business partnerships. Such favors demanded loyalty in return. With the general public, the Medici continued their soft-as-silk coercion with entertainments like this joust and by building an almost mythical image for themselves. Giuliano was so gallant and handsome, Lorenzo so witty and poetic, that there was a widespread affection for the young Medici brothers.

Perhaps recognizing the political blunder of undoing Giuliano de' Medici at the joust his family was footing, Morelli made a brilliant move.

He raised his leather-gloved hand and shouted, "Good Giuliano, in thanks for your gracious arrangement of this glorious day, I concede our round to you. And in commemoration of our valiant bout, I present you"—at this he signaled his pages—"my banner. Accept this in salute to your jousting prowess, to our great city's alliance with Milan and Venice, and to the honor of this joust's Queen of Beauty!"

The crowd's answering applause was rapturous. Morelli may have lost his match by the gesture, but he'd certainly won the hearts of Florence. He instructed his pages to drape the triangular pennant over the railing in front of Simonetta before he trotted off the jousting field.

Much as I liked her, I felt myself pout as I inspected the artwork. Could one woman possibly deserve all this attention?

The image—of a reclining nymph, asleep after gathering a bouquet of wildflowers, and the Cupid who crept up to wake her—was absolutely exquisite. Better, frankly, than the joust's centerpiece by Botticelli, I thought. There was something so real, so alive about their expressions. The Cupid youth looked upon the nymph with such tenderness, and she seemed so peaceful, as if entranced by the scent of the blossoms she held. Delicate shading around her cheekbones and eyes added such depth and naturalness to her face.

"Who painted this?" I asked Simonetta. "Do you know?"

"Maestro Verrocchio," she said.

"Really?" I was surprised. Trained as a goldsmith, Andrea del Verrocchio had become the Medici's favorite sculptor now that Donatello was dead. "I am amazed. I know Verrocchio's studio is one of the busiest in the city, and his sculpture much admired. But I did not realize he could paint so . . . such . . ."

"Haunting faces?" Simonetta finished my thought.

"Yes."

We both gazed at the pennant. "In the Medici palazzo

hangs a portrait painted by Verrocchio, which is quite lovely," Simonetta said. "But there is something different about this image, something new. I've heard it said that one of his older apprentices helped Verrocchio paint this pennant. A man named Leonardo, from the little village of Vinci. He's the illegitimate son of the Medici notary, I believe. Isn't it astounding that such promise emanates from so low a beginning?"

3

THE JOUST CONTINUED, ROUND AFTER ROUND, UNTIL THE
Piazza di Santa Croce began to darken with shadows as the
sun slid low toward rest for the night. That was when Renato
de' Pazzi rode into the lists on an enormous black horse.

Simonetta took in a sharp breath. "I have been dreading
this. Giuliano practiced daily for a month to ready himself
for today's tournament and sought out the very best horse
to ride. He asked his godfather, the Duke of Urbino, to lend
him this very mount that now enters under the Pazzi rider.
This horse has won countless jousts throughout Tuscany.
Any man who rides it into the tilting yard has a tremendous
advantage over his opponent."

"Why does Giuliano not ride it, then?"

Simonetta's fair face grew shadowed like the piazza. "His godfather wrote back saying the Pazzi family had requested the horse first. That was all. No apology. His own *godfather!*" Simonetta grew indignant. "It was a terrible insult to my Giuliano that his godfather lent this horse to someone else for his joust, but especially so since he showed the favor to a Pazzi son."

I knew the Medici were constantly having to beat back challenges to their power—some attempts to dethrone them worse than others. When Lorenzo had been a mere teenager, several families organized an assassination ambush of his father. Lorenzo had managed to catch wind of it and directed his father to travel a different route. But I had never heard it said that the Pazzi were part of that plot. So I asked, "Why is a Pazzi wanting the horse so bad?"

"Oh, Ginevra, the Pazzi are bitterly competitive with the Medici. Even though they do banking business together, the Pazzi hate that their family is outdistanced by the Medici, a family without noble lineage. They constantly try to undermine Lorenzo's influence in Florence and to build up alliances against him. Borrowing this particular horse from Giuliano's very own godfather feels like the Pazzi are trying to recruit the duke to some underhanded business. At best, it's simply a way to embarrass Giuliano that his godfather would favor someone else. But to me it feels more like retribution for Florence's last major joust. The whole thing smells of . . . of . . . well, it smells like horse dung!" She pursed her lips and crossed her arms on her chest.

"Retribution?" I asked.

"I forget how young you are, Ginevra. You would have been a child when this happened. When Lorenzo hosted a joust six years ago to celebrate his engagement to be married, he rode in it himself, as Giuliano does today. Francesco de' Pazzi hit him with such force during their tilt that Lorenzo was unhorsed. The Magnifico landed on the ground so hard that at first they almost stopped the tournament. But he managed to get up and continue riding. At the end of the tournament, Lorenzo still won the trophy. Everyone said he had competed beautifully and deserved it. But his win infuriated the Pazzi since one of them had unhorsed Lorenzo, which technically could have eliminated the Magnifico from competing further that day. Francesco has been grumbling ever since."

Florence was rife with such intrigues and rivalries. I looked at Giuliano, who was smiling as his pages handed him his helmet. "He doesn't seem upset about the horse," I said.

"No." Simonetta shook her head. "He is possessed of a gentle, cheerful disposition. He does not recognize guile or notice slights, or if he does, he shakes them off quickly. That is part of his great charm. I just hope it will not prove his downfall."

Her worries were interrupted by the call of the Pazzi herald. "Great Florence! The noble Renato de' Pazzi—whose family fought in the last crusade to Jerusalem and brought God's grace to our cathedral by giving it a flint chipped off Christ's tomb . . ." He paused to ensure that his listeners remembered the Pazzi were the knights to bring back a sacred relic from the clutches of the infidels. The Medici had no such history or pedigree.

The herald continued in a chant-like voice. "Renato de' Pazzi, the glorious, wishes to challenge the Medici's youngest son, Giuliano . . ." He paused again, glancing back at the Pazzi combatant, seeking affirmation of something. The Pazzi rider nodded and gestured dismissively to his servant to continue. "The great Renato de' Pazzi wishes to challenge *à la guerre!*"

"À la guerre?" Simonetta gasped.

In war. For this bout between the Pazzi and the Medici, there would be no pretense of polite competition. There would be no conceding the match. Points would not matter. Unhorsing a rider would be the aim and the only honorable way to win. And that could, indeed, kill one of them.

The obnoxious Pazzi man behind me stood, applauding loudly.

This time I put my hand over Simonetta's to quiet her. I knew enough about horses from my brother to recognize that the Pazzi's destrier was a type of horse bred to be taller, heavier, and stronger than Giuliano's charger. But I tried to comfort her. "Peace, Simonetta," I whispered. "Giuliano has speed and agility and valor. Those will win out against brawn and a villainous heart, I know it."

"Ah," she sighed. "So Lorenzo is right. You are a poet."
She glanced sideways at me and then back to the jousting
field. "Sadly, Ginevra, I have learned that poetry does not
always match reality. But you give me hope. And hope is
what elevates mankind above God's other creatures here on
earth, is it not?" Simonetta sat up a little taller. But she still
bit at her lower lip in nervousness.

A page crouched at the tilting fence line, the starting flag
he held now darkened to a bloodred in the late-afternoon
shadows.

Orso pranced and tossed his mane, his head armor
glinting even in the growing gloom.

The Pazzi horse pawed and snorted like the giant hell-
hound Cerberus.

I held my breath with Simonetta as the page snapped the
flag up and ran for the safety of the sideline.

Both horses leaped to a gallop. *Da-da-dum, da-da-dum,
da-da-dum.* No gentle, musical canter beginning to this rush
toward collision. The Pazzi horse thundered up the track,
kicking great clods of dirt. Orso raced, so speedy it was
almost as if his pretty hooves did not touch the ground.

CRRRAAACCKKK!!

With an enormous rip, both riders' lances tore apart from
the blow, up to the cone-shaped vamplate that protected the
hand holding the lance. Orso staggered as he trotted away.
Giuliano held his hand to his chest, as if he fought to breathe.

The Pazzi rider hurled what remained of his lance to the
sand, then turned to see what Giuliano's condition was. His

black horse bucked and stomped its way back to the start line.

A solitary tear slipped out of Simonetta's eye and slid slowly down her otherwise composed face. She stayed frozen, creating a convincing picture of having complete confidence in her champion. She knew Florence's gossips were watching. I discreetly entwined my fingers with hers and squeezed her hand.

Again the flag snapped its signal to start.

Simonetta clutched my hand so hard I thought she might crush a bone.

CRRRAAACCKKK!!

Again the two riders smashed each other, sending splinters flying. Both were knocked sideways in their saddles, making it a mammoth struggle to pull themselves upright. Retreating to the recess area, they yanked off their helmets to splash their faces with water from bowls their pages held up toward them.

Giuliano's shield was badly dented, and one of his liveried servants frantically pounded at it from the inside to straighten it. Giuliano patted the young groom's head to stop him and gently took back his shield and helmet.

The Pazzi rider snatched his headgear from his servant.

As Giuliano turned to reenter the lists, one of his men-at-arms dashed to his side. The Prince of Youth reined in Orso and leaned down to listen to his friend.

"What do you think they say?" I whispered.

Simonetta merely shook her head, unable to speak. I could feel her trembling.

Once more the flag flew up.

Once more the horses stormed toward each other.

Once more the heavy lances drew nearer and nearer and nearer to the riders' armored but mortal bodies.

Had I blinked, I would have missed what happened next. Within a few feet of collision, Giuliano kicked his horse once with his inside heel and pressed hard with his leg against Orso's ribs. Only a highly trained and trusting horse would understand what that meant, and then actually do it while running at such a breakneck speed. Orso took a sashay step outward, away from the fence. Then, within a stride, Giuliano pressed and kicked with his other, outside leg, to push Orso back into the center barrier. It was like an elegant dance move.

And it made the Pazzi miss.

Giuliano's lance struck him full-force at an angle.

The Pazzi man went flying.

Simonetta sprung to her feet, and I followed. She laughed and wept at the same time as the crowd erupted in riotous cheers.

The applause went on and on. No one seemed to care that it took quite a while for the Pazzi rider to stagger to his feet or for several men to catch his destrier, which raced round the piazza in confusion and fury.

Finally, Lorenzo de' Medici stepped out of the banner-bedecked dais and raised his hands to silence the crowd. Unlike his beautiful younger brother, Lorenzo was homely, with a jutting jaw and a long, crooked, flattened nose. But his richly embroidered clothes dazzled, and his words were honey. "Dear friends, good citizens of Florence! Giuliano de' Medici, my beloved brother and"—he paused and pointed at the crowd, sweeping his arm along the piazza's length—"your Prince of Youth . . ." On cue, the crowd interrupted him with cheers. "Your Prince of Youth has won the day over a field of virtuous and gallant men. We thank them all for braving the lists and displaying such mighty athleticism and chivalry." The crowd cheered again. "All these riders—every single one—are champions. Champions worthy of Olympus!"

I smiled. Oh, Lorenzo was good. He had the crowd enthralled.

"Please, my friends, please. Toast them all tonight. Recount the story of today again and again. Remember the heroism displayed in their battles! Their undeniable demonstration of valor and skill! Today is legend!"

He held up a parchment containing the final scores. "And now to share the complete results, but first . . ." Lorenzo gestured for a page to step forward holding the tournament's grand prize—a spectacular helmet, its crest adorned with Mars, the god of war. Lorenzo waited for the appreciative applause to die down before breaking the seal and unfurling the official tallies.

"Giuliano di Piero de' Medici won this joust by twenty-one points! He broke a total of fifty-nine lances! Fifty-nine!" Lorenzo shouted. "Behold our winner and your hero!"

The crowd roared.

Lorenzo embraced his brother. Awash in triumph and smiles, Giuliano walked the length of the stands, holding aloft the exquisitely decorated helmet so everyone could admire it. The piazza reverberated with cheers that echoed along the walls of the church and the surrounding houses. As I clapped, I cast my eye around the scene, memorizing the jubilant faces, the sumptuous clothing, the heart-lifting laughter, and the colorful, rich brocade banners festooning the usually modest, sandy-colored buildings of the piazza. It was as if a rainbow of happiness had fallen from the sky and laid itself out along the square. Tomorrow the piazza would be stripped and back to the grittier business of bartering and selling, cloth weaving and dyeing, while penitent pilgrims climbed the stairs of the grim, brown-bricked church of Santa Croce to prostrate themselves before dark, candlelit altars.

Tomorrow my life would be ordinary again as well.

I let out a resigned sigh as I watched officials and dignitaries cluster into typical end-of-celebration good-byes. Ragged Florentine boys dashed onto the field, searching the sand for the pearls lost from Giuliano's costume, knocked off by the joust's collisions. One child jumped up and down clutching a jewel in his hand, knowing his life had just changed for the better.

I turned to say my good-byes to Simonetta and to look for my escort home. "Oh my! Forgive me, Your Grace." I had almost walked straight into Lorenzo the Magnificent himself.

Though technically not a nobleman, Lorenzo honored me with a bow fit for a king's court. I curtsied. As I rose, about to congratulate him on the wonders of the joust, I realized that the man Simonetta had pointed out to me stood behind Lorenzo. "Ginevra de' Benci Niccolini, may I introduce you to the honorable ambassador from Venice, Bernardo Bembo?"

"My lady." The diplomat bowed low, sweeping his hand down and then out across his outstretched foot. Holding the pose, he glanced up at me with startling bright-blue eyes and a decidedly mischievous grin. He was even more handsome up close, despite the gray peppering his hair.

I felt myself blush and stammer like a new postulant at the convent. "G-good even, my lord."

"Ambassador Bembo is much praised for his oratory and knowledge of Petrarch and Dante," Lorenzo continued. "He longs to meet Florentines who share his love of poetry. I plan a dinner in his honor at our palazzo and am inviting guests who share his devotion to literature and the ancients. I, of course, thought of you. Before he died, your dear father and I often discussed the meaning of Plato's dialogues. I know you have inherited his interests. Abbess Scolastica has told me of your lovely verses. Perhaps you would share one of your poems with us that evening?"

I trembled at the honor of such a request. Lorenzo was lauded throughout Tuscany for his fostering of literature. He often invited artists, writers, and scholars to his country villas at Fiesole and Careggi to listen to music and poetry read

34

aloud. They discussed the nature of man's supreme good, his *summum bonum*, as explored within classical texts. He also sponsored a Platonic Academy within the city, led by the great philosopher Marsilio Ficino, who had been a friend to my father.

"Oh, sir, I would be delighted!" But then I realized that the invitation was not for me to accept. Trying to hide my annoyance with such societal rules, I demurred, "But first . . . first I must . . . I must ask . . ."

"Your husband?" Lorenzo smiled at me. "But of course, Luigi Niccolini will be a cherished guest as well. I know he will be thrilled to have his wife delight us with her poetry. The feminine voice is so moving. My mother writes fine devotional verses herself, as you know."

"Indeed, she will be honored to come, as will Luigi," spoke a deep baritone voice. My uncle Bartolomeo had approached our group. "We all are very proud of Ginevra's womanly virtues, particularly the needlework she learned to sew at the convent."

"You must attend as well, Bartolomeo," Lorenzo added graciously. "Your presence makes any event more festive." The twenty-six-year-old slapped my uncle on the back. Only Lorenzo was allowed such familiarity with men a decade older. Even more telling of how Florence's rules did not apply to him, the all-powerful Medici was four years shy of being eligible to have his name put into Florence's lottery for public office. Lorenzo turned to Bernardo Bembo. "Such tales I have to tell you about Bartolomeo. But they will wait until our dinner."

My uncle bowed in thanks, putting his hand to his chest. He wore a scarlet, knee-length wool *mantello*, the standard over-cape wealthy Florence merchants donned in cold weather. But I noticed that underneath he wore blue hose to match the Medici costume.

I looked to Lorenzo and back to my uncle. The two of them had brokered my marriage to Luigi exactly one year before, when I was sixteen years old. And so the evening was agreed to, like so much of my life had been determined up until then—negotiated and sealed by men and their ambitions.

But this time, I was rather happy about it.

4

THE NEXT MORNING, I BUSIED MYSELF WITH CHORES WHILE I hoped Lorenzo's invitation would truly come. I was on my way to check our granary supplies when I ran into my husband.

"Good morrow, wife." Luigi bowed his head.

"Husband." I curtsied.

"I trust you slept well after yesterday's festivities?"

"I did, sir. And you?"

He nodded. "A wonderful display of the city's cloth in all the banners and garments."

"Indeed, yes. I hope the brotherhood was pleased?" My husband was an important member of the cloth merchant guild, the Arte di Calimala. During the joust, he'd been seated with other prominent guild officials and magistrates. We had yet to discuss our differing experiences at the spectacular event.

"Immensely," he answered. "And you looked quite beautiful, my dear. I hope you received compliments on your garb?"

"Simonetta was very impressed with the roses and vines stitched into the mantle's border." It was delicate, artistic work, done by one of the female embroiderers populating the narrow streets that wrapped around Santa Croce. "She thought the blossoms particularly well executed."

That pleased my husband. I was, after all, essentially a walking advertisement for his wool shop and fabric trading business. In a city where people judged wealth and reputation on fine textiles, clothes were recognized symbols of status, ennobling the wearer. My husband oft quoted the popular writer Leon Battista Alberti, saying, virtue ought to be dressed in seemly ornaments.

The opportunity to display his goods at the joust was sweetened by the fact that I would be sitting beside Simonetta, an honor I was granted because my aunt Caterina was her mother-in-law. All eyes would be on La Bella Simonetta— and if my clothing was resplendent enough, I would catch those gazes as well.

So Luigi had carefully directed my attire, sparing no expense. My cape was of the softest wool, colored a deep scarlet with the costliest of dyes made from ground-up shells of the kermes beetle imported from Arabia and Persia. Its gold border—the color created with a dye of crushed marigolds and poetically named "Apollo's Hair"—matched the fabric of my dress underneath, which was embroidered with intricate flower blossoms of red and emerald threads.

I was both embarrassed and pleased when I had put on the ensemble and recognized how the combination of rose and yellow hues accentuated the gold and tawny brown color of my hair. I hadn't realized Luigi noticed such things.

"Did you enjoy the jousting?" he asked.

"Oh yes," I said. "The riders were all so valiant, the horses magnificent. Like something out of Boccaccio's *Teseida*. And the painted banners were exquisite. Especially the one with the nymph and Cupid that Morelli gave to Giuliano de' Medici when he conceded their match. Wasn't that an amazing gesture of chivalry? To give up the match and such a work of art. That flag was so . . . so . . ." I couldn't find the right word for the thrill that banner had sparked in my heart. "So . . . lovely." I felt my face flush.

Blinking the way he did to focus his eyes on a piece of fabric he was assessing, my husband observed me for a moment before smiling patiently. "Yes," he said, nodding. "Yes, it was all that." His tone was that a fond father might use with a spirited but slightly wayward child. "It was good for the *popolo* to enjoy such a celebration in the cold of winter and before the deprivation of Lent. Happy memories by which to stay warm, yes?"

Then he continued down the hallway to his study.

Yes, just so, I thought. I'd be holding mental images of the joust to me tight as just a few years earlier I cuddled a doll to my chest to soothe me as I slept. For I still slept alone, in a small antechamber to the house's main bedroom, where Luigi snored and flopped through the night. After a few awkward encounters to consummate the legality of our nuptials, our marriage had become a polite business union. Luigi did not seem concerned with producing an heir, despite Florence's emphasis on family fruitfulness. Mostly we passed our nights separately and peaceably enough. At meals, Luigi talked of cloth and politics. I listened. He had certainly never asked to read my verse. I'm not sure he even knew I wrote.

It was not the life I had envisioned or hoped for myself. I sighed and went about my business of running the household.

"Sancha!" I called.

A pretty, dark-haired servant girl scurried to me. She was the type of voluptuous, olive-skinned, Mediterranean beauty that some wives might fear could distract husbands. But Luigi seemed so unmoved by matters of the flesh, I had no such concerns. And even though they were a bit scandalous, Sancha's gossipy stories did enliven the house. Her family worked the dye vats along the Arno River, and she'd grown up hearing rumors and bawdy retorts exchanged as readily as the nobles discussed the weather.

Sancha wiped her hands on her apron. "Ready?" she asked, reaching for the broom—her own lance of sorts. The first day I'd taken up my wifely chores in the granary, a mouse had darted across my foot and up my dress in terrified confusion. Sancha had knocked it off me, and I'd crumpled to the floor in tears—overwhelmed with the commonplace feel of my new life. "There, there," Sancha had said stoutly, petting my head like a lapdog. "No rodent will dirty my lady's chemise, not when I'm around." She'd been the closest thing I had to a friend in my new home from that day forward.

"Were you able to see any of the joust yesterday, Sancha?" I knew she and the apprentices who slept in the Niccolini family workshop to guard Luigi's wares had planned to elbow their way to a space along the fences.

Sancha beamed. "Oh yes! We had such a laugh over the one lord whose hose were so tight that he couldn't grip the horse properly. Vanity!" She lowered her voice and winked. "But the tightness of his hose certainly showed off a comely leg."

Knowing the rider she described, I giggled. "I think that had been his idea, Sancha. But to land face-first in horse manure probably not!"

As she and I checked the levels of our oil jars, I tried to feel grateful for what I did have. After all, I had had a front-row seat to an event that had awed the people of Florence and would be legendary for years to come. Plus, Luigi was not a bad man. He was old, of course. All husbands were, it seemed, in Florence's arranged marriages—except Simonetta's. Her spouse, Marco Vespucci, was a young man her age.

My marriage was more typical in terms of the age difference. When I had been married off the previous January, Luigi was thirty-two, twice my years. But he was also a widower of only five months, so our betrothal seemed unusually sudden. The negotiation process, with all its pomp and ceremony, was rushed. Most wedding days were saved for the spring and its warm weather, but mine took place in the chill of winter.

The other oddity about my marriage was that a bride's dowry typically purchased her family something—nobility, prestige, or riches. I could still feel the pit-in-my-stomach shock when Uncle Bartolomeo announced that I was to marry Luigi. At first, I could not fathom any logical reason for it.

"But why a Niccolini, uncle?" I had blurted. "They rarely socialize with our circles. They have no noble blood."

"Nor do we, girl. Time for you to shed that uppity nature of yours. Luigi is a fine man, an influential guildsman. A better man than you deserve, frankly, given your immodest pride and inability to contain your opinions."

"Please, uncle, I will gladly serve my family in my marriage, but at least grant me someone I can discuss literature with, someone who has some connection with Florence's philosophic circles. I grew up listening to my father read Petrarch's sonnets about the beauteous Laura and Virgil's stories of Aeneas's escape from the plunder of Troy. I cannot survive on discussions about bolts of cloth! Please."

Uncle Bartolomeo glared at me. "I always told Amerigo

42

that he was a fool to turn the head of a daughter with reading."

How I longed at that moment to slap him. How could God, or the Fates—damn them—let my good father die and leave me under the thumb of this man? Lord, how I missed my father.

Not long after his death in 1468, I had been sent away to Le Murate's convent school, returning home over the years for visits and feast days. By the time I left the convent permanently to receive suitors, our palazzo was crammed not only with my mother, two brothers, and four younger sisters, but also with my uncles, their wives, their children, plus my step-grandmother and great-aunt. To my dismay, Uncle Bartolomeo, with his virile sociability, had surfaced as the new head of our family. With men, he was convivial and popular. With me and the other women of my family, he was cold, calculating, and brutal.

It was foolishness to appeal to his pity. He had none. So I changed my argument to one better suited to him. "Uncle, there is no business advantage to a union with the Niccolini. The family's cloth shop is respectable, to be sure, but modest. Not on a par with our family's banking interests. My marrying a Niccolini will not tighten our bonds with the Medici. And surely there is no concern for that, given our long history with the Medici. After all, my grandfather and Lorenzo's grandfather essentially grew up together, as apprentices at the Medici bank in Rome. As their fortunes grew, so did our family's."

My uncle was silent at that, so I had braved continuing. "Weren't we once listed in Florence's tax records as second only to the Medici in our riches? Thanks to my grandfather—your father—being general manager of all Medici banks, but also to my father running its Geneva branch?" I and my brother Giovanni had been very proud of our father's rank and the cosmopolitan attitude it brought to our dinner table conversations. Medici banks stretched across Europe from Naples to Antwerp, London to Rhodes.

But referring to my father's business success was a mistake. My uncle bristled. "Ah yes, your father, '*Saint* Amerigo.'" He smirked. "Well, your father is no longer with us, is he? And my little brother Francesco is a fool. Do you not understand the implications of your uncle Francesco stepping down recently from his post in the Medici bank in Avignon?" Uncle Bartolomeo snorted.

I frowned. So I was being used to soften my other uncle's fall from grace. But I still did not see how a marriage to Luigi would accomplish that. "But why a Niccolini?"

At that, my uncle had stood abruptly from his desk to tower over me. "Luigi is a friend. And the Niccolini family has a long history of serving as *priori* and *gonfalonieri* loyal to the Medici. I'll hear no more about it."

It was the reference to Florence's top lawmakers that finally made sense. Even though names were drawn from official lottery bags every two months—making it seem that any business-owning citizen had the chance to serve in the city's governance—everyone knew that the pool of names dropped into a *borsa* was controlled and presorted in backroom agreements.

I was being sold off for a better chance in a lottery.

I could not stop what came out of my mouth next. "A fourteen-hundred-florin dowry is a high price to pay for merely improving the odds of your name being pulled out of a leather bag, don't you think, uncle? Or perhaps it is in actuality . . . a well-priced bribe."

Uncle Bartolomeo's eyes narrowed like a lizard's. "Maybe I felt the amount was well worth it to rid this house of you and your insolence. And maybe it took that large a sum for any man to be willing to take you."

So I was married on a cold and sleety day. Few people stood on the street to view the traditional parade from the bride's house to her new home. I rode the customary white horse but was bedraggled and wet to the bone when I arrived at Luigi's house on via San Procolo—so much smaller and so inferior to my childhood's palazzo.

A few months later, Uncle Bartolomeo was selected to be one of the city's all-important eight priori.

"My lady." Sancha interrupted my bitter memories. "Do you wish to check the wine barrels?"

Hoisting my skirts, I followed Sancha down steep wooden stairs to the dank dark of the wine cellar. I felt moisture ooze into my slippers. Carefully, we held a torch up to each barrel, close enough to see if it leaked, far enough away that it didn't catch fire.

Through the floorboards came the drone of men above, bartering and cajoling for deals. My husband negotiated with all manner of craftsmen involved in the twenty-seven steps necessary to finishing wool—importers, carders, spinners, warpers, and weavers, all the way down to the men who worked the scalding, foul-smelling vats of dye and stretched the cloth out to dry afterward. Florence was a city where rich and poor were bound together in a trade, their fates the same in terms of the ups and downs of a good and its market. Even the humblest spinner might call my husband by his Christian name. Conversations were always animated, with little deference shown for rank.

Their feet shuffled above me. Voices rose and fell like plainchant. Suddenly, I felt like I was in a crypt. Was this tedium all there would be to my life? My checking supplies while men in other rooms made the deals that ran our city?

"The barrels are fine," I snapped, hastily clambering back up the stairs to seek the sunny warmth of our courtyard garden. Later in the spring, it would be scented with sage, rosemary, mint, onions, and leeks. But now all plants were dry and cracked.

How I missed the airiness, the colonnades and beautiful statuary of our large courtyard, the classically inspired lines of our Benci palazzo. To create it, my father had joined two large houses on via degli Alberti, one block from the Arno and one from the Piazza di Santa Croce. He constructed a beautiful Roman-like atrium in its center to match the Medici's. But in truth, it wasn't the no-nonsense simplicity of

Luigi's house that so bothered me. After all, I had spent years in the austerity of a nunnery. What disappointed me most was how barren of books it was. Luigi preferred his ledgers to any kind of poetry. Most of the books in our home were mine, smuggled in with my trousseau in the wedding chest all brides brought with them.

The night before my nuptials, as I hid Dante's *Divine Comedy* and Ovid's *Metamorphoses* underneath my linen chemises, my brother Giovanni had entered my room. Seeing that I trembled with anxious anticipation and—truth be told—outrage at my fate, he had tried to calm me. "Do not be afraid, sister. Or angry. You will be just a five-minute saunter away. I will check on you every day if you wish. And Luigi will not mind if you visit home. Remember, he and Uncle Bartolomeo were great friends in their youth. Luigi was often at our dinner table."

My brother continued, using the same soothing voice with which he'd calmed the injured horse at the joust. "We *know* him, Ginevra. Why, I recall when I was very young, crashing into him as I chased a ball. He just laughed—unlike Uncle Bartolomeo, who might have cuffed me for it!" Giovanni took my hand and concluded with his earnest, boyish smile. "Luigi Niccolini is no brute."

At that, I nodded. Florence was a densely packed city, a gossipy commune. Had Luigi been unkind to his first wife, if he had beaten her or . . . well, we would all know.

"Plus," Giovanni said more lightheartedly, "Luigi will tolerate your book learning. You know, sister, some men might find your snare-quick mind a bit . . ."

"What? Indecorous?" I couldn't help sarcasm. "Unfeminine?"

"Overwhelming," he had said gently, and pinched my cheek playfully.

"Ginevra? Did you know of this invitation?"

Startled, I turned to find my husband in the doorway. He held a beautifully scripted parchment in his ink-stained hand. The Medici coat of arms was at its bottom. It had come! The invitation was real!

"Oh yes, husband," I said, breathless with excitement. "It is in honor of the new ambassador from Venice. Signor Bembo seems quite learned and distinguished." Then—recognizing slight irritation on Luigi's face, which suggested he didn't like being surprised by such an important audience with the Medici or the fact that I knew something of a new ambassador he did not—I turned politic. "Isn't Venice the port through which you ship your finished fabrics across the Adriatic Sea to the harems of Turkey?"

"Yes," he answered, drawing out the word.

"And I have heard you say that the trade to Eastern markets is the most profitable part of your business."

"Yes." He nodded. "They can afford the most expensive of my wares."

"Well then," I said. "What better way for His Excellency the ambassador to learn of your cloth's sumptuousness? I hear the wife of Venice's doge is so extravagant she demands even her daytime overdress has no less than thirty *braccia* of fabric. For special events, her dresses are trimmed with peacock feathers and emeralds. What a sight she must be. Perhaps Ambassador Bembo can catch her ear for you." I smiled. "If he comes to know you."

Again that slow consideration of me before Luigi responded. "Then we shall go. You will wear your wedding dress, the taffeta. It is our finest."

I was giddy. A night of music, high art, and philosophic debate among Florence's most renowned and beautiful. A night I'd hear about all sorts of exotic things—like Venice, a city that lived on stilts in the sea. And the chance to share one of my own poems! Lord, which one should I bring?

I ran upstairs and lifted the heavy lid of my wedding chest, the traditional Florentine *cassone*, painted with a scene to encourage a bride in her marital duties. Some were romantic scenes, but most were historical or biblical, representing women's submission to the rule of husbands. For my chest, Uncle Bartolomeo had commissioned one of the most popular choices—the abduction of the Sabine women by Roman soldiers. I hated it.

As I always did when I opened that chest, I simply closed my eyes to the scene. That day I nearly fell into it, rummaging for the poems hidden at its very bottom.

5

SEVERAL WEEKS LATER, ON A COOL, EARLY MARCH EVE, MY husband and I approached the Palazzo Medici for dinner. The sun was setting, yet a handful of petitioners still sat on the rough-hewn stone benches carved into its fortresslike walls. One of them held a squawking, squirming chicken, another a thick roll of parchments. In all probability, they had been waiting all day, inching their backsides toward the inner courtyard as the man nearest the portal was granted access, creating a ripple of shuffling bodies as the line slid forward.

Every day dozens of citizens—merchants and craftsmen, magistrates and farmers—waited to speak to the Magnifico, seeking Lorenzo's help in resolving business arguments, brokering marriages, or securing a government post. The law courts of the Mercanzia might be where guild disputes were settled, and the Signoria where the *gonfaloniere* lived and the *priori* fashioned laws, but it was here at the Medici stronghold that the real business of Florence was done.

Tucked in the sleeve of my gown I carried my own supplication of sorts, one of my poems, as invited by Lorenzo. Would I dare present it in this place of power and sway?

A scribe emerged from the entrance's enormous carved wooden doors, followed by another servant bearing a torch. "No more today, signori. Come back tomorrow."

The merchant closest to the hallowed gateway protested. "But I have been here all afternoon!"

The scribe seemed to smile patiently, but even in the twilight I could see it was more a smirk. "Of course the Magnifico looks forward to speaking with you. But I suggest next time you return closer to dawn to be ahead of the line."

As he retreated inside, the merchant kicked the dirt with his soled turquoise hose and swore. "God's wounds!"

My husband caught the arm of the merchant as he stomped past in indignation. "Ludovico, what troubles you? Perhaps I can help? Is this a matter the guild can take up?"

"Luigi? Forgive me, my friend, I did not see you in the dusk." And as he said so, a Medici servant lit fire to the first in a series of torches held in iron rings along the palazzo. One after another, they cast a warm glow on us and long flickering shadows down via Larga and the houses facing it.

As the men conversed, I marveled at the enormity of

the formidable palace. Twenty dwellings had been knocked down to build this one. But of course, it never was meant to be just a home but a public forum of influence, carefully placed only one block away from the Duomo and Baptistery and on the major processional route for our feast days. The first-floor exterior consisted of taupe-brown unfinished boulders—nothing fancy or ostentatious to annoy the pragmatic Florentine business class. Simple, solid, strong. The second and third floors, in contrast, were elegant testaments to the Medici refinement—the stone smooth and cut in symmetrical blocks, punctuated with a parade of tall arched doubled windows. But one had to look up to see this.

Of course, I knew the real beauty lay inside. I itched to enter.

"Luigi," I began, and reached to tug at his sleeve. But I was interrupted by two more men exiting the palazzo.

"Master Verrocchio!" Luigi hailed the older of them.

Verrocchio! Was it the artist who'd painted that exquisite pennant of the nymph and Cupid?

"Signor Niccolini," Verrocchio greeted my husband in return. He was a round, happy-looking fellow, with a broad smile.

"What brings you here, lingering so late?"

"Ah. I have the pleasure of repairing a pair of ancient sculptures the Medici brought from Rome and placed in their garden. Both portrayals of Marsyas."

I could tell my husband had no idea who Marsyas was and decided to help him. Full well knowing the answer, I asked, "Marsyas? Is that the satyr who was such an excellent flute player that he foolishly challenged the great Apollo?"

"Indeed." Verrocchio turned to me with surprise. "Protect your gentle heart as you look on them, signora. One shows Marsyas in a moment of absolute agony, when he is flayed for daring to compare himself to Apollo, the god of music and manly beauty. Poor Marsyas hangs from a tree by his bound hands, his ugly face a grimace of unspeakable pain."

"Oh," I murmured. Such cruelty to capture forever in stone!

"And what work have you been asked to do on such a . . . a mutilated figure?" Luigi asked. I had come to know my husband well enough to recognize that he was baffled by the Medici spending hard-earned florins to restore a work showing a half goat/half man being skinned alive. To him there was no reason for such expenditure. He wouldn't understand that Marsyas was a powerful allegory, a warning against the dangers of hubris. His mind was set to ledgers and definable profits, black and white, simple tallies.

"Right now I am working on its mate," Verrocchio explained, "a very ancient work of Marsyas's head and torso that Lorenzo has come into possession of. It is badly damaged. I have found red marble that matches the original and am working on legs and arms to replace those that were lost." Verrocchio grew animated as he described his plans. "The red stone is laced with thin white veins. If I work carefully, I will be able to carve Marsyas's new limbs in such a way that

53

the stone's natural white threads will look like a man's underlying tendons as they appear after skin is torn away."

Luigi looked queasy. I was fascinated.

But even as I hung on Verrocchio's every word, I began to feel the eyes of his companion on me. Slowly, I turned my gaze toward him. He was veiled in dancing shadows. But I could tell from his form and the way he stood that he was young and athletic in build.

"Signor." I nodded at him.

At that, the man stepped forward so torchlight spilled onto him. Tall and lithe, with broad shoulders and a small waist, he moved with a swordsman's grace, even though clad in the typical plain smock of an artisan. His nose was prominent but finely boned, his face smooth, framed with a froth of tight, perfectly combed honey-colored curls that cascaded to his chest.

But it was his eyes that so captivated—large, dark, and quizzical. I could not pull my own from them. I felt myself blush at his rather impertinent stare and my utter lack of decorum in not turning away from it.

Verrocchio stopped chatting abruptly. "Donna Niccolini, forgive my lack of manners. I should have introduced Leonardo before. This is my former apprentice and now a *dipintore* and a member of the painters' confraternity Compagnia di San Luca—Leonardo da Vinci."

Leonardo bowed, sweeping out a hand like a courtier. "My lady. I am honored." It was a resonant, mellifluous voice.

Verrocchio chuckled. "This one should have been born

a noble," he said. He put his hands on Leonardo's shoulders, noting that Leonardo still stared. "But he was not. Were you, Leonardo?" He physically turned his former apprentice away from me and put his own arm over his shoulder. "We must go home now and let these good people pass. We have much work to begin in the morning."

Leonardo didn't budge. "She would make an excellent subject, Andrea. Her hands are lovely. Did you see how she held them to her breast as you described Marsyas's torture? Like a Madonna in her pity. You always say the hands convey the feelings of the heart. You should sculpt her. And her curls. Her curls look like swirling eddies under waterfalls—what a challenge they would be to paint!"

"Yes, yes." Verrocchio smiled and shrugged at me as if in apology for his former apprentice's bluntness. "Come, Leonardo, we really must go now."

As they retreated down the street, Verrocchio kept talking. "Lest you forget, Leonardo, we live by our brush and our chisel. First we must be asked to do a work and then promised money to do it—before we ever do a single sketch. Tomorrow, we start on a commission that will pay for my . . ."

His voice trailed off as Verrocchio and Leonardo disappeared into the dark mysteries of Florence's night streets.

I held up my hands in the darkness to consider them as oracles of human emotions. I had never really thought before of how much our gestures said of our feelings. Then my thoughts switched to Leonardo da Vinci, the illegitimate son of a notary, who hadn't bothered to wait until he was out

of my presence to analyze my appearance. What did that say
about him?

But there was little time for such musings. As Luigi and I
prepared to step into the Medici stronghold, a deep voice
boomed up the street. "Luigi! Wait! Let us enter together,
brother."

I froze. I was so excited to see the Medici courtyard
once again. I had not been in it or embraced by its art and
patrician aura since my father died. The last person I wanted
to share that delight with was my crass, calculating uncle.
But I plastered a smooth smile on my face before turning
toward him.

Uncle Bartolomeo quickly closed the distance between
us with his long, swinging stride. Lisabetta, his little pretty
wife, scampered to keep up. His first spouse had died in
childbirth while I was studying in Le Murate, and this new
bride was kin to Lorenzo's mother, Lucrezia Tornabuoni. As
I said, calculating.

Panting, Lisabetta reached for my arm to steady herself.
Her face was ashen, her hand trembling. She was afraid, I
realized. Poor lamb. I'd known timid girls like this at the
convent. I took her hand, as I used to my younger sisters'
to help them learn to walk. Together, like children, behind
our more important husbands, we walked through the portal
into the magical world of the Medici.

The inner courtyard was ablaze in torchlight. Fashioned
after a Roman villa, the palace framed this large, vaulting

square. Each floor of the palace's three stories had views down into it from colonnaded balconies so that visitors and residents could look again and again at the sculpture centered at its heart—an almost-life-size bronze of David, the young shepherd who felled Goliath with his slingshot. Donatello had created this depiction of the Old Testament's unlikely hero, the boy who won a battle against the Philistine army through cleverness rather than brawn.

David was a much-loved symbol for Florence, the little republic that defied monarchs. Cosimo de' Medici had commissioned this statue upon returning to Florence from political exile, having outlasted and outfoxed his foes. So David was also the perfect symbol for a family that ran things through charm and favors rather than armed intimidation.

Raised on a pedestal, Donatello's adolescent *David* stood triumphant, one foot on the severed head of the giant, one hand on his hip, the fingers still curled around a stone. The other hand grasped a sword that *David* seemed to lean on, causing his other hip to sway out jauntily. How many times had I seen my own brothers stand thus after winning a game of tag, with that self-satisfied look-what-I-can-do attitude? It was a powerful image of youth's promise and bravado.

It was also stark naked, *David*'s exposed manhood basically at eye level.

"Oh my," Lisabetta gasped.

Oh my indeed, I thought.

I had remembered that this figure was nude, except for his boots and a hat. How could a young girl forget such a sight, her first glimpse of the male physique, and one so ennobled in art? I also recalled my father saying how scandalous the statue was, since David had never before been represented in the nude. But I had forgotten how beautiful and sensual the statue was, with *David*'s ribs and muscles so lovingly cast, that slight smile and dimpled chin, and a wing from Goliath's helmet stretching up along the boy's inner thigh, almost as if stroking it.

"Holy Mary, Mother of God, cast down your eyes, Ginevra," my uncle hissed into my ear.

I laughed out loud in embarrassment, jubilation, defiance— I am not sure which. Lisabetta dropped my hand and stepped back.

"The *David* makes you laugh, Donna Ginevra?" Lorenzo approached, freshly changed from his daytime civic-leader mantle into evening splendor, the jewels sewn into the quilted and padded chest of his tunic twinkling in the torchlight.

Lord, what should I say?

I gestured toward the bronze boy, holding my hand in the air like a dance turn to buy a few seconds to collect my thoughts. "How could one not laugh in delight at this exquisite figure, Your Grace? I was just contemplating the boy's . . . face." I punctuated that word. "Why, look at his smile, do you not see glee there? Look." I pointed, forcing everyone around me to do so. "Look how his lips lift at the edge, ever so slightly. He is smiling. In pride perhaps. Or in surprise that he was able to conquer such a terrible foe."

"Are you certain?" Lorenzo asked. He and I moved away from Luigi, my uncle, and Lisabetta to the base of the statue to look up into the bronze face. "I always thought that perhaps he is reflecting upon the enormity of what he has done, weighing his conscience. He has, after all, just taken a life." Lorenzo's face carried a half smile as well. He was testing me.

"Perhaps that, too, my lord," I said slowly, carefully thinking through what to say next. "Surely, Magnificence, you have had similar mixed feelings? When you have had to make a terrible decision that negatively affected, sacrificed even, the one for the good of the many?" I turned my gaze from the *David* statue to Lorenzo. "I am uncertain, Your Grace, but did Caesar comment on that topic once?"

"Hmmmm." Bernardo Bembo joined us, hands clasped behind his back. How long had he been standing there, listening? "I must look it up, signora. I do recall that when Caesar conquered Pompey's armies within a mere four hours, he wrote home to the Senate in Rome, '*Veni, vidi, vici.*'"

I came, I saw, I conquered.

Something about the way Ambassador Bembo looked at me unnerved me. I took a step back as he bowed. "I think," he said as he straightened up, "that I must write home as well, but I shall report: *Veni, vidi, victus sum.*"

Lorenzo laughed heartily at the ambassador's shift in phrase: *I came, I saw, I was conquered.*

Oh my.

59

Bernardo Bembo smiled and offered his arm to escort me to dinner. I climbed the carved marble stairs to the hallowed *piano nobile* floor of the Palazzo Medici, my hand resting lightly upon the charming diplomat's arm, Lisabetta on Lorenzo's, and our husbands following behind.

6

Roasted pigeon, venison, and peacocks' tongues. Fish pies spiced with nutmeg and saffron, topped with dried dates and oranges. Pasta stuffed with goat cheese. Sugared almonds and chestnut cake. The trestle tables almost buckled with the lavish fare. I had not seen such a feast since my wedding.

But the greatest wonderment of the meal was a set of silver jewel-handled table forks Ambassador Bembo presented to the Medici. "The princes of Byzantium used them to keep their hands clean as they ate," Bembo explained, and demonstrated, stabbing a slice of meat with the tiny, two-pronged spear, then cutting it with his knife. "Muslims have created a great many things we would do well to imitate.

Forks have become quite popular in Venice—one of the benefits of our trade with the East."

With giggles and guffaws, we all imitated his use of the new table utensil. Sitting to my right, Bembo turned the fork to the correct angle in my hand and gently skewered an olive for me, his hand atop mine.

"I see no need for such heathen goods when God in his wisdom gave us fingers," the Medici's priest grumbled. "On the sixth day, God made Adam in his own image and saw it was good."

"But Father, God did not give us swords either, and certainly they have been useful in the Crusades," the poet Luigi Pulci said. He sat next to Lorenzo. The two were great friends, hunting and writing verse together. "Besides, if we are indeed thinking men, must we not sometimes interpret our biblical stories in the context of the real world? I suspect had we been there, we might have seen Moses simply open the floodgates of a very large pond to drown the Pharaoh's men rather than parting the entire Red Sea. And that is not to denigrate his accomplishment!" Pulci raised his cup. "To Moses and his defeat of the Egyptians."

The priest gasped. "You best mind your tongue. Such insolence borders on blasphemy!"

"W-w-we all might be accused for s-such, Father," said Marsilio Ficino, Florence's most renowned philosopher. Even with his stammer and stooped bearing, Ficino immediately commanded everyone's attention. A clergyman, he had translated Plato's teachings from Greek into Latin and helped found the city's famous Platonic Academy. His own writings promoted a belief that pagan Roman and Greek mythologies were, in fact, infused with Christian virtues and were therefore allegories for our faith. It had been quite shocking to his fellow priests, particularly since many mythological stories were lusty ones.

"Let us think about this using logic," Ficino continued. "If God created man with a godlike mind, then surely the fact that we have many religions—Muslim, Judaism, and Christianity—is merely an expression of our Lord's complexities, his infinite aspects. These religions are cousins of sorts." Ficino held up his hand to stay the priest's protests. "I believe our souls are capable of understanding many metaphors of God's word. Therefore, going back to our friend Pulci, w-whether s-sea or pond, Moses led the Hebrews to safety, following the edicts of his faith. Thanks be to God."

A few of us crossed ourselves in rote reaction to his thanksgiving.

Pulci, however, vindicated by Ficino and well into his cups, felt safe making yet another irreverent joke. "Well said, Marsilio! If only more churchmen could see this. Of course, too many of them spend their time draining off the communion wine so they cannot see a thing—except perhaps the lovely young sinner they ogle in the confessional!" He threw back his head and laughed.

The Medici family priest spluttered.

"Now, now." Lorenzo raised his hands to keep the peace, although he was clearly amused by the exchange. "Do not pay too much heed to Luigi, Father. Sometimes he fixates on a thing like a hunting dog on the trail of a boar." Lorenzo punched the shoulder of his friend. "Like an overly ardent hound, Luigi may get gored by that which he hunts someday."

Everyone laughed.

"I think perhaps you wrote of that very quality in your poem 'The Partridge Hunt,' did you not, my son?" Lorenzo's mother, Lucrezia, interjected herself quietly, obviously accustomed to taming her son's playful conversation. "Let us now speak of poetry, instead of . . . mmm . . . delicate church matters." She smiled. "Can you remember the stanza about our dear friend Luigi?"

"Yes, my lord, do recite it," Lorenzo's wife, Clarice, cajoled him. "I love to hear you speak your verse."

"Yes, yes," we all said.

Lorenzo closed his eyes and thought for a moment. He began, tentatively at first, and then gaining speed as if reading from a page in his mind:

"And where is Pulci, that he can't be heard?
A while ago he went into that spread
Of trees, perhaps he wants to spin a sonnet—
He's sure to have some notion in his head.
Watch out . . . if I'm not wrong,
He'll skewer you in some lampoon or song."

While Lorenzo recited his Tuscan verse, I tentatively inched my own bit of poetry out of my sleeve. I had tucked it in between my tight, brocaded outer sleeve and linen under-dress, which peeked out in poufs from slits in the over-sleeve. I smoothed the parchment out on my lap. My hands shook at the audacity it took to bring it to the Palazzo Medici.

We applauded Lorenzo, and his smile of gratitude almost made that misshapen face of his handsome. Pulci stood to take a bow, good-naturedly laughing at Lorenzo's teasing portrayal of him as the absentminded writer.

"What about you, Cristoforo?" Lorenzo turned to the poet Landino. Lorenzo had indeed invited Florence's greatest minds and writers to his table. "Ambassador Bembo is a true connoisseur of fine literature. I hear he owns an original manuscript by Petrarch. What can you offer us that is fit for the likes of Ambassador Bembo?"

Landino stood and recited in Latin about the glories of Florence: "'*Nunc tua maiori, praestans Florentia, versu . . .*'"

My husband nodded his head in approval of Landino's descriptions of battles and politics, cliffs and churches, impregnable gates and the waters of the Arno.

As he droned on, I looked down at my own neat handwriting. It was my best-turned verse, detailing my struggle to rein in my wayward heart to run quietly apace with my more reasoned and morally upright intellect. I reread it for the thousandth time.

My soul is as a poor charioteer
Steering two horses, one black, one white-gray.

The steady gray keeps his course, the black may
Instead overturn us—he bucks and rears
And against my reins he flattens his ears.
He is distracted, wild, and in his day
Has run through town, causing many to say
I lack direction, and at me throw sneers.

But we work together, these steeds and I,
The black is headstrong, and the gray is calm,
Dignified, beautiful, and like a psalm
In his devotion to keeping our course.
But at last, when the sun sets in the sky
I hope to guide them well, Christ as my force.

"Ginevra de' Benci Niccolini?"

Startled, I looked up, realizing with horror that Lorenzo must have already called my name several times by the way all the guests were staring at me.

"I think our Medici host would like to hear that verse you hold in your beauteous hands," Bembo said, leaning toward me.

Nervously, I cleared my throat in preparation for reading and glanced around the table. Uncle Bartolomeo was glowering at me, and I suddenly remembered how he had ridiculed me the one time I had shared a poem at our own dinner table. I hesitated.

"I—I—I—forgive me, my lord," I simpered, crushing the paper closed. While rereading my poem—waiting, hoping, thrilled at the opportunity to finally be sharing my creative work with like-minded poets—I had begun to realize that my verse stripped me as naked as the *David* in the courtyard. Laid bare were my misgivings, my fear that my tempestuous side might overtake my more contained virtues. What had I been thinking? Even though my poem was inspired by Plato's analogy of man's soul being a chariot, these important citizens could make all sorts of misinterpretations of my character from it. I could scandalize them. I could disgrace my family. Worse yet, they might not like my writing!

"I—I—I fear it is inadequate, my lord. . . ."

"Nonsense." Lorenzo tried to coax me to read.

But before I could find my courage, Uncle Bartolomeo—who had been seething with impatience at my clumsy hesitation—took over. "It's sure to be of dainty stuff, my lord. Instead give us one of your carnival songs. I can still remember following along behind a band of lusty youths shouting out one of them. Let's see. I believe it is called 'Song of the Village Lasses.'"

"Oh no, Bartolomeo! Not that one! Not at the table with—"

But Uncle Bartolomeo was already singing.

"We also have some bean pods, long
And tender, morsels for a pig.
We have still others of this kind,
But they're well cooked, quite firm, and big.
And—"

"Peace, friend, peace." Lorenzo held up his hands in surrender to stop my uncle continuing in his bawdy verse. He glanced in embarrassment at his mother before saying, "Now I will tell a story on you, Bartolomeo de' Benci." He turned toward the ambassador. "Let it never be said, Bernardo, that Florence does not have as much pageantry as Venice."

He looked mischievously at my uncle before beginning his story. "During Carnival 1464, Bartolomeo organized the most famous *armeggeria* in our city's history."

An *armeggeria* was a carefully orchestrated mini-tournament in which youths banded together, dressed alike, paraded through the city, and then fought pretend battles against other gangs of young blades. These parties-on-horseback were all about showing off riding abilities and lances, without getting hurt.

"For this brigade," Lorenzo continued, "Bartolomeo amassed four hundred men!"

"Four hundred riders?" Bembo asked in surprise.

"No, no, my lord, four hundred men total," Uncle Bartolomeo explained. "Florence allows us only a maximum of twelve riders—for fear more might cause mayhem in the streets. I gathered nine riders to my brigade. But each rider, out of honor, was allowed nine other youths around his horse and thirty liveried torchbearers. Then, of course, we needed musicians and pages. Luigi Niccolini was one of my riders." He pointed to my husband.

Luigi beamed. "Yes, that was quite the day."

I felt my mouth pop open in amazement. My husband

had been part of that riotous group? I was seven years old when that party descended on our palazzo, eating and drinking all our stores and leaving wreckage that took days to repair. My mother had locked her children into her bedroom for safety so drunken revelers would not trample us.

"What a spectacle, yes?" my uncle bragged. "Oh, the sweetness of the music from the trumpets and flutes. Do you remember the applause of the people as we passed?"

"Indeed," Luigi said.

"And what, pray tell, was the aim of this enormous *armeggeria*?" Bembo asked.

"To declare my chaste love and complete devotion to Marietta di Lorenzo degli Strozzi!" Uncle Bartolomeo blustered, as if offended that Bembo did not already know the legend of his exploits. "Once my entire *armeggeria* arrived at the Strozzi palazzo, and La Bella Strozzi appeared on her balcony; we each galloped at the lady's gate and broke our lances upon it. But the best was the float the pages pulled at the end of our parade. You should have seen it, Ambassador. This float was twenty feet tall and displayed a painting of the triumph of love. Atop it was a bleeding heart. We pulled it up underneath her window and set it aflame for her! It burned high and long."

Uncle Bartolomeo leaned back and clasped his hands behind his head, looking toward the ceiling. "She wept at the sight." He seemed transfixed at the memory, and the dinner guests surrounding him were as well. He sighed. "What a beauteous, rare thing she was in those days."

I could not help myself. I leaned toward the ambassador to whisper, "It should be added, my lord, that this was the year Cosimo de' Medici lay gravely ill and there was much conjecture about who would retain power in the city upon his death, the Medici or"—I paused—"the Strozzi."

"Ahhhh." Bembo smiled at me. "Clever."

Yes, very. *Clever* should be my uncle's middle name. The goodwill that extravagant display built between the Strozzi and the Medici via one of its most loyal allies probably did much to ease tension between the dynastic families. But looking at his lit-up face, I wondered for the first time if Uncle Bartolomeo had actually loved the Strozzi girl, even though he had absolutely no chance of such a match for himself.

"But, but, Bartolomeo, you leave out the best part," Lorenzo prompted gleefully.

My uncle frowned slightly. "Your Grace?"

"The snowball fight!" Lorenzo looked round at each and every face of his assembled guests to make sure he had our rapt attention. "Here the Benci had gone to such lengths to host one of the most splendidly attired and outfitted *armeggeria*. Ever! And it even snowed—as if our Lord himself wanted to add to the glory of the night by sending snowflakes to sparkle in the torchlight. Perhaps God meant it as a symbol of the pure soul of the Strozzi girl and snow-white purity of Bartolomeo's Platonic affections. But"—Lorenzo paused dramatically and extended his arm toward my uncle—"what does this man do?"

We all shook our heads, not knowing. "I will tell you,"

Lorenzo crowed. "Amid all that pageantry, Bartolomeo scoops up a handful of snow, packs it into a white cannon-ball, and hurls it at the maiden!"

All the men burst into laughter and cheers, pounding their fists on the table in appreciation.

"Well, she threw one back at me!" my uncle said.

This only made everyone laugh harder.

"And it was Luigi who actually hit her!"

Another wave of laughter and applause.

With wonderment, I turned to my husband, who was chuckling and nodding.

"And were there other lances broken that night?" Pulci joined in the manly teasing.

"Ho-ho!" Lorenzo roared.

At that, Lorenzo's mother rose from her seat. The men managed to suppress their guffaws to purse-lipped amusement like young students caught in a prank. "Good sirs," Lucrezia said graciously, "I think it time we ladies adjourn. Come, my dears. Let us to chapel to say evening prayers."

Bernardo Bembo caught my hand under the table as I started to stand.

"You must promise, La Bencina, to let me read that poem someday." Then he let go and nodded formally. I curtsied, hoping the candlelight did not reveal my blush.

As we exited, and Lucrezia closed the door on the dining room, it erupted inside with baritone laughter. She shook her head fondly as she said to us, "Boys. What's to be done?"

"Hail Mary, full of grace. The Lord is with thee.
Blessed art thou among women, and blessed is the fruit
of thy womb, Jesus. . . ."

IN THE CHAPEL, THE VOICE OF LORENZO'S MOTHER ROSE AND fell, songlike. Gray head bowed, eyes closed, she appeared so peaceful. I watched her pray and wondered if it had been hard for her to achieve that level of faith and calm. Lucrezia Tornabuoni Medici was a bit of a heroine for me—her devotional verses moved many to tears. How did she choose her words, her images, to so affect her reader? Plus, her family clearly adored her. On the way to the chapel we passed a painted portrait and a sculpted bust of her. How had she achieved that level of respect and honor from the men in her family? I almost laughed to think what Uncle Bartolomeo might do to such portraits of me. Luigi would certainly decry such expenditure of florins as frivolous.

"Ill things from us expel, all good for us procure . . ."

Kneeling on either side of Lucrezia, Clarice and Lisabetta harmonized, syllable by syllable in sync. Lisabetta's chest rose and fell with that slumber-like bliss of innocents at prayer that I had envied in new novices at the convent. I tucked the folds of my dress under my knees to pad them better against the hard inlaid marble floor and, lowering my face over my clasped hands, squeezed them tight to concentrate.

"O Lord we beseech thee, that all thy saints may everywhere help us . . ."

A candle flickered, spat, and fizzed. I looked up, distracted by the spluttering light dancing along an ornate fresco of the Magi. Across the entire chapel, in sumptuous lacquers of red, ultramarine, and emerald, marched a parade of kings, pages, and penitents on the long trek to find the newborn Christ child. First came Melchior, the oldest of the holy kings; then Balthazar, in his manly prime, his ornate gold crown festooned with feathers; and finally the youth Gaspar, with yellow curls and a tunic that gleamed with gilded gold highlights. Even the kings' attendants were resplendent. One had a cheetah in a jeweled collar, riding beside him on his horse's rump.

Following the three biblical kings was a closely packed

crowd of recognizable Medici faces. Lorenzo's father, Piero, rode a white horse behind Gaspar. Next came Cosimo, sitting atop a donkey, as he always did in life, no matter the wealth he amassed. I spotted the teenage Lorenzo because of his crooked nose. To his left peeked a beautiful young face—Giuliano. Nearby was Luigi Pulci, with his saucy expression, and Marsilio Ficino, his hand held up as if preaching. The painter had captured exactly the personality of the Medici conclave and made them almost as important as the Magi themselves.

I couldn't help going back to Balthazar, seeing something of the Venetian ambassador echoed in the powerful and handsome king. My heart beat a little quicker remembering the feel of Bembo's hand pressing mine, the melodious resonance of his whispered request to read my poem. He had called me La Bencina—delicate, pretty, little Benci. No man had ever talked to me like that before. My hands began to tremble and grow damp with nervous perspiration.

Thanks be to God . . . Amen.

We rose, they shaking out dust from their skirts, I trying to dry my hands on the fabric of mine.

"Shall we?" Lucrezia motioned for us to move next door to the main *camera*, Lorenzo and Clarice's bedroom. Typically the most lavishly decorated rooms in Florence's palazzos, bedrooms were the place friends were received. An enormous carved bed with a canopy of silk and fringed curtains dominated the room. We sat atop *cassoni* chests adjacent to it, and Lucrezia, stiff with arthritis, lowered herself into a carved wooden chair, arranging pillows around herself. "Now, what shall we discuss?"

She smiled in a warm, nurturing way I had always longed for from my own mother. Having birthed seven healthy babies and losing her husband immediately after the last child arrived, my mother always seemed so desperate to please her brothers-in-law. I knew widowhood placed her in that humiliating position, but I still resented her seeming so cowed. The only book she read was Alberti's treatise on the family, *I Libri della Famiglia*, which pronounced that women were by nature destined to be timid, slow, and weak—she certainly proved his thesis.

How I missed my father and our conversations.

As if reading my mind, Lorenzo's mother turned to me. "Ginevra, my dear, I am pleased you have come. I so enjoyed my chats with your father. Amerigo wrote several spiritual lauds I thought finely turned. You write yourself?"

Once again, I was overtaken with shyness. I nodded like a village idiot.

"I think my son frightened you by asking you to share a poem at supper. Perhaps you would share it with me now?"

Sweet Mother Mary, how could I possibly share a poem about my spiritual inconsistency with this noted poet of faith? I swallowed hard. "I think not tonight, my lady."

Out of the corner of my eye, I could see Lisabetta and Clarice startle at my rudeness.

"But," I hurried to add, "I would be grateful to return after I better chisel my verse." Lord, how could I be so presumptuous? But I could not stop myself. I was so hungry for such conversation. "If I might be so bold, my lady, tonight I would appreciate learning how you find your voice for your verse. I am sure that knowledge would help guide my quill."

"Why, God speaks to me, child." She patted my arm. "But it took me a long while to learn to listen well enough to hear."

"Really?"

"Certainly. Sometimes artwork inspires me, too. Do come back in daylight. I will take you into the garden to see Donatello's statue of Judith and Holofernes. It helped me write my devotional about the good widow Judith."

"Really?" I repeated myself, this time incredulous that she did something I often did for inspiration—gaze upon art, not the altar. I was about to ask more, but one of Clarice's servants entered the room.

"My lady, your guests are preparing to leave. Your husband asks that their wives join Signori Benci and Niccolini downstairs."

On the way out, we passed Lorenzo's study. Hanging there was another painted portrait—this one of a beauteous young woman in profile. Her hair was caught up in elaborate coils of thick braids, intertwined with pearls and flowers.

"Oh my!" I exclaimed, pausing in front of it.

"Lovely, isn't it?" Lucrezia asked, putting her arm through mine. "By Maestro Verrocchio."

"Is it . . . is that you?"

"Lord love you, child. No, not I. I was never that pretty."

I glanced toward Clarice to ask if it was she, but I could see for myself that her haughty face had not been the subject for this painting.

Lisabetta frowned at me in an expression full of warning. But I did not know of what.

"It is Lucrezia Donati," Clarice said, pinpricks in her voice. "Godmother to my son Piero."

Lucrezia Donati!

Like Simonetta was to Giuliano, Lucrezia Donati was Lorenzo's much celebrated Platonic love. Their very public idealized romance had entertained the people of Florence for years. According to Ficino's Neoplatonic philosophy, if a man could keep his ardor for a woman to a Platonic friendship—in a look-but-do-not-touch idolization—and only contemplate her physical loveliness as being manifestation of her virtuous spirit and absolute beauty, then his soul was purified. His love would, in essence, replicate the selfless love of Christ for us and bring the man closer to God.

With this kind of unconsummated love, it was entirely acceptable for the love object to be married to someone else. Perhaps even easier to maintain the desired chastity.

I stared at Lucrezia Donati's portrait. The painting felt like a shrine. What was it like for Clarice day after day to pass by a portrait of the woman to whom her husband wrote endless sonnets and to whom he saw as his way to heaven? Lucrezia Donati had actually been the Queen of the Tournament at the joust Lorenzo hosted to celebrate his engagement to Clarice! Pulci had written a long narrative poem about the event, spending stanza upon stanza on the beauty of Lucrezia Donati. Only in passing had he mentioned Clarice, who still resided in Rome at the time, portraying her as praying for her soon-to-be husband's safety during the joust.

Glorious for Lucrezia Donati to be such inspiration for the Magnifico, to be sure. But what was that like for his wife? I had never thought of that before.

The question must have been etched all over my face.

Clarice's smile was cold. "Come, it is late. Your husband awaits you." As we came to the staircase, she added pointedly, "When you return, I do hope Ambassador Bembo's wife will join us. Such a shame she was indisposed tonight. I think she would like you, just as much as I do Lucrezia Donati."

I had spent enough time with my sisters and other boarders at the convent to spot a cat's claws in Clarice's tone of voice. Before that moment, I had been thrilled and aflutter that a man of letters seemed so interested in my writing and my thoughts. But Clarice's remark about the ambassador's wife made me recognize what everyone else had clearly already understood about tonight—that Ambassador Bembo's interest in me might go beyond poetry.

At the bottom of the steps stood Lorenzo de' Medici, my uncle, my husband, and my new admirer, deep in conversation. As if sealing some deal, Lorenzo slapped Ambassador Bembo's back and laughed. When they noticed us looking down on them, the men abruptly stopped their banter. They bowed low, Bernardo Bembo keeping his eyes upon me as he did, his gaze so flattering, so inviting, Lord, so . . . so brazen.

I felt dizzy. What did it all mean? Stumbling, I put my hand on the marble rail to steady my wobbly legs.

As steeped as I was in ancient lore and biblical tales, there was so much to the world I did not know or understand yet. I was, after all, only a few years past childhood. I hadn't even begun bleeding—the mark of womanhood—until the previous spring.

Suddenly, I longed for the simplicity of my convent school years—prayers and psalms, giggles and gossip, innocent imaginings of what romance promised—and the wisdom of its Mother Superior. I wanted to nestle up against her and pour out my heart as I used to during my weekly confessionals. I needed her sage advice.

Tomorrow I would flee to that sanctuary, as fast as my shaky legs would carry me.

8

"GINEVRA, MY DEAR. WHAT A LOVELY SUR—OH!" ABBESS
Scolastica gasped as I hurled myself into her arms.

"Oh!" I cried out as well. I hadn't waited for her to put
aside her crewelwork before diving at her. Her long needle
lodged in my dress, attaching her stitched canvas to me by a
golden thread.

"Goodness, child, hold still." Scolastica plucked the needle out of my bodice. "How many times did I caution you
to move gracefully, like the lady of good breeding you are?
Were all our lessons in modest deportment and self-discipline
for naught?" But she smiled fondly as she said it.

"I'm sorry, Mother."

Scolastica put aside the exquisite piece she had been sewing—a colorful emblem of the Trinity surrounded by a garden of blossoms. How bent and crooked her fingers had become, how swollen the joints. "Mother, does it hurt you to sew with your fingers so . . ." Lord, she was right, I had learned nothing. I slapped my hand over my mouth, as if I could retrieve and lock in the rude question.

She patted my face before answering. "Embroidery helps me meditate on God's kindness in granting me the ability to paint in silk thread. I wish this piece to be part of my shroud when the Lord calls me, so that I may take some of this temporal world's beauty with me to heaven. It is not really allowed, but the Holy Father has been lenient in many things for us." Scolastica lowered her voice and said almost mischievously, "I have even secured permission for eating meat when a good-hearted patron provides it."

Indeed, the reverend mother was rather legendary for her power of persuasion with church leaders and outside patrons. She'd once been married and lived in a country villa adjacent to ours in Antella. After her husband's death, she changed her name from Cilia to Scolastica and entered the convent, bringing two of her young daughters with her. At her pleading, my grandfather had extended Le Murate's garden, walled in the convent perimeter, and built its main chapel and high altar. Then she convinced my father to spend even more on the convent, building its infirmary, kitchen, pharmacy, dormitory, and workroom.

Scolastica took my hands in her gnarled ones. "I hope

you still work your own fabric canvas, Ginevra. Your crewelwork was some of the finest Le Murate ever saw. I know I must promote embroidery as God's tool for morality, keeping women's hands from falling idle or meddling where they do not belong. But I also think it pure artistry, pure creativity, which is a drop of divine spirit in us, surely. I remember well that beautiful band of our gold thread you embroidered into the neckline of a brown frock, making a commonplace dress exquisite."

Blessed with such praise from her, I was doubly embarrassed to admit I had not done any needlework for weeks. "I—I have been distracted of late, Mother."

"Ahhhh. So that is why you have come. To tell me of a distraction? The world outside these walls is filled with those, my daughter. What is troubling you?"

My eyes welled with tears. "Oh, Mother, I am so—"

"Abbess Scolastica?"

I startled at the sound of a male voice. Scolastica cocked her head, assessing my face, before turning to greet three tradesmen and an apprentice who stood in the parlor's doorway, which led to the outside world. We sat behind a grate the Church required be between nuns and laypeople even in the convent's one public receiving room.

"Good sirs." She waved, beckoning them to enter.

They tiptoed toward her as if approaching a high altar. One was a scissors master, a whetting stone under his arm. Another was a *battiloro*, a gold beater, balancing paper-thin sheets of gold leaf. The third man brought yellow silk, and his apprentice carried a basket of empty wooden spools. All these things were necessary for the spinning of gold thread taking place in the workroom adjacent to the parlor.

"Reverend Mother." The men knelt. The apprentice, though, gaped at her. Obviously it was his first visit to the convent. He managed to spill most of the spools onto the floor as he bent his knees.

"God's blood!" he cried out.

His master cursed loudly and more graphically before cuffing the boy's ear, which sent even more spools spinning across the wooden floor.

Then they both froze and looked to Scolastica, their eyes filled with horror, realizing they had blasphemed in front of the city's most renowned nun.

But she merely burst out laughing. "Come, come, gentlemen, pick up your wares." Holding on to my arm as support, she stood, taking a long breath of pain as she did. "I will escort you in." Entrance to the inner sanctum of the convent was strictly forbidden—a rule that was bent for only the most important patrons and silk-thread tradesmen.

She smiled reassuringly at the apprentice. "Do refrain once inside from such language. My flock would feel the need to spend hours in prayer if they heard the Lord's name used in vain. After all, that is the . . . the . . ." She prompted the boy to finish her sentence.

"The third commandment," he squeaked.

"Indeed." She turned to the apprentice's master, her voice becoming stern. "No need for my chaste daughters to do penance for your weaknesses, is there, sir?"

"No, Mother."

"Recite one hundred Hail Marys tonight. And no wine for a week."

Scolastica put her arm through mine to lead the way into the workroom. The gold beater and scissors master shoved the reprimanded silk merchant behind them, making faces at him for his stupidity. Scolastica let out a slight snort of amusement.

In the workroom, warm light spilled through its windows onto several nuns cutting sheets of gold into narrow strips. Bathed in an adjacent pool of sunshine, two other sisters wound the gleaming strips tightly around a core of yellow silk to make golden thread. Their fingers were calloused from pulling and yanking the sharp-edged metallic strips tight to ensure that the thread was thin and supple enough to be cast through looms without snagging. One of them stuck her finger in her mouth to stop the bleeding from a new cut sliced into her flesh by the gold.

When studying at the convent school, I'd tried to write a poem likening the sisters to the Fates spinning a person's strand of life. I noted that they bled to produce beauty for others. The verse was embarrassing in its exaggerated and overwritten metaphor. But witnessing the familiar scene once more, I was again struck by its paradox—cloistered sisters, dedicated to self-imposed poverty and stark modesty, spinning the richest of gold thread for luxurious brocade cloth. They provided the cheapest labor to the city's merchants, allowing them huge profits and thereby stoking Florence's overall wealth.

Once a privileged laywoman living in the outside world, Scolastica had well understood the city's thirst for such beautiful fabric and recognized the potential benefit to her flock. Le Murate became the first of Florence's convents to produce gold thread and remained its best thirty years later. With the florins generated by its thread production, Scolastica purchased food and supplies but also books. She'd even managed to buy a portable organ for the chapel and hired musicians to teach her nuns how to sing the new polyphony—a rare touch of musical sophistication for a nunnery. That very moment I could hear voices trilling the psalms of David in the chapel.

"Ginevra!"

I turned to the other end of the room, where literate sisters were copying manuscripts.

"Juliet?" I rushed to hug a girl who had been one of my closest friends in the boarders' dormitory. We had spent many hours whispering through the night together. She had been the prettiest of all of us, with a mane of the softest hair falling to her waist. Any sane man would fall in love with her for her tresses alone. But she was the fourth daughter of her family, and there had been no dowry money left for her. Now, her wimple hid everything save her face, and I knew her head had been shaved underneath. All that silken hair was gone. But her lovely face was anything but sad.

"How I've missed you," she said. "Come, look what the Mother Superior is letting me do." Juliet pulled me to her table, and I gasped at the border of angels she'd painted on the margins of the manuscript—figures as gorgeous as anything I'd seen the day of the joust.

"Juliet, your illustrations are magnificent. I did not know you were so gifted an artist."

She beamed. "And look at this," she whispered, glancing toward one of the older, sourer nuns bent over her work to make sure she wasn't eavesdropping. "I am compiling a book of sayings for the abbess—quotes from Saints Augustine and Gregory but also from the likes of Seneca and Socrates!"

By her hand, birds of paradise nested around a snippet of Socrates's philosophy: *The unexamined life is not worth living.*

"And"—Juliet leaned close to my ear—"Mother Superior said I may also write a play from what I learn from the quotes to entertain our sisters when we celebrate Easter this year." She clapped her hands silently, like a child thrilled with a new gift. "I have learned so much reading these passages. My family never would have allowed me access to such books."

I couldn't help feeling a tug at my heart as I recognized that Juliet had become Scolastica's favored protégée—just as I had once been. I knew how much joy her encouragement brought a young, intellectually and spiritually hungry girl. I missed it.

"Is not her work marvelous?" Scolastica approached from behind, slipping her arm through mine for support. "I know the new printing press can produce many copies of a book at a time. A miracle indeed, and yet, what a shame to lose the glory of this handmade art."

Juliet's face lit up at the compliment.

"Come, sisters," Scolastica announced. "Time to go to the laundry and receive your clean tunics for the week." When the women glided out silently, heads bowed, she turned to me. "Now we have time for a chat, my dear. Help me to my cell, where it can be a private one."

Small, whitewashed, and ornamented only with a crucifix hanging on a wall, the abbess's cell contained a low bench-bed, a wooden chair, a washbasin, and a cabinet I knew hid her favorite books, sacred and secular. That was all. We sat down facing each other on the thin mattress. I had not forgotten how hard this bedding was despite the fact Scolastica had somehow obtained permission for wool rather than straw mattresses. Seeing how she grimaced as she shifted to get comfortable, I felt a flare of anger that she could not enjoy a real bed.

"Mother, I wish you could sleep with me on my feather bed."

"You sleep alone, child?"

I sucked in my breath. She always did cut right to the marrow.

"Yes, Mother," I murmured. "But I do not mind." How could I admit that even though Luigi's disinterest made me worry that I might be horribly unattractive, I was still relieved by my solitude? Luigi's touch had been uninspiring to the point of making my skin crawl.

"I hope you will be able to conceive children by him?"

I turned crimson. "I . . . I do not know, Mother."

"Ginevra," she said gently, "children are one of the greatest joys this world offers a woman. Especially in arranged marriages. Is your husband capable?"

"I . . . I suppose?"

"Is he able to perform properly?"

I shrugged and began twisting handfuls of my skirt in embarrassment.

"Child." Scolastica put her hand over mine to stop my fidgeting. "Do you suspect your husband is a Florenzer?"

"Indeed, Mother, he was born in Florence, you know that."

Scolastica laughed gently. "Perhaps we did our job in keeping you innocent of the world too thoroughly. Let me explain. Because of our city's attachment to the ancient Greeks and Romans and their idealization of the male figure and close friendships among men, some Europeans have started calling men who love each other—in all senses of the word—by the name Florenzer. Do you suspect that—" She stopped abruptly and studied my face. "Ah, I see. It is not your husband you have come to discuss, is it?"

This time I managed to wait until she opened her arms toward me before I cuddled up against her. I poured out the story of the joust, the Medici dinner, and the ambassador. "His Excellency seemed so taken with my verse, Mother. And he is . . ." I hesitated to admit how handsome and charming he was. "He is . . ."

"A man," Scolastica said with a small laugh. "And a

diplomat looking to seal a strong bond between Venice and Florence. Think with that brilliant mind of yours. What better way, my dear, to become fast friends with Lorenzo de' Medici than by joining in the Magnifico's poetry and philosophy circles and choosing a Platonic lover to idolize as Lorenzo does Lucrezia Donati, or Giuliano does Simonetta Vespucci?"

I pulled away from her in embarrassed disappointment. "You mean I am nothing but a . . . a pawn on a chessboard? That he really does not think highly of . . . of my poetry . . . or me?"

"Child." Her voice was full of affection. "How could he not be taken with your poetry? It is so fine. Or not enamored of that face?" She pinched my cheek. "Of course, these reactions of his are surely true. But Ginevra, you must also recognize forces that lie behind actions and roll them forward. And you must safeguard your virtue or lose heaven."

She grew serious. "Such—shall we call them—'unsanctioned' love affairs are commonplace in Florence, since marriages are essentially business deals for affluent families like ours. Peasants are more able to let affection or friendship guide who they marry, God bless them. We are not. But while a man grows in reputation for his conquests, a woman simply becomes of ill repute. You must recognize that and be wary."

"Am I to never know love then?" I said. Was I never to know the bliss described in the sonnets I'd memorized? Never experience the promise and surrender of a real kiss?

Scolastica's eyes twinkled bright within the constellation of wrinkles surrounding them. "I did not say that, daughter." She still had a young girl's dimples when she smiled. "After all, I had a husband and beautiful children myself before retiring here to devote myself to God. I knew love of all kinds—wife, mother, friend, and . . ." She lifted my chin so I looked directly into her eyes. "I knew a heart-stopping Platonic love myself, the height of chivalry. Never consummated physically and the most elevating of devotion. My soul is far richer for it. Some things are even better than"—she lowered her voice to a whisper—"or at least as good as a kiss and what follows."

I looked at her with shock.

She gently patted my face before continuing. "But Platonic love is a complex notion, my dear, fraught with pitfalls and dangers as well as glory for the woman. It is a terrifying thing to be—in essence—seen as responsible for a man's soul. After all, that is the individual man's responsibility, is it not, to lead a life that takes him to God? Too often a man can proclaim this Platonic ideal and use the show of piety and self-control it creates to hide and continue all sorts of behaviors that the Lord would not smile upon."

She paused a moment to make sure I had taken in her words. I nodded.

"Too often we women think that we can save the men we love from themselves, or that it is our responsibility to do so. All we can do is try to influence by our own behaviors and choices and keep ourselves intact spiritually and mentally. Now, that being said, my dear, there is love to be found within these truths with the right man. With the right man both of you grow, inspiring each other. With the right man, such love and friendship is genuine, born not of calculation or some sort of advancement politically or socially, but of understanding and giving. Like our Lord's love for us. Just be sure that it is this kind of Platonic love, Ginevra, before you give your heart."

I burned to know what man in her past she referred to, but her look told me not to dare ask. "But how will I know when it is real?"

"You will know it when you feel it, Ginevra. It is like nothing else. But heed the boundaries I described as best you can. Wear virtue like armor in a joust for eternity and for your own sense of self." She squeezed me tight and then pulled away to stand. "There is something I have wanted to give you."

From her cabinet, Scolastica pulled out a carefully folded black scarf. "Take this scapular. Wear it to mark yourself as a beloved *conversa*, a noncloistered laysister of our convent, free to come and go. As a Benci, Le Murate's greatest benefactor, you are always welcome to the room your grandfather made for your aunt Caterina. You may come here anytime for reflection and prayer. So many people see our walls as confinement, but you know the supportive community among our sisters, the study of thought possible for women in a convent's seclusion, released from men's politics."

She placed the dark scarf upon my shoulders. "Outside,

my dear, you may be placed within a gilded cage of men's perceptions of you. They will stand and admire you—which is a blessing and a curse. It can be a lonely thing to be turned into an ideal, especially when one is young and has a heart that beats and yearns. But don't forget that from that perch, you can see and experience the wonders of this mortal world, wonders that men control—its art, its literature, its music.

"Most importantly, you make the choice of songs you sing within the cage. With your mind and gifts, it can be an exquisite litany. Sing of us. Sing of yourself. Sing of what treasure lies inside women's hearts and minds if men but look beyond their preconceived notions. We think, we feel, we bleed when hurt. We have courage when tested. Someday men may laud rather than fear that. That is my hope.

"So sing, Ginevra. Make them listen."

9

"WHAT IS IT LIKE IN THE CONVENT?" SANCHA WHISPERED TO
me as we began the walk home. She had refused to let me cross
the city alone, tucking a kitchen knife in her belt to escort
me—a comical precaution, but I had been in too much of a
hurry to argue the point with her. Of course accompanying
me also allowed her one of her favorite pastimes—watching
people. Rather than entering Le Murate with me, she had
waited outside on via Ghibellina, amusing herself by assessing visitors coming into the city's northern gate, weary from
crossing the Apennines on the road from Bologna.

Her curiosity now turned from that parade of strangers
to the inner workings of Le Murate. "Is it all hair shirts and

floggings? And spirits and goblins pursuing the nuns?"

"Goodness, no, Sancha. What makes you think such things?"

She shrugged. "I've heard of strange goings-on inside." She yanked me away from stepping in ox dung. Florence's backstreets were narrow and crowded. Men jostled one another, relieved themselves in corners, and argued loudly—even throwing punches—over neighborhood politics. A pair of debaters in front of us shoved each other until one of them fell to the ground. Sancha kept me close to the sand-colored walls and stayed on my outside arm, dismissing men ogling her with a scowl.

She was a rare good soul, this fierce little protector of mine. I couldn't help but smile. "And what have you heard, Sancha?"

"Well . . ." She pulled me close, as if someone could hear her in that din. "My cousin works in the Medici kitchens. Once the great Lorenzo and some of his band climbed the garden walls of the convent at night and peeped in windows. And . . ."

I stopped. "He did what?"

"My lady, men do that on a lark and a dare all the time to see the nuns."

I was horrified. "I had no idea."

Sancha nodded, as if confirming something as obvious as the sun rising in the morning. "The Magnifico and his friends returned at dawn, hungry, and laid siege to the kitchen, where my cousin was beginning the morning meal.

She heard Lorenzo brag that he had seen the nuns at prayer. He said that over each hovered an angel." Sancha lowered her voice as if sharing a secret. "But one had a bloodred devil crouching beside her, whispering in her ear, as if they were friends conspiring together. It was later told that the sister confessed a sin to the abbess that required her doing terrible penance."

Sancha's expression was so earnest, I knew I could do little to shake her superstitions. But I tried. "It is not like that, Sancha. The sisters do pray, for their own souls and ours, and many do seem rather angelic. But in all the years I was there, I never saw a demon or a ghost." Of course, I did remember the novice who fled her new husband on her wedding night when he passed out from wine, daring to run away into the night disguised as a servant. She claimed she had been guided safely through the dark streets to Le Murate by a kind gentleman, who at the convent door revealed himself to be St. Peter. I always supposed she'd made up the story to prevent her family dragging her back to her marriage. Who could argue with an apostle?

But I was still incredulous at the thought of carousing men climbing the walls to spy on penitent women just for fun. "Are you describing the night the Magnifico spotted smoke coming from the convent's kitchens and rushed in to put out a fire?"

Sancha patted my arm. "No, my lady."

"But," I began, "he has been such a benefactor to Le Murate since the fire, rebuilding the kitchen and the laundry."

Sancha just shook her head. "Why do you think he was so nearby that he happened to see smoke and fire in the middle of the night?"

That silenced me. We continued our path home along via dell'Agnolo. I was about to protest her gossip again, when I heard her catch her breath and mutter, "My God, who is that?" Sancha quickened her pace and pulled me along with her.

I glanced up the street in the direction she was looking and spotted the back of a tall man with a mane of curls, wearing a rose-colored tunic. He had just emerged from a small corner row house. In the mustard browns of the surrounding buildings and the crowd of dirt-covered laborers who lived on the north side of Piazza di Santa Croce, the man's richly colored clothing made him stand out like a colorful rooster among chickens. But it wasn't until he turned to speak to someone ambling beside him that I recognized the beautiful, smooth-chiseled face. It was Leonardo da Vinci.

"He's a painter and sculptor," I said.

"Hmmmm. I thought from the looks of him that he was born of higher stuff." Sancha seemed pleased to hear he was not.

We trailed behind Leonardo, since we were heading in the same direction. He bowed and spoke to people as he passed. I have to admit I was curious myself. Although artists were regarded as mere craftsmen for hire, I still marveled at such talent milling about town like any ordinary person.

But as we approached our house, I slowed, ready to leave the street.

The bells of the Duomo began to chime the hour, a deep resounding tolling that rippled out along the streets from the cathedral, washing up against the walls in swells of sound, then crashing off them in echoes. Other church bells answered, one after another, so all of Florence pealed and throbbed.

"My lady." Sancha tugged on my arm without taking her eyes off Leonardo's retreating figure. "I feel the need to attend midday mass. May we go to the cathedral?" The Duomo lay a few minutes away in the direction Leonardo was walking.

I laughed at Sancha's thinly disguised motivation. She grinned at me. Why not? I thought. And so Sancha and I followed.

Another turn on a corner and the rich red bricks of the Duomo's legendary dome loomed over Florence's tiled roofs. I never ceased to marvel at it whenever it popped into my view. I stopped and shaded my eyes to look up at it.

The largest dome in all Christendom, it had risen under the direction of Brunelleschi, an artist-engineer renowned for his temper and strange habits. He based his design for the Duomo on his study of Rome's Pantheon—a pagan temple—which alone was enough to make most Florentines distrust its construction. Despite citizens amusing themselves by sitting at the cathedral's base to watch the laborers—and making bets as to when the whole thing would crash to the ground—Brunelleschi successfully finished the egg-shaped dome in fifteen years. The final touch was placing a golden orb and cross atop its lantern. Watching that gleaming ball being hoisted to its spot touching the sky was one of the last things I witnessed as a young girl free to be out on the streets of Florence, before I entered convent school. I remembered the scene vividly—Verrocchio had constructed the orb and overseen lifting it by cranes and pulleys.

I brought my gaze back down to street level, estimating that a young Leonardo had been part of Verrocchio's band of workers that day—probably the age I was now. Sancha tugged on my arm, and I resumed my gait, allowing her to pull me along so she kept Leonardo in sight.

Just as we stepped into the massive shadows the cathedral threw along its square, Leonardo stopped abruptly. He balled his hands into fists, putting them on his hips, and shouted angrily.

"What's he doing?" Sancha muttered. We both looked in the direction he'd yelled. A young man in two-toned hose and a tight doublet turned, searching the crowd for the shout. When he spotted Leonardo, he squared his feet and bit his thumb at him—the highest of insults!

Sancha laughed. "Now there'll be a fight."

But when Leonardo threw up his hands, spread wide in disbelief and challenge, the man waved him off dismissively and stalked away. Leonardo stayed rooted for a few moments, staring at where the man had been. Then he lowered his arms and stormed into a nearby house.

"What was that all about, do you suppose, Sancha?"

Watching that exchange, her expression had changed from delighted curiosity to gossipy interest and finally to disgust. "That man just dropped a letter into a *tamburi*."

"Really?" I asked. *Tamburi* were locked wooden boxes placed near major churches by the Ufficiali di Notte, the Officers of the Night. In those boxes, Florentines could denounce their neighbors for vice by leaving secret accusations of crimes against decency that brought arrest and trial in front of a tribunal of old men. The *tamburi* were notorious and much used—but I had never before seen anyone actually drop a denunciation into one. "What do you suppose he is reporting?"

"Well, it could be a number of things, my lady. Gambling, prostitution, lechery, a woman breaking the laws against seductive or overly showy clothes." She scowled. "Or any kind of bodily pleasure that is not procreative as prescribed by the Bible and could not bring about a baby."

Sancha spat on the ground. "May the Lord strike down that man! My own father was accused by some willy-wag gossip of debauchery. Not that the jackass didn't deserve it. He was constantly wasting his wages at the brothels, carousing and buying ale for others to appear like an important man and doing disgusting things when drunk. Imagine the humiliation to my mother. And doing that when he had children to feed! The Officers of the Night tribunal had him beaten until his ribs cracked. But what help was that to us?

He was never able to manage the hard work of the vats again. That's when I had to leave home to work for your husband. My mother started mending clothes. It ruined her eyes."

Her face smoldered with hatred. "If I ever discover who denounced my father, I am going to find some piece of trash about that man that will stick to him and drop letters in every *tamburi* I can find. I will—"

Sancha was interrupted by Leonardo emerging onto the street again.

Verrocchio appeared at the door, shouting at his former apprentice's back.

Clutching a large hammer and sculpting chisel, Leonardo was marching toward the *tamburi*.

"Leonardo!" Verrocchio called again, louder and more authoritatively this time.

Leonardo ignored him.

Verrocchio threw a cloth he had been wiping his hands with to the ground and ran after Leonardo as fast as he could, his belly jiggling. The older artist didn't reach his former apprentice until Leonardo had already inserted the chisel up under the lid of the *tamburi* and raised his hammer to strike.

Verrocchio nabbed him from behind by his arm and yanked so hard the taller and stronger Leonardo had to turn around to face his master. He shook Leonardo's arm as he spoke. Leonardo listened for a moment before pushing Verrocchio away with such ferocity the artist nearly fell. But Verrocchio managed to steady himself and then took a step forward to slap Leonardo across the face.

I gasped. Verrocchio was in his rights to discipline an apprentice that way, but a free man?

Leonardo raised his hammer as if to strike his old master. Again Verrocchio held his ground. He spoke in a voice too low to overhear, gesturing to the box, to the house. Leonardo's arm fell. Verrocchio grabbed him by the collar, like a mother would a child's ear, to drag him back inside. That's when Verrocchio realized people had stopped to watch them. He spoke urgently to Leonardo and took a step toward the house. But still Leonardo resisted.

More people gathered and began whispering to one another behind their hands.

"Someone is going to report him trying to break into the *tamburi*," Sancha muttered, "if that older man doesn't get that saucy one off the street fast."

I looked at Sancha, who nodded at me grimly, and then back toward Leonardo and Verrocchio. I'm not sure what got into me. I put my arm through Sancha's and walked us toward them.

"Maestro Verrocchio," I called out, and smiled. "How wonderful to meet you again."

The pair of artists froze, mid-curse. Then a small smile spread across Verrocchio's face. He let go of Leonardo's collar and patted his chest. "Look, Leonardo, it is Luigi Niccolini's wife. We met her outside the Medici palazzo." He bowed, elbowing Leonardo to do the same. "Remember?" Leonardo merely nodded at me.

"And how are you today, my lady?" Verrocchio asked.

"Well, thank you. On our way to mass, although I think we are late for it now."

"I trust that you enjoyed your evening at the Medici palazzo?"

"Yes, indeed, I did."

As Verrocchio and I exchanged these pleasantries, we both watched Leonardo out of the corner of our eyes. The way he held his body made it clear he was poised to return to his dangerous attack on the *tamburi*. Some of the crowd surrounding us lingered, nosiness keeping them there, watching.

I was determined to keep talking until Verrocchio figured out what to do with Leonardo. "I was disappointed, however, Master Verrocchio, not to see the Marsyas statue you described. I would have very much liked to."

Verrocchio's smile broke into a full-fledged grin. He whacked Leonardo's chest to get his attention, but he spoke to me. "Perhaps my lady would like to see what we are working on right now in my studio? I am expecting a visit from a patron, praise God in all his mercy. But . . ." He elbowed Leonardo again. "Master Leonardo can show and describe some of our ongoing work to you."

"I would love that, sir. Thank you." I smiled and looked up into Leonardo's face expectantly.

Verrocchio cleared his throat loudly and spoke sternly. "Leonardo, I know you wish to wipe gossip and hypocritical moralizing out of mankind's character. But smashing the *tamburi* box is no way to do it. And"—he nodded toward me—"Donna Ginevra is waiting."

With palpable irritation, Leonardo relented, sighing and handing his old master the chisel and the hammer. "My lady," he finally addressed me, and swept his arm toward the house.

10

STEPPING OVER THE THRESHOLD INTO THAT WORLD OF HEAV-
enly beautiful art, I nearly retched from its earthly stench.
Varnish, sweat, urine, stone dust, cow dung, charred ox
horn, billowing smoke. I covered my nose with one hand.
The other flew to my ear against the pounding and ham-
mering, the chisels scraping stone, the shouts of apprentices
as they dashed about the yard.

Leonardo took me by the elbow to guide me through to
the studio proper, Sancha trailing behind. We passed a young
boy, in a swirl of dust, sweeping scrapings into the street.
Another knocked chickens off a nesting roost in a great flut-
tering of wings to collect eggs. A third stoked a fire to a

hellish-high blaze within a red-glowing furnace. The child was covered in soot, but he grinned and waved at Leonardo.

Inside, a slightly older youth sat at a grindstone, smashing lapis lazuli into a powdery pool of blue. Next to him, another applied cream-colored gesso to a wooden board, just the right size for a portrait. A little army of small plaster statues of draped cloth marched beside them on the bench. I paused and cocked my head, wondering why they had no heads or arms.

"These are exercises," Leonardo said. "Master makes his apprentices do these studies so we know how to sculpt and paint clothing in folds that imply the movement of the human body underneath. Know the bones and muscles underlying the clothes, he always said. That way the cling of the cloth shows a walk. The direction of a gesture conveys the emotion of that moment."

"Ahh." I nodded. Leonardo still held my elbow with his pincer-strong hand. He unceremoniously jerked me out of the way as the boy who'd plucked eggs from the hens darted past. Cradling a half-dozen in his arms, the boy looked as if he might drop them in his haste to deliver them to the youth grinding colors. That apprentice took the eggs one by one, cracked them, separated them, and dropped the gold yolks into a bowl to mix with water. Next he sprinkled in the ground lapis, creating an eddy of bright blue that slowly spread out into an azure paste as he stirred.

"Take that paint to Perugino, boy," Leonardo instructed the youth, who hurried the bowl of vibrant blue to an adult artist in the corner, painting the dress of a Madonna.

I'd known nothing before of the process of making art. Enchanted, I pulled my elbow away from Leonardo's grip, slowly turning around to take it all in. The studio was crowded with worktables littered with bowls, knives, papers, and charcoal bits. Along its walls hung tools and sketches. I caught my breath when I recognized a long triangular drawing of a reclining nymph and a Cupid trying to awaken her—the beginning sketch for the joust banner.

I approached to get a better look. Gazing at the drawing, I began to understand how the figures on the painted banner had seemed so lifelike, their faces so expressive and the contours of their cheeks so real. The effect seemed to be achieved with contrasts of light and dark. The nymph and Cupid were sketched in black chalk against the warm, creamy color of the paper. Their faces were made of soft smears and rubs of the chalk. There were no hatch marks or bold strokes until the elaborate braids in her hair and the millet stalks surrounding Cupid. Inching closer, I got practically nose to nose with the nymph and could see the cool white accents within the dark smudges on her face that at a distance created the dimple in her chin, the fullness of her lips, the rise of round, high cheekbones from the thinner jawline.

Leonardo had come up behind me as I marveled at the technique. Once again reading my curiosity, he said, "Maestro Verrocchio wet the laid-in chalk with a brush to make those grays and white."

"The illusion is . . ."

"Extraordinary. I know."

I turned round to look at Leonardo and caught his profile. His eyes remained fixed on the banner drawing, giving me a chance to study him better. He had a high broad forehead, full arched eyebrows without the wild scraggle common to men, and large dark eyes that drooped slightly at their outside corners. His nose was long but straight, his mouth soft and etched in supple red, his chin and jawline clean and strong. It was a lovely face, somehow pretty and masculine at the same time. What was most remarkable about it, though, was how perfectly proportioned it seemed, one element flowing into the other without a bump or bulge or pockmark to interrupt it. Flawless, as a perfectly measured and executed statue might be.

Unaware of my staring, Leonardo reached over me to point at places in the drawing where dark and light blended seamlessly. "The trick is to blend the shadows and light without any clear borders or strokes, like smoke seeps into the air. *Sfumato*. That's how the maestro created the swell of her facial bones as effectively as he does in his sculpture." He didn't move his arm as he murmured more to himself than to me. "I wonder." He paused. "I must find a way to do this better, more consistently, with paint. Egg tempera dries too quickly. Perhaps . . ."

Arm still extended, Leonardo inhaled deeply and then sighed, his breath warm on my cheek. He was completely transfixed by the drawing. I was riveted by his face, no longer by its physical features but by his expression. I fought

107

my breathing, fearing to interrupt. I knew I was witnessing creativity, a thought trying to fight its way out of a cocoon to light.

Sancha giggled from the corner.

Startled, Leonardo stepped back, dropping his arm. The spell was broken. I shot Sancha a look of annoyance. She lowered her head, bobbed a curtsy, and retreated to the doorway.

I tried to retrieve the magic. "I am intrigued that the maestro included this millet." I pointed to the little forest of grain shafts. "Millet symbolizes fidelity, yes?"

Verrocchio's hearty laugh answered me. He was crossing the room toward us. "You know your mythology, my lady." He threw his arm over Leonardo's shoulders. "But my dear former apprentice includes the millet for a different reason, eh?" He playfully knuckled Leonardo's ribs. "This one is not as interested in classical symbolism as our dear friend Botticelli is, for instance. Go on, explain yourself."

Leonardo frowned at Verrocchio, and then assessed me, his eyes narrowing a bit as he considered. I bristled at what was implied by his analyzing expression that I might not be intelligent enough to understand his reasoning.

"My family owns several Alberti treatises, and I remember the author writing that painting contains a divine force that can make absent men present and the dead seem almost alive. Is there something about the way an artist presents millet that improves this divine capability?" I spoke with some arrogance in my education, thinking it would impress

Leonardo. But I was still careful to smile sweetly as I challenged him to answer my question and not brush me off as incapable of such philosophic and artistic dialogue.

Humph. Leonardo nodded slightly. "Well . . . if you are truly interested . . . I think nature is an all-encompassing force that dictates our earthly life. So to not include it in artwork, to present man standing all alone in a void, is idiocy."

Verrocchio roared with laughter and clapped his hands together, creating a little volcano cloud of stone dust. "Leonardo is as blunt as he is talented. Look there," he said, gesturing to the millet. "Leonardo drew the millet, not I. To get it right, he brought armloads of the grain stalks into the studio to study before drawing. I swear they look as real as the plant in terms of the construction and details. But he goes beyond that. See how the millet's lowest leaves swirl as if being tickled by the wind? So alive! Astounding! I am making use of that eye of his in one of my more important commissions. Come."

Now he took my elbow and walked me to an alcove at the far end of the studio, where light spilled in through a window and the stone floor was washed clean of dust. He pulled a cloth back to display a large painting of St. John baptizing Christ.

"How lovely," I said, instinctively crossing myself in reverence at seeing the depiction of the momentous biblical moment.

Verrocchio considered the painting. "I have taken far too long to complete this. It was commissioned for a church high altar many years ago—there have been so many other lucrative works ordered in between. After all, I am responsible for feeding all these boys." He gestured back toward the studio's large room, swarming with busy, hungry youths. "And I will admit, signora, this painting has taught me that I am a far better sculptor than painter. I just could not get it quite right until recently. Leonardo has helped with that, particularly with the landscape."

He pointed as he spoke. "Look at the delicacy of these ferns and grasses, how transparent the water is and how it ripples away from Christ's ankles as he steps into the river. Look how Leonardo has rendered the wilderness behind John and Jesus. The perspective! The scene seems to stretch back toward infinity."

Indeed, the meandering river and the mountains behind the holy pair became vague and paler as they receded, conveying a sense of distance—the hills in particular vanishing into the misty horizon, like smoke into air, just the way Leonardo had described. The scene also captured the imposing vastness of nature. I had seen many religious paintings that might have distant hills seen through windows or archways. But I had never before seen earth presented as a powerful, mythical force in its own right.

Verrocchio put his hand to his chin and rubbed back and forth in thought. I waited for him to speak, and my eyes drifted to a pair of angels kneeling to the left of Christ. Their robes were still being finished. But I felt my hand cover my heart as I looked at their faces. One of the angels turned to

110

witness the baptism with such rapture and awe.

Verrocchio shifted his gaze to the angels. "Ah, you see. I am painting this one." He pointed to the angel on the right, which was lovely, too. There was a true sweetness to his face, but somehow that angel didn't possess the palpable look of adoration the one on the left did. "Leonardo is completing the angel to his left," he said. His usual convivial smile faded to a rueful one. He crossed his arms and went silent as he looked over the work. "There was a time when Leonardo's and my technique blended perfectly, like mirrors of each other. I did a Tobias, depicting the scene in which the angel Raphael tells him to burn the gall of a fish to cure his father's blindness. Leonardo painted the fish in Tobias's grasp and added the little dog said to have accompanied Tobias on his journey. The two figures added so much life to the painting, and echoed the look of the angel and boy I created. Now, though"—his voice lowered to a murmur—"in this painting of St. John and Jesus, it is clear that a hand other than mine painted that angel."

"Maestro!" A loud, merry voice pealed through the studio.

"Ahhhh." Verrocchio brightened. "There's our patron," he said, and winked at me before shouting out, "Your Grace!" He threw open his arms to greet the newcomer. "Welcome!"

In strode Giuliano de' Medici, grinning with his confident exuberance and obvious delight in the world that had earned him the title "Prince of Youth." His waves of midnight-black hair were swept back from his handsome face, one hand jauntily atop the hilt of his sword to keep it from bumping along his thigh as he walked. Everyone stopped whatever he was doing to bow, one boy dropping a hammer to the floor in a clatter. As they straightened up, they froze again—this time to gape at La Bella Simonetta, who swept in behind her champion in a wake of apricot silk.

Like a queen receiving courtiers, Simonetta remained serene as apprentices stared and Verrocchio hurriedly wiped his hands on his tunic before kissing hers. But then she spotted me. "Ginevra!" she squealed, and rushed toward me, holding her hands out for me to clasp. Kissing my cheeks, she whispered, "You are certainly well met." I pulled back and looked at her quizzically. She giggled and squeezed my hands. "Prepare yourself, my dear."

"For what?" I whispered, charmed as always by her affectionate and conspiratorial girlishness.

"A surrrrr-priiiise." She warbled the word. Raising her perfectly plucked eyebrows mischievously, Simonetta Vespucci put her arm through mine. She turned me to face the threshold, just as Ambassador Bernardo Bembo entered.

II

WHILE GIULIANO MOVED WITH AN INFECTIOUS AURA OF JOY and gleeful anticipation of what the world was about to present him, Bernardo Bembo's stride was jauntier, more of a grand entrance. It wasn't swagger, exactly. It wasn't a prowl. And it wasn't pretense. It seemed honed, built by successful adventures—of a man sent to foreign kingdoms to charm old enemies into friendship, a man from a city-state that defied logic to create itself in a bog as the gateway between Christendom and exotic lands to the east. His bearing spoke of a place that bred men of resolve and improbable vision, men who did not take no for an answer.

When Bernardo blessed me with that broad smile, that

quick sweep of appreciation in his sea-blue eyes, I knew the word I sought to describe him. *Audacious.* I felt my legs go wobbly again, as if I stood in a boat bobbing on the Arno.

Simonetta hugged my arm closer to her. "A pleasant surprise, then, I see," she whispered in my ear. "The ambassador was talking about you and asking questions all the way here." She raised her voice to a musical lilt. "Look who I have found, Ambassador, my dear friend and cousin, Ginevra de' Benci Niccolini. I believe you two know each other?"

"Indeed." Bernardo moved quickly to bow before me, though never taking his eyes from my face. "And I hope soon to have the honor of knowing her better."

"Well then," Simonetta said, "here is a perfect opportunity, surely sent by the Fates." To my horror, she extricated my arm from hers and slipped my hand into Bernardo's offered one. I made my eyes big in protest and glared at her. She just smiled regally at me, although her eyes danced with mirth.

"Come, let us join Giuliano." She gestured toward another corner of the studio, where Verrocchio and Giuliano circled a terra-cotta bust of a young hero in classical armor. "He is here to view a sculpture portrait Master Verrocchio is creating of him to commemorate the joust. He wanted my opinion, but I would more value yours, Ambassador. I know you are quite the collector of art yourself. Giuliano told me that when he traveled to Venice several years ago, you showed him what is thought to be a portrait of Petrarch's Laura?"

"Really?" I interrupted. What a treasure! "Oh, how I would love to see that. Is she quite beautiful? Can you see the nobility of spirit Petrarch praised her for?"

A pleased laugh rumbled up from Bernardo's chest. "Yes, she is enchanting. But not as fetching as you two ladies."

Simonetta's smile was unruffled. She must have been so accustomed to such compliments. I was not. I blushed and spluttered, saying nothing coherent.

"I did not know that Laura sat to be painted," Simonetta offered, clearly to give me a moment to collect myself.

"In Avignon's cathedral, there is a fresco of St. George and the dragon. Laura was reportedly known by the fresco's painter and was his inspiration for the princess St. George saved," Bernardo explained. "I had her copied when I was ambassador to France."

"Oh my, what an honor to have one's likeness used to represent a legendary personage," she said.

"But Simonetta, you have already been such. Botticelli made you Pallas in the banner Giuliano carried into the lists." Did my envy leak into my voice?

"And so she was!" Verrocchio boomed, beckoning us to join him. "Botticelli's portrayal of La Bella Simonetta as the warrior goddess was magnificent. And I have made sure to keep the symbolism of Pallas in Giuliano's armor. See?" He pointed to a snarling face in the center of the armor. "Just as Pallas's breastplate carried Medusa's head to defeat her enemies in war, so does Giuliano's. This way I continue to mark him as your champion." He smiled, obviously pleased with himself. "Now, look at my sculpture and tell me what you think, Signora Simonetta. Did I capture your beloved in this clay face?"

Giuliano beamed at Simonetta so she could compare.

"Oh, *carissimo*," she said. "The maestro has re-created you!"

Indeed, the terra-cotta looked exactly like Florence's Prince of Youth. The same expectant tilt of the head, the slight boyish smile, the smooth face, the arched and expressive eyebrows, the long but chiseled nose, the chin-length mass of curls.

She turned to Verrocchio. "It is exquisite. It is so very like Giuliano I wish to kiss it. May I?"

"Gently!" Verrocchio laughed. "The clay is still soft until we put him into the furnace."

"God's wounds, Andrea!" Giuliano swatted Verrocchio playfully on the shoulder and joked, "That sounds like a prophecy of damnation!" The men laughed as Simonetta leaned in to press her pretty lips to the statue's. When she withdrew, she coughed lightly.

Now Bernardo added his appraisal. "Your image in this bust, Giuliano, looks exactly how I imagine Alexander the Great."

Giuliano appeared pleased with the comparison.

So did Verrocchio. "Yes, yes, exactly! Very much in my mind as I carved. His head is tilted to the left, you see. Plutarch wrote that the youthful emperor always held his head thus!"

"How clever of you, maestro." Bernardo thoughtfully surveyed the bust before asking, "Giuliano, how old are you?"

"Twenty-two," he said. "Why do you ask?"

"Because the parallel is astounding. That is precisely the age Alexander the Great was when he left Macedonia to begin conquering the world. I can see you riding out, just as Alexander did, to unite Italy someday. I would happily guide Venice to follow such a magnanimous and virtuous champion."

Oh my, I thought, his words were honeyed, but appropriately and charmingly so—no wonder Venice chose this man to be ambassador.

Giuliano laughed heartily and modestly dismissed the idea. "Bernardo, you are a man of dreams and myth." But the younger Medici held himself taller, his chest swelling from the compliment.

"Perhaps we should show Lorenzo this representation of you as a warrior, so he stops trying to convince the Pope to make you a cardinal," Simonetta murmured.

Giuliano's happy grin faded.

"A cardinal?" I asked with far too obvious surprise.

When, oh when, would I learn to stop speaking my mind? Giuliano was many admirable things, but pious was not one of them. But of course, such high offices in the church were mostly about political influence and power, not necessarily about the spiritual. Many a second son of wealthy families who would never inherit its full riches was sent into the cloth. And the celibacy required of priests and nuns did not seem to be a rule they followed. I remembered Abbess Scolastica speaking of a pope who had a herd of illegitimate children he called his "nephews and nieces."

Fortunately, Simonetta ignored the hint of incredulity in my voice. "It's true, Ginevra! Oh, my heart will break if Giuliano is sent to Rome."

Giuliano gently took her hand and kissed her palm, then held it against his cheek as he spoke to her. "It cannot be helped, my love. It is for the family. For Florence. The Vatican and the Papal States question Florence's holding of certain provinces and mines. And there is talk of the Pope no longer wanting the Medici as the Vatican bankers. He looks to favor the Pazzi bank instead, which would ruin us. Our Rome office is our main bank, from whence come the majority of our Medici wealth and our ability to pressure the papacy to Florence's benefit. One of us needs to know what is discussed within St. Peter's walls. And Lorenzo is already married."

"But my dear . . ."

Giuliano kissed her lightly to stop her speaking.

The sweetness between them brought tears to my eyes. Was this love?

"I have an idea, Andrea." Giuliano turned to Verrocchio. "I had been contemplating asking you for a work, and now I realize it might also assist my brother's quest to have me ordained. I would like to commission a Madonna and child from you, using the virtuous Simonetta as the model for the

Virgin Mother. She would be the sweetest of Marys, don't you think?"

Verrocchio's face lit up. "Marble or bronze or terra-cotta, Your Grace?"

"I think a painting this time, Andrea, that I may hang in my *camera*."

Verrocchio's face clouded a bit. He glanced toward his painting of St. John baptizing Christ. I think only I really knew what he was considering, what he was questioning about himself. "Perhaps," he began, "you would prefer Leonardo do that for you, Your Grace." Verrocchio motioned for Leonardo, who had been standing respectfully at a distance as his old master had conducted the commonplace business aspect of art—showing wares to a buyer.

The four of them retreated to an inner garden to sit and talk, Leonardo looking thrilled but trying to mask it with nonchalance. That left me alone with the ambassador.

Bernardo turned to me with an expression I could only compare to the delight I'd seen on Luigi's face when a client was purchasing a large bolt of his best cloth.

"It dawned a foggy morn, but I feel awash in warm sunlight now that I am in your presence," he said, his voice as velvety as his expensive cloak. "Tell me, La Bencina, do you feel the clouds disperse as well? The flaming wheels of Apollo's chariot riding through our horizon and lighting it up?"

Too quick. It was all just too quick. I withdrew my gloved hand from his and responded carefully. "Yes, Your Grace. I am bathed in the glow of . . . of . . . of this glorious art. My heart races with the warmth of wonderment." I turned away from him toward the painted baptism and fixed my gaze on Verrocchio's work, hoping he couldn't sense that my heart raced.

From the corner of my eye, I saw Bembo nod slightly, his expression amused, as if to say, *Ah, I see the game.* He changed tack. "Speaking of the sun as Apollo's chariot," he said, "the other night, I was dazzled by your poem about your soul being a charioteer, struggling to guide two horses to pull together in harmony."

"But how could you be?" I asked, startled. "I did not read it aloud." Then I blushed with irritation at myself, remembering how I had unfolded my sonnet under the table across my skirts to read and reread, and then lacked the courage to share it with the dinner guests when invited.

"Ah, you have found me out." Bernardo lowered his voice. "I could not help seeing and reading the riches held in your lap."

Sweet Mary, Mother of God. I was untested in such courtly banter, but not so naive as to not catch the flirtation in his wordplay. Flushed, flattered, yet still a bit frightened, I backed away, regaining my composure in the distance between him and me.

"And what did you think of my poem, Your Excellency?" I emphasized *poem.* "I would value your opinion."

Again that slight nod and small smile as if entertained by my determined innocence. Another change of tack. This time he steered to my intellect.

"I was impressed by your metaphor of horses to represent the duality of human nature. Pray, how did you think of that image?"

I tried to read that handsome face, lean and strong, in its absolute prime, neither soft with youth nor slack with age. But Bernardo kept his thoughts masked in a polite attentiveness he'd no doubt learned as ambassador. Was he testing to see if I had actually read the dialogue by Plato that had inspired my poetry? Did he doubt that I, as a woman, was capable of reading ancient philosophy and had simply picked up the image from table talk?

I hesitated. What had my brother warned me against? Displaying my education and appearing "overwhelming." Although I had just used my reading to goad Leonardo into answering my question, annoyed, if I was honest, that a man of lesser breeding might doubt my intellect, I didn't want to offend the ambassador by appearing to show off.

Then Scolastica's command filled my ear: *Make them listen. Sing of what treasure lies inside women's hearts and minds.*

Yes. Yes! I thought. But I fought the urge to rush in clumsily, brandishing what I knew, like a too-ardent foot soldier charging a battlement only to be the first killed. I took a deep breath and spoke as casually as possible. "Why, it is not new to me, Ambassador. I read the allegory in Plato's *Phaedrus*. My abbess gave it to me. I am sure you know this dialogue."

Bernardo smiled, oh so graciously. "I am afraid I am more a scholar of Aristotle and the Muslim philosopher Averroës."

He glanced over his shoulder toward where Giuliano sat. He lowered his voice. "I would be grateful if you would educate me more in Plato's thought, as it is clearly of such importance to my hosts, the Medici."

I hesitated. I had witnessed Bernardo exchange all manner of Platonic concepts with Ficino at the Medici's palazzo the night of the dinner. And yet I smiled back at him in spite of myself, charmed that he was pretending I could help him by sharing my knowledge.

Sing of us. Make them listen.

So I answered. "Even though Plato believed women needed to be educated in order for a republic to be truly strong, I would not presume to *teach* you, Ambassador." I allowed a little flirtation to slip into my voice. "But certainly I will share what I know in order to learn more myself. I believe Socrates suggests this, yes? This give-and-take." I hastened to add, "Of ideas."

Goodness, this was rather fun.

Bernardo clearly heard the shift in my tone. His face lit up like a sailor spotting land he recognized. He took my hand again, his own leathered ones swallowing it up. "Please. Instruct me."

I looked up at him. This close he seemed so tall, so enveloping. "Well," I said, pausing to assess his face once more.

He nodded. "Please."

"Well, Plato used the chariot, its driver, and horses as an allegory of the human soul. The charioteer represents intellect and reason. He must steer his chariot through life, trying to keep to the path of enlightenment to find truth and earn immortality. He drives two horses. One is rational and moral, peaceful. The other is passionate, full of earthly appetites, erratic. The task is to blend the two elements, to create harmony between the two different steeds so that they keep apace and work together."

"Aaaaahhhh." He nodded. "Just like your poem!"

"Oh, well, I, but . . ." I frowned. Lord, what a nitwit I was being. "I would not presume to compare anything I might think of to the great Plato. I tore up the verse."

"What? Oh, that was a crime, La Bencina! It was an exquisite poem. I was about to ask if I might have it as a"—he smiled warmly—"a token of our new friendship. But I am grateful to you for my better understanding of Plato now. I so like the ancients' concept that earthly pleasure is not completely forbidden or viewed as evil that must be killed off—as our priests teach." He leaned even closer toward me. "But rather a force to be harnessed for its energies and guided by the more noble in us."

I laughed nervously. "Yes, most men do like that concept when they hear of it."

That telltale rumble of mirth in his chest grew to a chortle just as Giuliano, Simonetta, Verrocchio, and Leonardo finished their discussion and approached us. Embarrassed, I pulled back quickly from Bernardo, but he let go of my hand reluctantly, keeping his extended like a statue's gesture of disappointment. Verrocchio and Giuliano were too busy discussing how Leonardo should paint the Madonna offering a red carnation to the Christ child to notice. But Simonetta's playful smile and Leonardo's disapproving glower told me the two of them had.

Her expression I understood and felt bolstered by. But Leonardo's seemingly negative judgment bothered me. I stiffened as I nodded formally at him, seeking some expression or gesture to explain his thoughts. Leonardo did nothing in response.

The business between patron and artisan was done. It was high time for me to get back to my house. I had been gone far more hours than I had planned, and I was queasy with hunger and a swirl of confusing emotions. I said my goodbyes hastily and awkwardly, not daring to meet Bernardo's gaze again. I swept up Sancha, who was chatting amiably with one of the older apprentices.

As I hastened out the door, I heard Bernardo proclaim with gusto, "What news I have, Giuliano. What a glorious day! Ginevra de' Benci's inner virtue and beauty are just as her outer loveliness promises. I have found my Platonic love. I have found my Simonetta."

12

St. John's Feast
June 1475

I DID NOT SEE LEONARDO AGAIN UNTIL THE FESTIVAL OF ST.
John the Baptist, when I spotted him sitting on a rock beneath
a tree, sketching. He was smiling. I realized Leonardo was in
heaven in terms of subjects. Before him paraded some of the
most majestic horses in all of Italy. Snorting, pawing the earth,
prancing, tails and heads held high, they strained against their
lead lines to nip at one another as their grooms walked them.
They were gathering in a meadow just outside the city's west-
ern walls for the *palio*—a tumultuous race from one end of the

city to the other, right through its main streets.

One of those magnificent steeds belonged to my brother—the infamous Six Hundred. Giovanni wanted to speak with his jockey one last time before he and dozens of other horses and riders would squeeze through the narrow gates of Ponte alla Carraia to start the breakneck dash to glory or disaster. The jockeys rode bareback, and many a horse crossed the finish line without a rider, the man having fallen or been pushed off somewhere along the five-minute course. Many horses were injured, too, squeezed up against the stone walls of palazzos or kicked brutally in the rampage of panicked animals straining to pull ahead of the pack.

"There he is." Giovanni pointed to his horse, Zephyrus, at the far end of the field, on the other side of the bucking herd. "Good. I told Apollonio to keep him away from the others." He kissed the top of my head, something he'd started doing right after my wedding when he finally grew taller than I, shooting up four inches within a year. "Will you be all right waiting here, sister? I don't think you should try to navigate that horde with me."

"Of course I will be, brother."

He hesitated. No other woman was in sight. And there were a great many men milling about, stumbling from the wine they'd just consumed at the midday feast meal.

"Go on." I laughed. "You can see me from over there. If I am threatened, you can jump on Zephyrus and rush in to save me!"

"It's just . . . I need to tell him . . ."

"I know, my dear, I know. If the jockey needs to pull up or turn a corner sharply, he must not saw on Zephyrus's reins, as the bit would damage that tender Barbary mouth."

He smiled. "Stay right here then." Giovanni wagged his finger at me. "Keep a sharp lookout for a horse breaking away from his groom. I don't want to have to explain some mishap to Luigi—after all, he did entrust your safety to me for the feast day."

"And hasn't it been grand fun?" I said. "Like old times. I am so grateful that Luigi was chosen to be one of the *festaioli* to oversee this year's festivities so that we were able to enjoy the events together, brother."

Giovanni pulled a tendril of my hair playfully before jogging away to see his horse.

I smiled, watching him go. At eighteen, Giovanni still moved with that childhood gladness, a boyhood joy in motion that we women were denied in our heavy dresses and society's requirement for calm deportment. I used to ache to run alongside him and his horses, to feel my legs skip. But that day I was so flush with the festival's colors and music and vibrancy, I felt nothing but happiness.

How could I not? Florence had nearly a hundred public holidays during the year, but St. John's Feast was its grandest— a two-day extravaganza celebrating both our material successes and our earnest piety. Another paradox, but Florentines explained away this contradiction by beginning the celebration with a government-ordered *mostra*—a lavish display of the city's riches as homage to the blessings our patron saint bestowed upon us that resulted in such robust economic well-being. Festooning their shops with colorful banners, merchants put out their best merchandise—gold cloth, silver plates, painted panels, tapestry, jewelry, carved wood, embroidered leather.

After a morning of everyone ogling such elegant wares, Florence's clergy donned elaborately embroidered vestments and processed through the streets with Florence's holy relics—a thorn of the Holy Crown, a nail of the cross, a finger bone of John the Baptist. Following them came the city's secular dignitaries dressed as angels and biblical figures, with musicians of all sorts playing and singing.

But the most important parade occurred the morning of the feast's second day. The city's guildsmen circled the Duomo cathedral to approach the ancient, octagonal Baptistery and its gates of paradise—huge bronze doors decorated with scenes of St. John's life. Carrying painted candles, they slowly marched under blue canopies painted with stars and lilies that were stretched across the streets to replicate the night sky.

All this pageantry was about to be capped off by the thrill of the *palio*.

I breathed in the warm summer air, cooling now in the late afternoon with a breeze blowing off the Arno. I did not often venture to this side of Florence near the Ognissanti monastery. I caught the fragrances of clover, summer-supple grasses, and olive trees in bloom—foreign scents within the clogged city streets where I spent most of my time. With pleasure, I took in the fragrance as my eyes wandered along the cavorting horses, the distant hills of Antella where we Benci had a country villa and I had frolicked as a child, and finally back to Leonardo.

He continued to sketch furiously, looking up at the horses and down at his drawing, up and down in rapid succession. With surprise, I noticed that he openly drew with his left hand. *Con la sinistra*. The Latin word for left, which had evolved to mean *sinister, of the devil*. Le Murate's nuns would never have allowed us to write so. Such a proclivity was often used as evidence that a woman was a witch.

As I watched, he stopped, mumbled to himself, flipped the page, and began anew on the paper's reverse side. He looked up and surveyed his choices before fixing his eyes on one horse to draw. Another few minutes and he was done with that particular sketch and scanned the field again—this time coming to rest on me. I instinctively smiled and waved at him.

Leonardo sat and stared in answer.

The man was infuriating. I stamped my foot under my billowing dress and turned my gaze back to the horses. I ignored him. But then I realized he was still looking at me. And he was sketching.

I am not sure which it was—vanity, curiosity, or fury— that propelled my legs. I marched myself toward him. Realizing what I was doing, Leonardo snapped out of his drawing daze and, appearing rather horrified, scrambled to fold up his sketches and pocket his chalk. In that fluster, he fell off his rock—just as I arrived at his side.

There he lay, sprawled at my feet, like a beetle flipped on its back. For a moment Leonardo was aghast at the indignity of his position. I felt a strange sense of power, for once towering over a man, and then a flood of concern for an artist being reduced to such embarrassment. But I knew my helping him up would only worsen his consternation.

I was frozen. So was he.

Then suddenly that beautiful, sculpture-perfect face of Leonardo's lit up with a smile. And he laughed. Laughed at himself—a rich, rolling belly laugh. I pressed my lips together, still uncertain what to do, trying to hold back a laugh myself. But then I giggled. And giggled. Our mirth harmonized and filled our little corner of the meadow, echoing the trumpetlike whinnying of the horses. We laughed so hard, we struggled to catch our breath.

"Zounds, man!" Giovanni came across the grasses. Helping Leonardo to his feet, my brother began laughing himself. "What happened, signor, did you take my sister on in a game of checkers? I seem to recall her once punching me so hard after I beat her that I fell off my chair!"

"Giovanni!" I couldn't help punching him lightly to shut him up.

"You see!" He threw his hands up in playful exasperation.

Leonardo chortled, but clearly did not know what he should say next.

"Giovanni," I said, realizing that now I needed to direct the conversation, "this is Leonardo da Vinci, an artist once apprenticed to the great Verrocchio. Maestro, this is my brother, Giovanni de' Benci."

The men bowed to each other.

"Is that your horse?" Leonardo gestured to Zephyrus.

"Indeed," Giovanni said. "Is he not magnificent? I have great hopes for him today."

Without a word, Leonardo pulled out a sheet of paper and handed it to my brother. The others he hurriedly tucked into his satchel, including one that showed the beginning outlines of a woman. On the page Giovanni held were multiple images of the same horse—rearing, standing, lunging, and shaking its head. Those images were juxtaposed with close-up studies of legs and their flexing, bulging muscles.

"Why, this is astounding!" Giovanni exclaimed. "This is my beautiful Zephyrus, is it not? The way you have captured his head, here"—he pointed—"is just the way he carries himself when he readies for a battle. I swear the horse loves to win. And look at the power of his hind legs—you have replicated it exactly." He shook his head in amazement. "I have never seen anything like it before."

Leonardo beamed. He stepped forward so the two men were shoulder to shoulder. "I am trying to portray how the horse propels itself forward with such speed," he explained. "I rode as a child, my uncle's horses, but none moved as fast as these. I remember the power felt like it came from his hindquarters. Is that right?"

Giovanni smiled. "Well, not exactly. A fine horse such as Zephyrus is a miracle of proportions. Every part of his body works together to produce his speed. He is a piece of art in his own right, maestro. See the angle of the shoulder here? The supple strength of his back? And the slope and stance of his hocks, knees, and hooves?"

Leonardo persisted. "So then it is not one particular part of the animal but how all the parts are put together?"

"Precisely! See, look at your drawing here . . ."

As they talked, I noticed more rich and powerful men coming to speak with their jockeys—including Lorenzo the Magnificent. I knew he had a stable full of racehorses and a phalanx of grooms. But it was said that Lorenzo exercised his own four horses himself whenever he could in the cold morning air and that his most famous racehorse, il Morello, would refuse food from any hand but his. The horse nickered happily upon spotting Lorenzo.

Then another figure caught my eye—Bernardo. He was talking to a jockey trying to calm a jittery chestnut just beyond il Morello. My heart began dancing like the horse's feet. I had encountered Bernardo twice since seeing him at Verrocchio's studio, each meeting bringing a brief, titillating exchange of banter and compliments from him, but no lingering conversation. Perhaps today, I thought as I watched him, surprised when I felt hope well up in me.

"Sister? Daydreaming again?" Giovanni interrupted my thoughts. He smiled at Leonardo. "So often this one would almost bump into walls as she read some book while walking to dinner. Always her heart and head somewhere else." He took my hand and threaded it through his arm. "We should probably make our way to the grandstand now, sister, to take our seats before the race begins."

Leonardo followed my gaze to Bernardo and the jockey. "Placing a bet," he said to me, reading my curiosity yet again, just as he had at the studio. "Many lords have been here in the meadow to lay a wager." Leonardo raised his eyebrow and shifted his gaze to another corner of the meadow, where a richly dressed merchant was glad-handing a jockey. "Or trying to bribe a jockey to hold back to fix the race." He shook his head. "Florence is full of intrigue, even on a saint's birthday."

He turned on his heel and walked away.

13

GIOVANNI AND I HAD PLANNED TO WATCH THE RACE WITH our mother, sisters, and younger brother, since Luigi would be sitting with city officials. But Lorenzo gathered us up at the meadow along with Bernardo to join him at the Medici's grandstand at the *palio*'s finish line. On the way, we passed hundreds of citizens dressed in their most festive clothes, waving banners and flags, pushing and shoving one another for a space in front of the crowd along the race's path. But they always parted to make way for the Magnifico. He and Giovanni talked excitedly about the horses entered in the race, while I walked behind with the ambassador.

"Have you enjoyed the Feast of St. John, Your Excellency?" I asked.

"Bernardo," he corrected me. "Surely you must take pity on your most ardent admirer and call me by my Christian name."

I nodded.

"Say it," he insisted.

"Bernardo," I said, testing the word. The sound was sweet.

"Yes, I have enjoyed the festivities, Ginevra. Is it permissible for me to call you Ginevra?"

I didn't know. So I sidestepped the question. "I would suppose surrounded by the sea as Venice is, you do not have races or many horses?"

"Well, La Bencina." He smiled and kept to the affectionate but more formal way of addressing me. "I actually enjoy nothing more than a good canter around my villa, near Padua. My favorite horse is named Pegasus. He is a gorgeous steed, much like your brother's in temperament and markings. We cannot race horses in Venice, no, but we do have our own feast day, for St. Mark, and our own grand procession in Piazza San Marco—an enormous space, modeled after the imperial forum in Constantinople. There we parade in front of our basilica. It is adorned with many treasures from Byzantium, including the pride of Venice—four life-size gilded horses that look down from the basilica's loggia onto the square below."

He drew in a deep breath and sighed a bit. It was obvious how much he loved his home city, and I could feel myself falling under its spell as he continued in his descriptions. "Our greatest ceremony is the Feast of the Ascension, when all the city's boats are taken into the lagoon. Our head of state, the doge, sails out in the state barge to throw a gold ring into the sea to symbolize Venice's marriage to the waters."

"Oh, how romantic," I said. "Do the sea and Venice have a good and happy marriage?"

He laughed. "Sometimes."

I had never traveled to the coastline of Italy to see the ocean wrapping around it. "Is the sea like the River Arno, just wider?"

"No, no, my dear. It is a vast horizon of unpredictable gray-green, sometimes as placid and alluring as sleep, sometimes as terrifying as God's wrath. It stretches and stretches, pulling your heart and your imagination with it, knowing that beyond where you can see are completely foreign lands, uncharted possibilities, and absolute freedom on the way there. There are no rules that man can make to tame the sea. He must brave it and ride it out, always alert for opportunity or threat. On the sea, man lives his fullest, his most alive."

"And what is Venice like?"

"Ah, Venice is beautiful and as mysterious as its waters." He stopped walking and closed his eyes. "It smells of brine and new boats and sails wet from sea winds. There is always the sound of unloading or loading cargo, ropes straining and sliding through winches and pulleys, fresh fish just dropped from nets and flopping on the decks. Men shout, berate, curse, and laugh, in a whirl of German, Turkish, Portuguese, Yiddish, as well as Italian. They smell of spice and sweat and sweet liquors, ripe fruits from the East packed in baskets, sitting in the sun, ready to devour."

He opened his eyes. "On the wharves, merchants and travelers, armed condottieri and beggars alike, all mingle together. They bring in exotic wares—ivory from Africa, furs from Mongolia, tea from China, slaves from Serbia. And such amazing animals are shipped in—monkeys, camels, giraffes.

"Oh, and the most magnificent thing I ever saw," he added, "a tiger from the Talysh Mountains just off the Caspian Sea. A sultan visiting the doge had hunted the beautiful creature down. He said that when his hounds cornered her, she did not panic and she did not show fear. She kept her ground with such dignity that he decided to keep her as a pet. He brought her to Venice as a gift for the doge." Bernardo shook his head. "But in the end, the sultan could not part with her. There was something about that tiger's eyes, her stare. I don't think she blinked. Everyone in the court would circle her cage and try to imagine her past and her thoughts, listening to her rumbling breathing—half purr, half growl—as they looked into her amber-gold eyes. Poets wrote of her, musicians sang of her. . . ."

"What happened to the mountain tiger?" I asked breathlessly, having hung on every word.

"I don't know." Bernardo shrugged. "One day the sultan just disappeared. So did the tiger."

We had arrived at the Medici's grandstand.

"Ambassador!" The poet Cristoforo Landino strode toward us.

But before the two men could truly greet each other, the great baritone bell in the tall tower of the Palazzo della Signoria tolled. One . . . two . . . three.

"Quick, up into the seats, all of you!" Lorenzo shouted, over the deafening cheer of people lining the streets.

The race was on!

I found myself plopped down in the shade of a blue-fringed canopy beside Lorenzo's mother and his wife, Clarice, on chairs covered with red satin. Behind me perched Simonetta and Lucrezia Donati, Lorenzo's porcelain-fine Platonic love. Their husbands sat with Giuliano on the far side of the dais. The odd assemblage of women clapped and smiled, a happy unit, it seemed. I joined in, leaning forward to watch down via dell'Oriuolo toward the edge of the Duomo, which the horses would skirt in their dash.

The race came to us in waves of sound. Within a minute of the old bell tolling, we could hear distant cheering, rippling louder and louder toward us with each passing second. Two minutes and we could catch individual shouts within the squall of voices, punctuated with collective gasps signaling that a rider had fallen and heartbreaking whinnies of pain from injured horses. Way down the street a rainbow of small pennants began to wave furiously. There was a shower of red flower petals hurled into the road, and the roar of excitement surged toward us.

My heart began to beat faster, and I glanced toward Giovanni. Had we been together I would have held his hand to soothe him. I could tell he was about to bite a hole in his lower lip in anticipation.

Now I could hear the torrent of hooves, pounding the hard-packed dirt of Florence's streets.

"There!" Simonetta pointed at the first horses rushing along the Duomo's base. "They are coming!"

Unable to contain their anticipation—or perhaps worried over their bets—many men scurried into the street, craning their necks to see which horses were in front. They pushed one another and pranced nervously, trying to time their exit from the race's path before being run down. I noticed Leonardo across the way, watching them, strangely quiet and still amid the mayhem.

"MOVE!" Lorenzo stood and bellowed, waving his arms at the men standing in the street. Somehow one man heard him over the cacophony or noticed his wild demeanor. He elbowed his neighbor, who elbowed his. The men scattered.

Now I could see the leading horses, legs flying, dirt churned up and sprayed, jockeys hunched and clinging to handfuls of mane. They had little hope now of steering their mounts, frenzied by the competition, frantic at the mass of humanity and their guttural shouts of encouragement.

Two were pulling ahead. I shielded my eyes from the sun

and strained to identify them. They were so lathered with sweat it was hard to tell their coloring.

Giovanni jumped up. Lorenzo started cheering.

It was il Morello and Zephyrus! Lorenzo's and Giovanni's horses, neck and neck. And right behind them, snapping at their flanks, another three, jostling one another angrily, teeth bared, nostrils wide to suck in air.

Out of the corner of my eye—as everyone on the dais jumped out of their seats to clap and urge the horses on—a few more men darted into and then out of the street. And then I saw a body dash across after them, stooping to gather something up. Was he mad? I followed the fool's sprint and realized it was Leonardo. He threw himself out of the way just as the storm of horses crashed across the finish line.

There was no time to wonder about Leonardo's risky behavior. Which horse had won? I couldn't tell. I looked to Giovanni, whose face was frozen in anticipation. Lorenzo was watching for a sign from the judges.

Cheering drowned out the pronouncement, but Lorenzo turned to my brother and clapped him on the back. Zephyrus had won!

The next hour was a blur of jubilation. Giovanni received the trophy—an enormous swath of the best scarlet velvet, in several parts stitched together with gold trimming as wide as a man's palm, the whole thing lined with squirrel belly fur and edged with ermine. Zephyrus was wiped down with cooling water and then loaded onto a cart decorated with flower garlands and a carved lion on each corner. He would be paraded around the Duomo in triumph.

Giovanni grabbed my hand so that I might walk behind the victory cart with him. Now, I thought, let's see what Florence will have to say about the Six Hundred! Certainly it was clear that my brother had spent his florins well.

Before our parade could begin, though, we had to wait for Lorenzo's contingent to assemble behind us and then all other dignitaries like Luigi, as the feast's organizer. My husband was beaming. He'd done good work—the feast was an obvious success. I watched Lorenzo congratulate him. Uncle Bartolomeo, of course, appeared out of the crowd in a great show of friendship with Luigi in order to join our little circle of victory.

Then Bernardo approached Luigi as well. I felt my smile evaporate. Why would he do that?

"Do not worry, my dear." Simonetta took my arm. "I know what that conversation is about. The ambassador is so taken with you and so impressed by Verrocchio's studio, he wishes to commission a portrait of you. To celebrate you as being his chosen Platonic muse."

I gasped. "Really?"

She giggled. "Yes, my dear, really."

"Just like you?" I couldn't help asking.

"Indeed! And if we are lucky, perhaps we shall meet regularly at the studio when we sit for the maestros. That would be such fun. Also"—she drew herself up tall, placing her hand above her heart, looking down modestly—"you can help me know how to appear like the Virgin Mother. You are so spiritually serene."

I turned to her with surprise. Was that how I appeared? If only she knew how those very different horses within my soul combated each other.

Beside me Giovanni shouted and waved, beckoning someone to look at him. It was Leonardo, still standing and observing. Giovanni cupped his hand to his mouth to shout over the celebrating crowd so Leonardo could hear. "What were you picking off the course?"

Leonardo approached, holding out his hand. In his palm were spikes called caltrops, shaped like crow's feet so that a point always stood straight up. The Romans threw the devices in front of enemy cavalry to puncture the soft insides of horses' hooves. It brought the chargers to the ground in horrible pain. Italians still used the wicked things during battle.

"How cruel!" Simonetta said.

"Who would do such a thing?" I asked.

"I can certainly imagine who." Simonetta spoke with uncharacteristic anger. "They are such sniveling, dishonorable rivals. They never have the courage to challenge the Medici directly. They spread lies behind Giuliano and Lorenzo's backs. They connive and lay traps. This is precisely the kind of underhanded trickery they might resort to."

"Who?" Giovanni and I asked together, although I could tell Simonetta suspected the family that had tried to thwart

Giuliano's triumph at the joust.

"Who? The Pazzi, of course!" She almost spat the name. "Mark my words, someday they will manage to do something terrible."

Leonardo shrugged. "I did not see the man. I just noticed the caltrops drop onto the race's course."

Giovanni cursed loudly before reaching out to embrace Leonardo. "Thank you, signor. I am totally indebted to you. Those spikes could have crippled Zephyrus."

"Let the parade begin!" Lorenzo approached, holding up his hand to signal the procession.

As we began to move, Bernardo caught up with me to speak into my ear. "Tomorrow, La Bencina, I will come for you and escort you to Maestro Verrocchio. Your husband allows me the honor of commissioning a portrait." He smiled and stood back and let the crowd swallow him from my sight.

A portrait of me. I still couldn't believe it. Me! From the legendary studio of Andrea del Verrocchio.

Of course, I already knew which artist in that studio I hoped would paint it.

14

THE NEXT DAY I AWOKE WITH EXCITEMENT. I DRESSED MYSELF in one of my best, most colorful day dresses long before the sun arose. When our house echoed with the sound of someone pounding its heavy ring knocker, I ran down the steps, skirts hoisted to my knees, to answer it myself. But when I pulled open the heavy wooden door, a different messenger than I expected stood there—Abbess Scolastica's son, a Franciscan monk.

"She is sick and requests you." Beneath the shaved crown of his head and its fringe of hair, Friar Don Ugolino's round face lacked the composure expected of a monk. His expression told me that his mother's illness was grave.

Despite the heat, I donned the cloak required of women when they stepped out of their homes into the city. I followed him through the streets, still littered with bits of festive flags and haunted by stray dogs sniffing out scraps of holiday sweets.

When we arrived at Le Murate and entered its familiar gate, I heard soft chants and weeping. I took in a sharp breath. Under Scolastica's leadership, Le Murate's numbers had grown from twenty women to more than one hundred fifty. Many of them were educated young women like my friend Juliet, enticed into becoming cloistered nuns by Scolastica's promise of being able to study and grow as scholars as well as brides of Christ, unmolested by earthly concerns. But the mourning I was hearing went beyond the respect such a leader and mentor was due. Scolastica was loved like a real mother, not just a spiritual one. When I heard the depth of sorrow emanating from those walls, my heart sank. She must be dying.

I was led to her cell by one of the older nuns, Sister Margaret, who had always berated me for my impatience and pride. She kept silent until we reached the door, where she grasped my sleeve. "Do not tax our Mother Superior too long. There are many who long to say their good-byes, who have cared for her daily and have remained faithful to our Lord Savior."

My face aflame with the rebuke, I entered Scolastica's room.

"Ahh, my dear." She motioned weakly for me to come to

145

her bedside. I knelt and took her hand. At first her eyes had the distant, watery look of the very ill, but then that intrepid spirit, that keen mind I so loved in her flickered. She looked at me carefully and reached out to touch the ribbon threaded through my sleeves, a dark-blue striping through peach-colored challis wool. Despite her Spartan surroundings, her years devoted to spiritual simplicity, the woman who had once been named Cilia and dazzled onlookers with her beautiful face and lavish dresses awoke. "What a vision you are, Ginevra, so full of life and color. That garment makes you look like our hoopoe bird in spring plumage. Such a compliment to the high color in your cheeks. You are glowing." She smiled. "Perhaps my prayers for you have been answered? Tell me, my dear, are you with child?"

"Oh no, Mother, I am not." I felt my cheeks flush red again.

She shifted on her stiff pillow to see me better. "Such a grand dress. Did you don that for me?"

"I—I—no, Mother." I shook my head. "I was already dressed when your friar son arrived to summon me here."

She nodded, pressing her lips together in thought, and fixed her gaze on mine. "Is there anyone outside the door, Ginevra?"

Over my shoulder I could see an edge of Sister Margaret's white habit beyond the doorframe. She hovered, waiting to swoop in and hurry me out. "Yes."

"Go close the door, child."

I looked at her in horror. I knew the wrath that would

146

await me with Sister Margaret if I did so.

"Go on, child, I know you are braver than that." She smiled. "Do not forget that the Benci crest of lions decorates our gates. You have some sway here." I swallowed hard to suppress sudden tears, wondering how I would get by without her guidance.

I rose and shut the door in Sister Margaret's face. God forgive me, I did feel satisfaction doing it.

I settled back down beside my abbess.

"Ginevra," she said, "I wish to speak to you now as your spiritual adviser, of course. But also woman to woman, a mother to a much-beloved daughter. I see it in your face, child. The man you told me of, the allure of his admiration is much upon it. Am I right?"

I nodded.

"As you go forward, then, remember this: Most men are hunters and collectors. You must come to know the difference between those who do so out of true appreciation and affection, those who do it for sport, those who do it for prestige and to possess what others admire and desire, and those who do it desperate to use a woman as a shield. The fourth man is hiding something, Ginevra. The third man can be like a dog that teases others in its kennel with a bone it will never share. That kind of man might tear his object of affection to shreds, without meaning to, just as a dog would a bone. The second man can amuse you with the game of the hunt, if you do not take him too seriously. And the first? Well, if you can find the first kind of man, you have found heaven."

She shifted herself and grimaced a bit. "But no matter what, do not lose the core of who you are. That inner poetry we talked of." She flinched and sighed. Her voice dimmed to a whisper. "I wanted to ask a gift from you, child. And only you will be able to do it for me, without worrying about breaking a sacred rule of the convent."

I leaned closer to hear.

"Go to my cabinet when you leave and find that embroidery you saw when last you visited. I have finished it. Find a way to put it in my casket with me. I wish to present it to the Lord on my day of reckoning. My thanks for his giving us this beautiful world. My own bit of poetry. Do you promise?"

Now the tears came. I could not hold them back.

"There, there, child. It is all right. I have lived a full life, with many different roles that have brought me fulfillment. Now go and do what I ask." She smiled. "I promise the only danger you will face in completing this task is getting it past Sister Margaret!"

I laughed. She laughed—a final little peal of earthly mirth. "Le Murate is always a home for you, Ginevra," she whispered. "And remember the wisdom I just passed to you. I had to learn it for myself long ago, and it may save you some pain."

As I stepped out of Le Murate's protective walls, Abbess Scolastica's embroidery tucked carefully into my dress, I was surprised to feel the bright Tuscan sun. Florence should be dark and gloomy, in mourning with me.

"Wife."

I startled at Luigi's voice. "Husband! Why are you here?"

"To walk you home," he said matter-of-factly. "I heard the news of the abbess's illness. I knew you would be sad."

"Thank you," I said, taking his arm. We walked several streets and were nearing Santa Croce when I thought to congratulate him on the festivities of St. John.

He nodded his thanks. "I wish to discuss something else with you."

"Yes?" I guessed at the topic but had no idea what Luigi's reactions to Bernardo's proposal would be. I braced myself.

"Ambassador Bembo and the Magnifico talked with me yesterday about His Excellency commissioning a portrait of you. Are you aware of this?"

"Yes, husband," I said carefully.

"And what do you think of that?"

I glanced at his face. Beyond recognizing the studied look of concentration he often had when bartering a labor deal with his workers, I could not read it. I chose the safest answer. "I should like to know your opinion, signor."

"I think it an excellent opportunity."

"Opportunity?"

"For my shop and for the Niccolini family. To have one of us noticed by the Venetian ambassador and to become part of the Medici patronage of the arts, well, that certainly elevates us above other wool merchants. Times are difficult. Weavers in the Netherlands and England are beginning to compete with our work. Worse, silk is becoming the preferred fabric of the upper class. My brothers and I are not set up to make that shift. So to stand out as a wool merchant, it is not enough to be a *priore* anymore or influential in the guild. To be seen as part of the Medici inner circle will be critical to our survival. Do you understand, my dear?"

"Yes, completely."

"Also, the ambassador has promised to introduce my fabrics to the doge and his wife, just as you suggested he might. That could open a lucrative client for me."

"So I have your permission to sit for the portrait?"

"By all means!" Luigi stopped and stood still for a moment, to pat my hand and look into my face for the first time since we began walking from Le Murate. "I know you will do the Niccolini—and the Benci, of course—great honor, my dear. As Lorenzo the Magnificent and your uncle Bartolomeo explained the Platonic love ideal to me, you are the perfect subject. Someone who inspires others to virtue." Then he started walking again, mumbling to himself, considering which dress to put me in, which jewels to pick from my dowry trousseau.

I thought of Scolastica's words and felt fairly certain which of her four categories of men she would put Luigi into. The question for me to determine, of course, was which type Bernardo was and how that might affect my virtue.

15

"LOOK OUT, SIGNORA!"

Leonardo called out too late. Just as he released a pair of doves from their cage, Sancha and I stepped through the gate into the inner garden of Verrocchio's studio.

"Oh!" I cried, shielding my face. The birds flew straight for me on their way out to open sky. But when I felt the fan of air from their wings and heard the rhythmic swoosh of each flap, I dropped my hands to look up into their snowy plumage as they fluttered past me.

"For God's sake, man! How many times have I told you not to do that in here!" Verrocchio whacked Leonardo with his cap as he hurried toward me. "Are you all right, signora?"

"Yes," I replied as Sancha fussed with brushing off my skirts, muttering curses and looking for bird droppings. I laughed, a little breathless. "In truth, that was rather extraordinary. I have never looked up straight into a bird in flight that close up. It is a wonderment, isn't it, that they are able to lift themselves off from the earth like that."

Leonardo strode toward me, his handsome face alight with questions. "What did you see?"

"It was as if they swam in the air, pushing and sweeping it as a man can the water."

He pulled out a small notebook and scribbled.

Verrocchio sighed with exasperated affection. "Leonardo thinks he can build some contraption that will allow man to fly. I have suggested he visit the Duomo's stone relief of Icarus plummeting to earth, the sun having melted the wax on the wings he built for himself. Man's vanity!" He swatted Leonardo once more. "God did not give us wings."

"But he did give us minds, Andrea, and the ability to imagine," Leonardo said.

"Bah." Verrocchio waved him off and spoke to me. "Always, this one has other ideas in his head that pull him from the work at hand. He's interrupted sketches of the Madonna and child that Giuliano de' Medici awaits with fantastical drawings of . . . I struggle to know what to call the thing. An enormous turtle shells with wheels . . ."

"That is an armored wagon to protect soldiers as they attack a castle!" Leonardo protested.

"And who has commissioned you to do that?" Verrocchio

laid his hand on Leonardo's shoulder. "Yes, God gave us minds and imaginations and hopes and dreams. But he also gave us stomachs, Leonardo! I know you like to understand the causation of things. Well, think on this: to purchase food requires coin and coin comes from work and work comes from commissions. By all means, go with your flights of fancy, but do so after you have finished your paid work. It is not as if we work the dye vats. Our paid work is tremendously fulfilling. We create art, Leonardo, art!"

Verrocchio turned to me. "And that brings me to you, my lady. We have been asked to paint you." He put his hands to his hips and gazed at me intently. Leonardo did the same.

Under their scrutiny I felt horribly shy. I looked toward the studio, hoping to see Simonetta inside so that she could be my guide to survive being gazed at so pointedly. She must have been so used to it by then. "Is Simonetta here? She told me that she would be sitting for you today."

"She was," Verrocchio said. "The poor lady was coughing so badly, she had to go home."

"And why was that, maestro?" Now Leonardo had the upper hand. "Is that not because of the mess of dust and stone chips you make with your chiseling that cloud the entire studio? The poor woman could not breathe."

"Come, Leonardo, I do not think that such a racking cough could be caused by my sculpting."

Leonardo swatted Verrocchio this time, prompting dust to plume up in a cloud and Verrocchio to sneeze. "No? Why, look at you, maestro," he teased. "You look more like a baker, you are so plastered with marble dust! By contrast"—he held out his arms and turned himself around so we could inspect him—"a painter sits before his work well dressed, as he applies delicate colors. No dust clogging his home. Plus, no crashing hammers!"

Verrocchio laughed. "But sculpture better captures the contour of a thing, its motion, its proportion. Painting cannot reveal the flex of muscle, the expression of a human face, or the direction of his gaze as well as sculpture does."

"Certainly it can! With a little more study of the layers of muscle underneath our skin, I will be able to. Besides, sculpture cannot include nature's variety of colors," Leonardo countered. "A painter can suggest distance. He can paint mists on snow-capped mountains, and fishes playing among underwater plants and even pebbles on the sand of a river bottom."

"So which is the better art?" I asked, joining the banter.

They both answered and contradicted in the same breath. "Painting!" "Sculpture!"

"Perhaps we should put it to the test," a deep voice spoke from the gate. It was Bernardo. Honestly, the man moved with the stealth required of stalking rabbits in a thicket. Almost all our encounters seemed to begin with his having listened and watched me without my knowing. I didn't like it. But my heart still did a little flip at the sight of him.

Bernardo joined the artists. "Let us use the lovely Ginevra de' Benci as a way of seeing which type of maestro—sculptor or painter—can best capture her beauty."

Verrocchio was delighted. "A marvelous idea!"

I knew Verrocchio was also tallying the florins that would come from two commissions over one. For me, the idea was flattering beyond compare. With all the attention lavished on Simonetta, never had she been sculpted as well as painted. I felt like preening. Still, I demurred. "But good my lord, that will be terribly expensive. I do not want you expending so much on me."

"Ah, La Bencina, your modesty becomes you."

"But I mean it, Your Excellency. Truly, I do not warrant such grandiose expense." As delighted as my pride was with the suggestion of two portraits, it also me made me uncomfortable, beholden to Bernardo in a way I was uncertain that I wanted to be.

"No, no, we must have both!" Bernardo swept his arms out in a gesture of largesse. "Mustn't we, maestro?"

Verrocchio knew how to close a deal. "Let us talk inside about what you would like, Your Excellency." He quickly ushered Bernardo toward the privacy of the small adjacent room where he did business.

I started to protest once more but realized it was futile— these men had decided what to do with me, and that was that—as always. My mouth snapped shut. I looked instinctively toward Sancha, who stood in the corner, as the only other woman present. She seemed to beam with pride and a sense of adventure. Well, I thought, escorting me back and forth to the studio would make her life more interesting than house chores.

Why not, then? I felt myself shrug as a voice inside me told me to relax and bask in the attention. Besides, if Bernardo ordered two portraits of me, Leonardo would certainly be responsible for the painted version. That was what I had hoped for, after all. I turned to him expectantly.

Leonardo watched Bernardo and Verrocchio exit, disdain on his face. I knew it was not directed at his old master, whom he clearly adored. "You do not like the ambassador much—why?"

Surprised by me for once, Leonardo mulled over his answer before speaking. "I happen to know the ambassador placed a large and losing wager on the *palio*. I doubt he has the florins for two commissions of art. I saw a great many gentlemen like him come to my father for notarizing legal documents. They seemed inordinately impressed with themselves, calculating, and blind to the effect on those they used to achieve their aims. Braggadocios all. Quite often they did not have the money they claimed to."

I noted with concern the statement that Bernardo was a betting man but knew it was unseemly for me to ask for more details. Leonardo might think me a gossip. Sancha could find it out for me later. "So you did not think of becoming a notary yourself?" I asked instead to make what I thought would prove polite conversation.

He snorted. "As an illegitimate son, I am not allowed to go into the law."

I blushed at my thoughtlessness. "Pardon me, signor, I forgot that restriction."

Leonardo caught his breath. I was sure it was in anger at my rudeness, and my face flushed even more. When he reached toward my cheek, I flinched, having endured Uncle Bartolomeo slapping me for insolence when I was home from the convent. But Leonardo cupped my chin and tilted it up so the sun spilled along my face and cheeks. "I must find a way to capture all these layers of color—rose, violet, cream, tan."

As I stared at him in bewilderment, his eyes refocused from my skin tones to me, the person. "*Scusa*, Madonna." He stepped back abruptly. "But your face's flesh, the blush and cream of it, will allow me to show precisely what I was talk- ing about being the painter's particular gift—the ability to use colors, shadow, and light to represent transparent and luminous surfaces, where the life of something emanates from within."

He backed up and continued to assess me.

I fidgeted, feeling aflutter under the unyielding scrutiny from an artist and from such an attractive and vibrant young man. As all girls in Florence must, I had grown accustomed to being appraised by older men and relatives—like a horse being readied for market—especially regarding the fit of my gown and coif of my hair. But Leonardo's lingering evalua- tion felt different, very different.

Only Sancha's chortling in the corner finally interrupted his concentration. He turned. I turned. She held several sketches in her hand. Sancha had been snooping.

Even with the heaviness of my dress, I got to my servant

before Leonardo moved. "What are you doing, Sancha? Those are private to Maestro Leonardo."

"But look how funny these are." She pointed to a smattering of faces on one page—men with enormous noses and jutting jaws, with great jowls hanging from their chins, toothless grins, and mirthless frowns. All roughed in lightly, with urgent stroke marks, as if Leonardo had drawn one after another while they passed him on the street.

I couldn't resist. I reached out and took the stack from her. In my hands were such complete miniature scenes—cats washing themselves, dogs barking, men arguing, all so alive. I recognized the horses, prancing and straining, from the meadow before the run of the *palio*. Underneath them was a page with a petite maiden pointing to a unicorn. Her face was round like an apple, framed by a froth of tight curls, the rest of her hair swept up and back. Her pointing hand was delicate, its fingers long and thin.

"My lady!" Sancha gasped. "That's you!"

Indeed. The sketched maiden appeared very like me.

"An idea from the day of the race," Leonardo said quietly. He had approached and stood by as we looked at his drawings, complimented by our rapt examination of them.

I was too moved by the image to look up from the page at him—both for the prettiness of the depiction and because of the symbolism inherent in a maiden taming a unicorn. It was one of Florence's favorite metaphors for goodness.

A silence hung between us as I kept my gaze on the paper, but I could sense Sancha looking from me to Leonardo and back to me. There was one last page underneath the maiden. I pulled it out. I had never seen anything like it—a pure landscape, no human being upon it, dated 5 August 1473. The Feast Day of Holy Mary of the Snow.

"Ah, yes." Leonardo seemed relieved to switch the conversation. "This is overlooking the Arno Valley near my village of Vinci."

The drawing included a waterfall cascading into a gorge, rocky cliffs crowned with trees, and a walled fortress on a hilltop. I could feel the expanse of the view, could smell the sweet fragrances of new grass and budding trees carried on the wind, could hear the song of clean, rushing water. Looking at it, I remembered the feel of lying in a field in Antella, basking in the sun, rolling down a small incline, gathering wildflowers in my skirts. No one telling me what to do, what to say, or what to wear. "How lovely," I murmured. "Your drawing brings back the childhood happiness of my family's country home."

He nodded, pleased.

"Have you read Petrarch's 'Ascent of Mount Ventoux'?"

"I do not like Petrarch's works."

Surprised, I looked up at him. No one who wanted favor among Florence's elite should admit that. He shrugged.

"Well, this drawing of yours is extraordinary, signor, for many reasons. But I am particularly struck by the difference from Petrarch. He climbed Mount Ventoux and was inspired to look inward to examine his soul. His essay is all about man's perceptions of nature and using that to find God. But this . . ." I tried to find the right way to describe something that would seem so radical to Lorenzo and Ficino's Platonic society. "This has nothing to do with man."

Leonardo grinned. "Precisely!"

I laughed.

"I had a thought, signora, about your portrait, having watched you in the meadow the day of the race. I would like to put you in front of a landscape like this."

Leonardo seemed unaware of how inappropriate it was for him to say he had been watching me or to suggest a portrait in which a gentlewoman be presented out of doors. We were domestic creatures, our definition coming from the houses we occupied and our roles within them. I had seen female portraits that included glimpses of the wide world, but only through windows behind the human subject. I asked if that was what he meant.

Frowning impatiently, Leonardo waved his hand as if to rid himself of a fly. "No, no. I am doing that for Giuliano de' Medici's Virgin and child. In fact, I will ask if I can paint Madonna Simonetta in the Medici palazzo, in front of those arched windows, to avoid her suffering from the dust Andrea makes with his chisel here. No, I would like to paint you as if you are out in the world, part of it. I have been thinking that a woman's ability to conceive and bear children is very like nature's ability to regenerate and create new entities." He pointed to his drawing. "Just as this waterfall carved the rock over time to give birth to the riverbed."

I laughed nervously, startled, even though flattered, by

how he glorified childbearing. I stuck to the theological point. "But doesn't the Church say God created all that we see in seven days? You don't believe that?" I wasn't so sure I did either but certainly would not admit it out loud.

Leonardo made a face. "No." He snorted before continuing, "I do believe God, or some eternal force, set our world in motion. But I think nature continues that motion, changing the earth constantly."

I stared at him. What Leonardo suggested was so unorthodox. And what he was saying about women so ennobled us. How I wished I could tell Abbess Scolastica that the man who was to paint me saw women in this way.

Sing of us, Ginevra. Make them listen. Sing of what treasure lies inside women's hearts and minds.

Leonardo seemed to hear our song already.

So I nodded. "Yes, let us do that then." I agreed just as Verrocchio and Bernardo stepped back into the room, having negotiated the scope and price of the commission. Outwardly, Leonardo and I slipped back into our prescribed roles—he the hired craftsman and I the docile subject matter. Inwardly was another matter altogether. We, together, were creating something entirely new.

16

Abbess Scolastica Rondinelli died that week. Her funeral was as well attended as that of a state official. Le Murate's main chapel was packed with dignitaries: Lorenzo and Giuliano de' Medici with all their kin, ambassadors from every foreign land, including Bernardo, and the richest of Florence's merchants. As I waited for the service to begin, I overheard murmurings of worry about whether the convent would continue its thread production, its embroidery, its sewing of delicate linens for rich family's trousseaus, and its illuminated manuscript copying now that Scolastica was gone. Nothing about her the person. I wanted to swat them all on the head.

I looked up to the chapel's second-floor choir loft, where the nuns watched services. Behind an ornately carved grating, the sisters of Le Murate were as densely packed as the laypeople below. Scolastica had governed them for thirty-six years, allowing such freedom of scholarship even while strictly directing their religious piety. Their worries that morning, unlike those of the city officials below, were real ones, coming from the fear of not knowing who would next control their lives. I was afraid myself. Le Murate was my second home, but mostly because Scolastica had been the mother who had awaited me there.

Turning back to face the high altar, I gazed at a painted Annunciation—a depiction of the angel Gabriel announcing to a virginal Mary that she was to give birth to the son of God. I let my eyes wander over it, remembering how oft I had prayed in front of it, kneeling on the stones of my father's tomb. The Benci crest of two lions was included in the elaborate frame of the large painting to mark who was its patron.

My grandfather had commissioned the deeply spiritual work from Fra Filippo Lippi and paid dearly for the expensive gold leaf and aquamarine paint that made it so vibrant. What I liked most about it, though, was the scene's drama. Most Annunciation paintings depicted Mary passively kneeling in prayer, head bowed, accepting the angel Gabriel's announcement that she would mother a child without first knowing a man. Lippi's Annunciation showed the Blessed Virgin rising, reaching out for the lily the angel held toward her. Lippi's Mary was making a choice. I always wondered if Scolastica had insisted upon that presentation of a decisive Mary.

I smiled, thinking on Scolastica, relieved I had been able to honor her last request to me. Inside her casket, underneath her robes, was her exquisite embroidery. I had managed to tuck it there for her. Knowing I might need to charm my way in, I had worn the simple brown dress Scolastica had mentioned during my visit—the one embroidered with Le Murate gold thread along its neckline—and the long, scarf-like scapular she had given me. Both items of clothing clearly marked my devotion to the convent.

Thus clad, I arrived early for the service. Sister Margaret had tried to block me. But I had already thought of something clever to argue my way in. "Why, good Sister Margaret," I said, "I would be so grateful for a moment to say my prayers for the soul of our beloved abbess. I would also like to kneel at my father's crypt to ask for the continued well-being of my family—and that I might convince my uncle to keep up the Benci's annual gift of one hundred forty-four bushels of grain and sixty barrels of wine to you and the sisters of Le Murate." That had done it.

As the service began, Bernardo turned toward me. He was so tall I could see his face over the heads of the dozens of people in between us. I nodded toward him in reply but did not return his gaze for more than a moment. I could sense his staying on me. God help me, there in that sacred place, my mind wandered to things other than church, to romance beyond Platonic admiration. Luigi had always been so disin-terested in me, and here was this influential, eloquent, and exceedingly handsome man who celebrated my mind and my beauty. It was beyond flattering. It was totally disarming. I feared that under the right—or the wrong—circumstances, I might allow the boundary walls of Platonic inspiration to crumble. Oh, how I would miss Scolastica's good counsel.

I shook my head to squelch such thoughts and focused on the service.

The priest droned on, we recited prayers, and still I felt Bernardo's gaze. My heart began to thud heavily in my chest and pound in my head. I decided to answer it by going from my mentor's funeral to see Verrocchio and Leonardo, knowing that Scolastica had wanted me to stand up and accept the possibilities offered me. When her funeral ended, I slipped away down the streets with Sancha while Bernardo lingered to talk with the Medici in the customary discourse about the beauty of a church service after it was concluded.

The studio was in its usual flurry of activity. The great furnace was roaring as it baked Giuliano's bust. Verrocchio stood in front of the flames, timing the cooking of his masterpiece.

"Good afternoon, maestro," I called out as I approached.

Verrocchio turned, and I had to stifle my laugh upon seeing his face. It was as red as the baking terra-cotta, awash in sweat and grime. Sancha, however, did not curb her amusement.

"My lady!" Verrocchio wiped his face with his billowing sleeve, leaving a smear of black soot on the white linen. "Forgive my appearance." He waved at the furnace. "Today we complete the Medici bust." His gaze darted from me to the fire and back again. "I am sorry, I . . ."

"It's all right, maestro. I can see you need to watch your kiln. I just thought I might speak with you about scheduling sittings for the portraits. I can return another day."

"No, no, my lady," he hastened to say. "Leonardo is inside, working on his Madonna and child. You two could discuss the painting he plans." He grinned. "Leonardo must plan a great deal to be able to create something as lovely as the sculpture I envision of you."

His jovial competitiveness was such an antidote to my sorrow. I felt myself revive. Verrocchio clapped his hands to get one of the apprentices' attention. "Paolo, take the signora to Leonardo."

Inside, Leonardo leaned over a large sketch attached to a gessoed wooden board. He had stabbed pinpricks all along the outline of the drawing and held a small cloth bag of charcoal dust, poised to pat it along the pinpricks. It would leave a powdery trail, the skeleton of his painting-to-be. On the paper, I could see a beautiful Mary with great twists of braids and curls like the joust banner's nymph. She held a carnation to a wiggly, fat Christ child, who reached out for the blossom.

It was such a lively, endearing image, aglow with Mary's obvious enjoyment of showing a blossom to a delighted baby, I spoke without waiting for Leonardo to notice me standing there. "Ah, maestro, what a sweet portrait of Mary's love for her child!"

Leonardo dropped the bag, making a splat of black dust on his drawing.

"I am so sorry!" I cried as he grimaced and blew on the dust to scatter it away. Would I ever manage to encounter him without doing something to make our meeting awkward?

After a few moments of blowing and wiping, Leonardo straightened up. I could tell he was planning a formal greeting, but when he looked at me, he blurted out instead, "Is that what you plan to wear for your portrait?" His eyes traveled from my feet, up my dress, lingering at my waist and my bodice before rising to my face.

"Oh, no," I said.

Leonardo stepped toward me and bowed to catch the end of my scapular, which reached to my knee. Lifting the cloth, his face was quizzical.

"My abbess gave it me to signify my being a laysister of the order. It allows me access to the convent when I desire its serenity. It was a great gift and honor she did me," I said, choking on the last sentence. "She was a magnificent lady. Most of what I am I owe to her."

He fingered the edge of the scapular. "I have never seen this before. It is very . . . somber."

"Yes, it is. Do not worry. I will not be wearing this for my portrait."

He let it go, and the velvety black scarf dropped back down to rest along my dress. "Why not, my lady," Leonardo asked, "if it is a marker of something that is important to you?"

I paused, taking in that concept: *important to me.* "Well," I said slowly, "it would cover the lily pattern of the scarlet brocade gown my husband wishes me to wear and certainly would distract from my trousseau necklace of gold and pearl." The outfit would be a beautiful combination of riches, fit for a duchess.

Humph. Leonardo snorted, still assessing my face, considering something. He was careful when he spoke again. "It is not for me to say, signora, but as I look at you in this attire, I think the finery you describe would overtake your portrait and distract from your"—he paused—"your lovely face. It is quite open and uninhibited."

"Hah, you are one of the first to think my inability to mask my emotions a good thing," I said. But I blushed at the compliment.

"And that, there." He pointed at my cheek and spoke with a hushed voice. "That is a lovely quality, so natural. As I said before, I want to capture that coloring. But I would also like to convey that intense reaction of yours to the world, your steadfast curiosity and openness." His eyes met mine. "The two together would be proof of painting's superiority."

I laughed self-consciously. "I am glad my annoying tendency to turn red will be useful to you, maestro!" Surely he would take my cue and keep to more general dialogue.

But Leonardo could not stop being an artist. His eyes drifted down from my face to linger on the cut and color of the dress's bodice. "Yes," he murmured, talking more to himself than to me. "The blue ribbon threading the bodice together is just the hue of the afternoon sky. Mmmmm. That and the deep brown of the dress will be a wonderful echoing of the natural hues of the landscape backdrop I am planning." He seemed pleased with himself.

He stared at my bosom. Although mortified, I also found myself proud of my new womanly figure as he did so. I was more aghast at the idea of not being bejeweled for the portrait. Not to present the riches of my trousseau—the clothing that still marked me as a Benci and tied my identity to my father and his success, financially and intellectually. Not to represent the social status, or the trade, of my husband. This dress was the simplest of wool, dyed the dullest of brown *monachino*, the color of monks' robes. "But—but—signor, even your Madonna there seems to wear a sumptuous dress and a large brooch at her breast."

"Yes, she must wear such," he said, "because she is a Medici Madonna."

I looked at the sketch and realized the gemstone and its setting resembled jewelry Simonetta had worn at the joust. Leonardo including that brooch would identify whom this particular Virgin Mary was inspired by and who commissioned it.

Leonardo still gazed at me, now focusing on my neckline. "The stitching on your dress is also splendid, so fine. Its gold thread matches the lighter strands in your hair. It is perfect. Simplicity provides the highest sophistication, the greatest elegance, after all. Your attire will be the perfect framing of you, so that the viewer focuses on what your face can tell us about your inner being rather than tallying the costs of your finery or speculating as to your family's wealth."

I was relieved that he finally had said something I could respond to rather than continuing to sit, annoyed with myself for being atremble with a disquiet that his incessant gaze produced in me.

"Do you realize, Maestro Leonardo, that what you just described is the perfect representation of me as the Platonic love of the painting's commissioner? If indeed my outward self represents inner virtues that are to inspire others to a more godly life? The ambassador must have described the philosophy to you?"

"No," Leonardo said. "Besides, I find it foolishness, this idea that a rose is merely a momentary expression of the absolute truth of beauty that we can only recognize through contemplation. I believe reality is rooted right here on earth, in nature. I also believe we come to understand our universe through active observation brought through our senses, not praying or meditating. It's our senses that allow us to watch and hear and feel and then comprehend the processes behind the phenomenon of light, water, a body's movement, a bird's flight, or"—he paused and gestured toward me—"the blush of a woman's face."

I stared at him. "You express Aristotle's philosophies, maestro. Have you read his translated works?"

"I cannot really read Latin, my lady. I was never taught and am trying to learn it a little at a time now. However, Master Verrocchio can and has told me some of these philosophies. Even so, I find experience to be a truer guide than the words of others."

His intellect was extraordinary given his lack of formal book learning. I mulled over his suggestion. Leonardo already planned an unprecedented setting for this portrait—a woman sitting outside her home, encased in the uncontrollable power of nature. His suggestion for my clothes would push my portrait even further beyond tradition. In such a dress I would be stripped down to my basics, the bare-boned facts of my face and thereby, as he called it, the motions of my mind, my heart, my soul. That certainly would be new to Florence's high society.

I weighed the consequences of such a portrait. Wearing the black scapular and a dress whose only adornment was the embroidery I had done with gold thread spun at Le Murate would allow me to pay homage to my beloved abbess and the world of learning and creativity she had fostered for women within the convent's walls.

Sing of us. Sing of yourself.

"All right," I said. "So be it."

17

"Ouch!" I yelped the next day. "Oh please, Sancha, rest a moment."

She had been plucking my hairline to give me the appearance of a high forehead, a mark of intelligence in Florence. Many a woman was tortured this way with tweezers when God had not thus endowed her—especially for important occasions and portraits.

Flopping onto the edge of my bed as I rubbed my head to sooth the sting, Sancha eyed the clothing she'd spread out for me to put on for my sitting. "I think you have gone mad, my lady. This is a dress my mother might wear!"

Her face puckered with disapproval at my brown dress.

"Why would you choose such a garment, when you have this?" She reached for the rich red dress punctuated with a delicately loomed pattern of white lilies. It rustled and shimmered as she lifted it, and the sunlight played along its different weft and weave. Indeed, the dress was its own work of art. And its detachable sleeves! They were even more beauteous, a midnight-blue velvet, embroidered from wrist to shoulder with one full-bloom lily in pearls and gold thread and tied to the dress with long silk ribbons of red, gold, and white.

Looking at the dress that morning, I wondered myself if I was insane. I had agreed to the simple brown frock, mesmerized by Leonardo's glowing enthusiasm. Away from him, it seemed a foolishly Spartan choice, perhaps even disrespectful of my station and my husband. I did look so pretty in that red dress. But I had said yes. I would not be some simpering, foolish woman and back away from a promise.

"It will be all right, Sancha. A magnificent dress would distract from what Leona—the maestro—wishes to accomplish. He wants to focus not on the details of luxurious clothes or jewels, but instead on what my face says about my soul, my inner thoughts."

Sancha frowned. "I don't know about you, my lady, but I have plenty of thoughts I prefer no one know about. I would think twice about inviting people into my head."

I laughed. "But Sancha, it is such a good head you have upon your shoulders. I am grateful for its wisdom."

That brought back her protective smile. "Well, my lady, I do not agree with you, but I will defend you like a mare would her colt if asked about it." She lowered her voice to a fond teasing. "And I will respect what you decide with Leona—oh!" She held her hand to her mouth and fluttered her eyes like a courtesan. "I mean . . . the maestro." She grinned at me.

"I—I—what do you mean by that?"

"Oh, nothing." She was still amused with herself. But then she quieted. "The ambassador is another matter. There is something about him. It's clear he has his own plans about you. You know that?"

I, too, sobered. Bernardo was a disquieting, alluring mystery to me thus far. All I knew for certain was that this portrait would solidify his friendship with the Medici, just as a hunting party brought men fellowship. And that he was a gambling man, of what degree Sancha had not been able to determine from her sources of gossip.

"What will you tell your husband about your dress?" she asked.

That I did know. I had lain awake all night planning my reasoning. "I will say it is a perfect way to draw attention to the beauty of simple wool, the mainstay of Florence's trade and his shop."

Sancha snorted. "Godspeed with that, my lady."

But that conversation went better at breakfast than either Sancha or I had anticipated. Luigi seemed flattered by my concern for the state of his beloved wool trade. I actually felt a twinge of guilt as he nodded and thought over my justification for the plain brown dress. It was the first time I had sought to convince him of something by using an argument I had fashioned and that suited needs of my own that I did not reveal. It felt disingenuous.

Luigi popped a fat sausage into his mouth and chewed loudly. "In truth, wife"—he splattered sausage as he talked—"there are sumptuary laws being passed that might make your choice of modest brown better politically for me. I sense a growing discomfort among magistrates with the grandeur of display by Florence's wealthiest. There is a law prescribing the number of buttons women may have on their dresses. Buttons!" He shook his head. "A woman is now allowed only twenty-two gilded silver buttons on her everyday gown. As if buttons were the sin that led to Satan. Plus, legislators just passed an edict prohibiting fur trim except on state occasions and special events like weddings. The *tamburi* boxes are stuffed to the brim with accusations of vice and sexual misconduct."

He wiped his mouth with the back of his hand. "Hopefully this mood is temporary. And certainly there are ways to get around all this if one knows how." He paused and considered for a moment. "But perhaps it would be wise for me and my brothers to display a godly reserve in our cloth business and to emphasize how rich one can look even in the simplest gown—if it is made of the finest-quality material."

And so later that day, I sat in the afternoon sun while Leonardo sketched me. For almost an hour there was no sound save the scratch of his drawing, the song of a chaffinch, and the flirtatious laughter of Sancha and an apprentice in the front courtyard. And then Bernardo, the handsome master of grand entrances, stood in the archway of the studio's inner garden, his voice booming into the quietude like a cannon. "*Carissima!*"

Leonardo startled and looked toward the door with annoyance.

Bernardo's arms were filled with dog-rose blossoms. He swept in and knelt by my feet. "My Bencina," he crooned. "How lovely you are. I have brought blooms for you, my own flower."

He held the thatch of pink blooms toward me. As I gathered them up, a thorn stabbed me. "Oh, ouch," I squeaked.

A little teardrop of blood glistened on my thumb. Before I could move, Bernardo clasped my injured hand to wipe away the blood, turning my thumb upward to make sure no more blood would form. Then he kissed it, holding his lips to my flesh for one, two, three, four, five spellbinding seconds before looking up into my face. "There now," he said, his voice warm, his eyes caressing, "all better."

I knew I should withdraw my hand from his. But I was frozen, enthralled by Bernardo's smile. When I finally made myself slide it out of his grasp, I lifted my hand to my heart and cradled the bouquet of roses close to my chest with my other arm.

"Oh my, look at that, Leonardo. What a picture."

I glanced up and realized that Verrocchio had entered

behind Bernardo and now stood beside his former apprentice. He beamed.

"Forgive me, my lady, but if I may . . ." Verrocchio slowly circled me. Bernardo rose from his knees and stepped back to allow Verrocchio to study me from every angle. Verrocchio stopped, frowned, stuck out his lower lip in thought, and then circled me again in the opposite direction.

He looked to Bernardo. "Your Excellency, I have always believed that hands and gestures, the movement of a body, suggest a person's emotions. I have been able to do that with my narrative sculpture." He pointed across the studio toward an enormous wax figure, still being formed for bronze casting. "I am creating a sculpture of Doubting Thomas. He will be stepping forward, his hand extended to touch the wounds of the risen Christ. I believe his gesture will convey Thomas seeking proof and help the viewer feel his crisis of faith.

"Portrait sculpture, on the other hand, has always stopped with the shoulders. It does not allow such expressiveness. With your permission, I would like to sculpt Donna Ginevra from the waist up, with flowers, so that we see her lovely hands and how she cradles the blossoms with such tenderness. If I can re-create the sense that she has just plucked the flowers from a field she is walking in . . . Well"—he nodded as he spoke, more to himself than to anyone in the studio—"that motion would say so much about her *leggiadria*, her inner harmony and grace. And certainly it can hint at her *vaghezza*, that powerful attraction a woman has on a man's soul."

"Magnificent!" Bernardo clapped his hands together. "I have not seen anything like that before."

"No, indeed not, Your Excellency. I believe it will be the first portrait sculpture of its kind in our great city of Florence." Verrocchio smiled with palpable pride. "Thanks to your beneficence. But"—he reined in his enthusiasm—"I will need a much larger piece of stone to carve such a statue, my lord. It might double the cost of the marble."

"*Psssssh*." Bernardo waved his hand impatiently. "No matter. Find the best and purest slab of marble in all of Tuscany. If I must, I will borrow the money!"

18

"Read that to me again, sister." Giovanni leaned back in his chair and put his hands behind his head.

For about the hundredth time, I unfolded Bernardo's letter. Inside was a poem he had commissioned from Lorenzo's old tutor and friend, Cristoforo Landino.

> "And so I shall play with Bembo's chaste affections,
> so that Bencia will rise up, made famous by my verses.
> Beautiful Bencia, Bembo marvels at your loveliness,
> which would overcome the heavenly goddesses',
> which great Mars could prefer to Venus's love . . ."

I looked up at Giovanni and smiled with embarrassment.

"Well, well, sister. Mars could prefer you to Venus? Are you ready to make . . . war?"

"Shut up!" I laughed.

He grinned. "Keep going. It is a beautifully turned verse."

"But he, awestruck, marvels more at your modest heart,
your old-fashioned virtue, and your Palladian hands.
He is inflamed with holy love, and the infections
of foul extravagance are not able to touch him.".

I sighed heavily, with rapture.

To have such a poem written to me and about me by one of Florence's most renowned poets was like being fed ambrosia. Poetry, after all, was my greatest passion.

"Wait. He is inflamed with a holy love?" Giovanni sat up abruptly. "Ginevra, my dear . . . you know Bernardo Bembo is rumored to have fathered at least one bastard child back in Venice?"

I felt my happiness falter. "No, brother, I did not know that."

"He has been ambassador to many nations. He has traveled a great deal. He surely has known many women." Seeing my disappointment, he softened that news. "But none as exquisite or fascinating as you, sweet sister. I do not doubt that he is besotted with your beauty and your soul. All of Florence should be."

I brightened. "With the right inspiration, men can reform their ways."

"Yes," he said cautiously, "*some* men."

"His Platonic love for me could better him. If the rumor you've heard is even true. It might be that some idiot has invented the tale to heighten Bernardo's reputation for virility and sport to impress a certain type of man. Besides, all the ambassador desires from me is inspiration, to be his muse. Here, listen to this as proof:

"And so, noble Bencia, having mastered such conduct,
you arrive as a role model for Tuscan maidens.
I admit Paris's love and madness for Helen is famous . . .
But now, Bencia, you are more beautiful than Helen, and
your rare modesty makes you famous the whole world over."

I looked up from the paper with pride. "Think of how many times Uncle Bartolomeo berated me and derided the joy I find in books and learned conversation, my shunning of superficial flirtations. Here is a worldly man who lauds those qualities." I smiled at my brother. "You of all people, Giovanni, must understand how this lifts my heart. Do not spoil my newfound happiness."

There was a knock on the door of Giovanni's suite. He rose to answer it, kissing me on top of my head as he passed. "How can I argue with a lady who is famous the world over and lovelier than Helen of Troy, whose beauty was so stunning it sparked a war?"

I laughed, my good humor restored.

It was Leonardo. Verrocchio's studio was crowded with work as he prepared to cast the Christ figure in his statue of St. Thomas's doubting. To get away from that fray, Leonardo had asked to paint my portrait at my home. But the light was poor in my narrow row house. Indebted to Leonardo for spotting the caltrop spikes at the *palio*, Giovanni offered a corner of his rooms in our childhood palazzo. I was to sit in the light of a second-story window facing into our center courtyard, where afternoon sun was gentle and rose-gold.

"Good day, signora," Leonardo greeted me. "How is your Zephyrus, signor?" he asked Giovanni.

"Full of himself! Especially since winning St. John's *palio*. He seems to believe his own legend now. I hope to enter him in Siena's race."

They continued to chat about horses as Leonardo set up to paint. He had brought with him a board of poplar, sanded smooth and prepared with gesso. He unrolled the sketch cartoon he had already pinpricked. He would pounce the outline onto the board and begin painting after he mixed his colors.

"Mind if I stay?" Giovanni asked. "I have never seen a painting being created before."

"Of course, signor. Although it will not be interesting for a long while. Your sister's image will be revealed slowly, layer upon layer."

"Well then, maestro, you will have need of my company. My sister is not a patient lady."

"Giovanni!" If my eyes could throw daggers, my older brother would have been bleeding all over.

But Leonardo laughed. "I think impatience is the mother of stupidity. But I am often guilty of it myself. It is the bedevilment of an inquisitive mind."

I smiled and nodded. "Indeed, maestro."

Leonardo approached me, carrying a single dog rose. "Please hold this in your hand." Taking my right hand, he lifted it and placed the sprig between my thumb and forefinger in front of my bodice, just as Verrocchio had me cradling flowers in his sculpture. He fussed for a few minutes to settle my hands the way he wanted them, his hand brushing against my breast several times. Leonardo seemed oblivious, his focus solely on getting the pose of my hands correct. I, however, cringed self-consciously, and my face flamed red.

God love my brother. He knew me well and saved me with joking, "Ah yes, we must not forget to feature those Palladian hands!"

Leonardo straightened up and turned to Giovanni. "Palladian hands?"

"One of her many lovely qualities eulogized in a poem written by Landino. The ambassador commissioned it. According to him, my sister is the model of modesty for all Tuscan maids!" Giovanni's voice was full of playful affection. I relaxed.

Leonardo studied us for a moment. "I would have liked to enjoy the company of a sister," he said.

"Good Lord, you can take some of ours then, can't he, Ginevra? We have a plethora, signor. Four more sisters to find marriages for! Plus a household of cousins."

But I heard the longing for family in Leonardo's voice. "Do you not have siblings, maestro?"

"Well, as you may know, my father did not marry my mother after siring me. I lived with his parents before coming here to Florence. My father is on his third wife now and has yet to produce a child other than me—although I hear she might be pregnant. Perhaps he should have married my mother after all! She has had five children by the man she wed after my father rejected her. She still lives in Vinci, but I was not allowed to really know my half siblings."

"Then you must spend time with us," Giovanni said. "I will call you Leonardo from now on, as you will be a friend and part of the family. We have children and joyful noise aplenty here! Rarely is there a quiet moment."

As if on cue, a servant knocked on the door loudly. "You see?" Giovanni laughed and hurried to take what the man held.

It was another poem by Landino, sent from Bernardo.

"Oh, give it to me, brother," I pleaded, exasperated to be frozen dutifully in the pose Leonardo had set.

"No, no, you must remain positioned. I will read it to you. Hearing it might inspire Leonardo's work as well." He skimmed the page before beginning. "Oh my, sister, hark you this.

"But if you should behold Ginevra's neck and shoulders,
by right, you will despise the shining snow.
Purple flowers beam in springtime,
but they are nothing compared to your mistress's pretty lips.
What shall I say about Bencia's fair forehead and her ivory
* white teeth,*
and her dark eyes above her rosy cheeks?"

He looked up at me, absolutely delighted. "There is more, something about your countenance being a mixture of lilies and roses. Shall I?"

"No!" I exclaimed. At that, I could no longer sit still. I stood and tried to snatch the paper from him. Laughing, Giovanni pulled it from my reach and held it high above his head. I jumped up and down trying to grab it until he hugged me and swung me around. "Peace, sister. It is a sweet poem for a sweet lady. Here." He handed it to me and put his arm around my shoulders.

Looking to Leonardo, he kept the moment jovial. "It is a marvelous thing to be immortalized so, is it not?"

Leonardo answered in similar good nature. "Yet I will do it better in painting than this poem does!"

I laughed, enjoying the banter. "Nothing is better than poetry, signor."

"Nothing? Are you sure? A poet cannot do with the pen what the painter can with his brush." Leonardo went back to mixing his colors as he spoke. "The poet addresses the ear, while the painter engages the eye. The eye is the nobler sense. It is as simple as comparing a puppet that has been torn apart and lies in pieces to a fully united body. A poet can only describe a human figure bit by bit, consecutively, and using a great many words. Neck, shoulders, lips, brow, teeth, eyes. That's how Master Landino's poem goes—only one thing at a time. While a painter"—his voice swelled deeper and louder as he spoke—"a painter can present all parts of a being simultaneously, as a whole. It is far less tedious than poetry."

My mouth popped open in indignation. "Tedious? You know, signor, that I am a poet? Well . . . I write poetry."

"You need not extend your modesty that way, sister. You are indeed a poet," Giovanni said, "and a gifted one."

Leonardo looked at me matter-of-factly, one hand holding a pot of resin, the other a pot of walnut oil. "Yes, I know you are a poet."

"Did you mean to insult me?"

"No." He shook his head. "Simply stating a truth."

I stared at him.

"I think people should be honest with one another," he said. "I do like word games and puns. But in conversation, you can trust me to never say anything false—neither honeyed to seduce you nor critical solely for the purpose of hurting or manipulating you. Unlike many, I find no thrill in deceiving someone or getting away with a secret. I do not believe in such sport. I simply say what I mean."

I could see in his eyes that he was sincere. I started to quip that dealing with a completely honest man would be a novelty. But the jest stuck in my throat—his pledge held such promise, such freedom and such safety at the same time, a glorious paradox.

He kept staring at me. And I did not turn away.

Giovanni laughed. "Watch out, Leonardo. She always beat me in staring contests when we were children. I swear the girl never blinked. She was like a house cat watching a bird."

But neither I nor Leonardo responded to him. I couldn't. I was transfixed.

"Do you believe eyes are the window to the soul?" Leonardo asked in a hushed voice. "Yes, your physical features—those pretty lips, fair forehead, and ivory teeth, as the poet writes—are beautiful. But it is the eyes that let one into that sanctum, into a person's essence."

Indeed, pulled in by those enormous, luminous eyes of his, I felt myself teetering at a threshold to something wondrous and disturbing. I did not break my gaze but still kept my foothold on safe terrain—books. "Cicero said something like that. And the Bible implies the same."

A glimmer of irritated disappointment clouded his face. "I know it from my own observation. Have you ever risked witnessing something yourself?" he challenged. "Not just read about it in a book?"

Still we stared. Now I burned with defiance.

"Yes, I have observed it, not just been convinced by someone else's writing," I snapped. And to prove it, guessing what Leonardo might hope from me, I answered before he asked to show my courage. "And yes."

"Yes, what?"

"When I was at the Palazzo Medici, I observed a Flemish portrait Lorenzo had procured, in which a woman was not in profile but instead gazed out in a . . . mmm . . . three-quarter pose." I turned my left shoulder back a bit so my torso shifted slightly but my gaze on him remained steady. "Like this."

"I have seen that portrait as well," he said. "But even then she is not looking directly at the viewer. She looks away to the side." A smile spread slowly upon Leonardo's handsome face. "Verrocchio's sculpture will have you posed as if the viewer has interrupted as you gather blossoms, and you turn to look at him—in reaction, in a kind of conversation. If you direct your gaze forward for my painting, you will become a living presence, not just"—he paused, searching for the right word—"a symbol, or an object. Signora, are you suggesting that . . . ?"

I nodded.

If that Flemish woman could turn outward, I could certainly dare to. And I could go one step further. I, the poet. I, the pronounced model for Tuscan maidens. I, the Platonic muse of an ambassador from one of the most powerful city-states in Europe. I, the educated protégée of a woman who changed her name to Scolastica and liberated the minds of cloistered women. I, who had the chance to make men listen—and see—what women had in their hearts and minds.

As a bird in a gilded cage, singing? No, too limiting. A house cat watching a bird? No, too domesticated. I wanted a different, larger metaphor for myself. I searched my mind.

Ahhhh. Rather I would look out and demand a return gaze like the Caspian tiger Bernardo had described, brought to the Venetian court by a sultan. My eyes would gaze unblinking to allow people to look into them and wonder about me. I, a mountain tiger, like the one that showed no fear when hunted, whose fierce dignity prompted imaginings about her soul and her courage—a creature with her own past and own story.

"Yes," I spoke once more, smiling with a strange new confidence.

Leonardo clapped his hands together as if to break our trance. He could barely contain his excitement. "Please sit, then, Ginevra de' Benci. I must sketch you anew!"

19

Il dado è tratto—A SAYING FROM CAESAR WHEN HE REBELLED against the Roman Senate—kept repeating in my mind. *Our die was set.* We had, like Caesar, crossed the Rubicon. There was no turning back in my insurrection with Leonardo. The fall and winter passed in a whirl of work, with a heady sense of doing something daring, forbidden even, something entirely new.

Oh, we were so full of ourselves. We laughed. We debated. I tried to convince him of Plato's metaphysical philosophies. He countered with his careful observations of the tangible world—the power of swirling water, for instance. "You know, I have found the remains of seashells up in the hills. I cannot help but think the seas were once much higher and then slowly receded, leaving them there," Leonardo said.

"Yes, in Noah's flood," I said.

"You don't believe the seas could carve mountains and leave behind its skeletons in a mere forty days and forty nights, do you?"

I opened my mouth to respond but closed it again without saying anything. I hadn't thought to question the biblical story before. He rattled my church teachings again when I patted the curls framing my face to make sure they covered my ears.

When he reminded me to sit still and asked what I was fussing over, I explained that Sister Margaret had admonished me to always keep curls covering my ears, since the Virgin Mary was impregnated with baby Jesus when the Holy Spirit spoke in her ear. Leonardo looked at me with such bemusement I had to laugh. Maybe our Holy Mother could conceive through her ear, but a normal woman would not!

Leonardo was full of such challenges and surprises. Constantly trying to expand his knowledge, he kept lists of words he wanted to add to his vocabulary. He had even recorded two dozen synonyms for a man's private parts. "Want to hear a really funny one?" he asked me one afternoon as he mixed his paints.

Taken aback, I frowned, unsure what to say. A virtuous woman would never admit being curious about such things. But of course, I did want to hear, particularly since he seemed so amused by it.

He smiled mischievously and told me.

As for me, I recognized that I could feed that intellectual hunger of his, at least in sharing knowledge I had gained from my reading. A few weeks into his painting, I asked, "Maestro, I know you struggle to read Latin. But do you know the content of Ovid's *Metamorphoses*?"

He put the brush he was using between his teeth and picked up another to put a dab of contrasting color to the panel. "No," he mumbled.

"Ovid opens with the line: '*In nova fert animus . . .*'" I quickly realized my rudeness in quoting a language Leonardo did not understand. "Ovid begins," I corrected myself, "with 'I will speak of forms changed into new entities.'"

Leonardo peered around the propped-up board so I could see his face. Slurring around the brush in his mouth, he said, "Like we are doing right now! Tell me more. It suits our work."

Precisely the reason I had brought it up. So I shared the legends Ovid recounted in his long poem tracing the evolution of man. I repeated Ovid's tales of human foibles like Narcissus's destructive self-infatuation and Julius Caesar's tragic fall from power because of his hubris.

All the while, Leonardo grunted and nodded. He was particularly taken with the story of Pygmalion, a Greek sculptor who carved a beauteous female figure out of ivory. "Ovid says Pygmalion was so put off by the prostitutes of his city that he foreswore mortal women and fell in love with the statue he was creating, its purity of spirit. He sighed and longed for his statue to become real. Upon hearing this, Venus took pity on him. One night he kissed the statue's lips, and they felt warm. He touched her breast and it softened from ivory to flesh under his hand. He embraced her waist and the figure melded to him." I stopped abruptly, realizing Leonardo had ceased painting and was staring at me.

"Go on." His voice was raspy.

"With his caresses, she became mortal. They loved. And had a child." I stumbled over my words, suddenly embarrassed, feeling a tugging at my heart and, well, elsewhere.

Leonardo seemed to shake himself and disappeared back behind the panel and into his painting.

Some days we were mostly silent, as Leonardo struggled to work with the oil paint. He and Verrocchio's other apprentices were well schooled in tempera. But Leonardo was one of the first in Florence to attempt using the oils preferred by northern painters in Flanders. Oil paints did provide subtler, more varied, and translucent tones but were difficult to mix evenly and to spread with the brush.

A few afternoons, he threw away his paints with a curse, as they ran or hardened on his palette. He apologized repeatedly about the smell. Eventually, he determined that the best recipe was combining one part oil with two parts turpentine, then stirring in the powdered color pigment. He continued to experiment with which oils to use—nut, linseed, balsam, or mustard seed.

Thus, he built my portrait, brushstroke upon brushstroke,

color upon color, layer upon layer. He re-created the blush on my cheeks by blending rose hues with violet, the highlights of my hair with browns, golds, and whites. Several times, he had not waited long enough for the undercoat to dry before applying the next. The paint bubbled, wrinkling the surface, because the top layer dried faster being exposed to the air. Sometimes Leonardo used his fingertips to flatten the surface and better blend the two layers of color.

He also found early evening light better illuminated the natural colors of my face and hair. "See," he said to Giovanni one late afternoon, as my brother watched Leonardo paint, "how much more graceful and sweet her face appears in this gentler sun?"

Always one to bring us back down to earth, Giovanni squinted in my direction. "Sweet?" He frowned. "If you say so, Leonardo!"

We all laughed.

Of course, Bernardo visited often. He and Leonardo discussed the portrait's composition and the choices Leonardo made as he painted. Bernardo approved Leonardo's decision to place me in front of a juniper bush *ginepro*, and to include the hint of a limpid pond, a distant town and hills beyond. Bernardo had described his own country villa near Padua, and Leonardo created a landscape that echoed Bernardo's memories. They seemed to connect well over their enjoyment of nature and horses.

Of the juniper, Bernardo had exclaimed, "Ah, *perfetto!*

The *ginepro* is a well-known symbol of chastity. It will heighten the statement of your virtue, *carissima*."

"Its emerald foliage will also create a lush halo of green behind her head, Your Excellency, and provide a color contrast that will accentuate the gold of her hair and the paleness of her face," Leonardo said.

"Of course, of course. Your eye is as keen as a falcon's, maestro," Bernardo said. "The combination of colors will be extraordinary. And the placement of her in such a magnificent natural landscape . . ." Bernardo turned his attention to me. "It will make you, and all of us, immortal, my dear."

I smiled. "That is thanks to you, my lord."

"Is she not a sweet, pretty, gracious little thing, maestro?" Bernardo asked. He kissed my hand.

I had learned that when Leonardo did not like a statement or a question he simply did not address it. And that is what he did now. "You'll note, Your Excellency, that the *ginepro* is also a pun on her name, a way of identifying Ginevra de' Benci for all eternity, as long as my painting survives."

"Indeed! Meaning upon meaning!" Bernardo beamed in appreciation. He circled the painting. "I have intended to ask you, maestro, how you will identify my patronage of your work? Master Verrocchio's sculpture will feature my beloved holding the rose bouquet I brought her, which conveniently is the blossom contained in my coat of arms. But what shall we do with your painting?"

Leonardo hesitated. His silence told me the thought of marking Bernardo's ownership of my image had not occurred to him before. After all, the portrait he and I had conceived was intended to show me as my own being. Leonardo also had a rather large ego about his work being unique and better than that of his Florentine brother artisans and, therefore, immune to outside suggestion. Sharing credit for his ideas was not something he would do readily. This was a man who told me he wrote his thoughts and observations in backward script so that they could only be read in a mirror reflection—his way of preventing others from stealing his insights or designs. And despite Verrocchio's teasing, Leonardo foolishly remained unconcerned with the niceties necessary to placate patrons and generate income from his art.

Bernardo's face clouded.

I didn't want Bernardo disappointed. But I also felt protective of Leonardo, not wanting one of his first patrons to find him lacking in deference or ideas. Such a reputation would discourage wealthy Florentines from giving him commissions in a city well stocked with thirty talented and more compliant master painters as well as fifty marble workshops with hungry workers to feed.

I spoke up hastily. "We have been discussing that, my lord."

"Ah, and what have you discussed, my Bencina? Something poetic, I am sure." Bernardo knelt and took my hand. "Perhaps you should hold one of my books, adding to our celebration of your exquisite mind. No, no"—he shifted his thoughts—"that would not do it clearly enough. You have books of your own." He paused. "Perhaps the backdrop should be changed to the sea with a Venetian ship on it. Yes, that would do. The sea and a ship."

I looked over Bernardo's shoulder at Leonardo, whose face contorted with aggravation—I knew he was already halfway through painting the landscape he had envisioned.

I turned back to Bernardo, whose lips were dangerously close to mine suddenly. "The ship can be sailing toward you, my dear," he whispered, drawing even closer so I felt his breath on my mouth, "its beloved harbor."

I caught his meaning of a ship putting into port. It was an uncharacteristically obvious wordplay to make in front of someone else. Shaken, I stood. "I think a sailing ship a bit too . . . too . . . nautical a theme, my lord."

Bernardo sat back on his heels, chuckling.

My mind raced, trying to come up with a viable alternative. "Oh! What about the verso? Something on the back of my portrait." Leonardo's relieved smile steadied me. "Yes, that's it. An emblem on the back. Maybe a winged horse like your Pegasus, my lord."

"Mmmm." Bernardo nodded. "I have seen paintings with a front and back during my ambassadorship to the Burgundian court."

"Perhaps a maiden with a unicorn," Leonardo suggested.

I thought of the sketch Leonardo had done in the meadow the day of the race. That certainly would be a flattering emblem. "Oh, that would be lovely, maestro. How kind of you to suggest such a symbol."

But something about that exchange annoyed Bernardo.

He didn't like the switch of emphasis away from his horse, Pegasus, which would unequivocally mark his commission. But I also sensed he did not like Leonardo picturing me as capable of taming a unicorn—one of our strongest symbols of the power of chastity to overwhelm even wild, magical animals—or that I was so flattered by Leonardo's appraisal of me.

Bernardo stood, crossed his arms, and said rather sternly, "Apt, very apt, for our lovely Bencina. But that says nothing of me, maestro, or the affection between my lady and *me*." For the first time I heard a mean-spirited and condescending tone in Bernardo's voice. "I hope you are able to think of something more specific than that? If not, perhaps I can consult with your master, Maestro Verrocchio."

Leonardo fumed.

Was Bernardo jealous? The situation was souring fast. What to suggest? I paced, definitely not maintaining the self-contained deportment Le Murate had schooled me in. Ah, schooling. I stopped. "Good my lord, let us devise an emblem that signifies both your learning and your generous encouragement of art and literature. Perhaps an emblem you've used or might use in the future, perhaps a stamp in the manuscripts you collect."

Oh, Bernardo was devastatingly handsome when he was pleased.

And so the three of us designed a wreath wrapped with a favorite motto of Bernardo's—*Virtus et Honor*—for the verso. Bernardo suggested the wreath be made of laurel and palm, both symbols of intellectual honor and virtue. I pointed out that the palm was also associated with victory and innocence, triumph over earthly temptation. Bernardo laughed and murmured, "Indeed, my love, indeed. But let us not forget that Apollo, the god of poetry who often wore a crown of laurel, succumbed to passion once or twice." He grinned meaningfully at me.

Leonardo looked back and forth between Bernardo and me. He had the strangest look on his face, a mix of anger and something else. Then he suggested that the background appear to be porphyry, a stone noted for its endurance and resistance to outside elements. "It will symbolize her resolve to remain pure and unsullied."

Sweet Jesu, this was idiocy on Leonardo's part. Was this really concern about my chastity, or simply a rebel's dislike of authority?

Bernardo frowned and eyed Leonardo. His lighthearted humor was gone. He spoke to Leonardo with cold imperiousness. "Finish the emblem with a sprig of the *ginepro* juniper—our symbol for Ginevra—in the wreath's center. Stretch the scroll carrying the motto across the wreath from side to side. But wrap it once around the stem of the juniper in its center, as I would encircle the waist of my beloved to kiss her. Thus."

Bernardo grabbed my waist and reeled me in for a sudden, brusque kiss. Then he let go so abruptly I almost fell backward. It was Leonardo who reached out to steady me.

For a tense moment, the three of us stared at one another,

I in the center of the two men. Bernardo's eyes narrowed as he looked at Leonardo. Then he bowed to me with great ceremony. *"Ciao, bella."* He headed for the door, saying nothing to Leonardo.

"Ambassador?" Leonardo called after him.

"Yes?" Bernardo turned and squared himself with the swagger a younger man might adopt right before throwing a punch. "What is it, signor?" His voice was dismissive.

"There is the matter of payment. Painting the reverse will require more color powder, resin, and oils. It will take more work, more of my time."

Bernardo smirked. "Yes, of course. Craftsmen do require payment." And then he was gone.

20

"SIMONETTA!" I CRIED. "HOW GOOD IT IS TO SEE YOU."

I was sitting for Verrocchio as he began real work on my sculpture portrait. He had already hammered away angular corners of the slab, and now a smooth forehead peeped up over the top of white stone, rounded elbows protruded from the chipped and chisel-scratched sides. As he explained what he would carve away next, Simonetta came in on the arm of Giuliano, there to see the progress on Leonardo's *Madonna of the Carnation.*

Oh, what a terrible difference there was in her from the last time she and I had really talked at length, at the Feast of St. John's *palio,* many months earlier. Then she had been so full of vivacious, playful humor. Now La Bella was still, but pale, her exquisite face grown thin, her enormous amber eyes entrenched in dark circles. She smiled when she saw me, but that was quickly followed by a shaking cough.

Shielding her mouth with a handkerchief, she reached out her other hand. "Dearest Ginevra, come sit with me a moment, while Giuliano speaks with the maestro."

Leonardo was nowhere to be found, so Giuliano went to inspect the painting with Verrocchio. Simonetta and I retreated to a quiet corner in that busy studio and settled down in a thick waterfall of dark- and light-blue skirts. I noticed one of the apprentices stop dead to look at the pretty picture our dresses, and certainly Simonetta, made.

"How are you?" I asked. Simonetta had been ill enough that she had rarely left her home, so I had heard only worried rumors about her. "Your cough?"

"I fear it is phthisis."

"Consumption? Oh no! What can be done?"

Her smile was wan. "They have bled me several times to rebalance my humors. And Giuliano has doctors scouring manuscripts from Hippocrates and Pliny to find some ancient antidote. But"—she shrugged—"my life is in God's hands. I have faith in his mercy and judgment, whether to keep me here or take me to him." She took my hand in her feverish one. "I would rather talk of you. I tire of discussing my illness." She leaned toward me and whispered, "Now tell me all." Her eyes still danced merrily despite the dark shadows under them.

"About?" For her amusement, I smiled mischievously and arched my eyebrow.

"Aha! Then it is true! You blush with love, my dear, and are even more beautiful for it since last we met. How is it with the ambassador? All of Florence is talking about his adoration of you."

"There is talk?"

"Of course! You two are the subject of many dinner conversations at the Medici palazzo, great philosophizing, sighs and dialogue about the power of pure, chaste love, and how beauty and a godly soul can inspire others to find the divine." She leaned closer and whispered in my ear, "And speculation, of course. Particularly among some of the ladies, who would give anything to be so lauded. They are jealous."

"Speculation?" I asked, taken aback. I don't know why the news surprised me, but it did.

"Yes, my dear. What did you expect?" Simonetta patted my hand. "But do not let it bother you. The things people have said about me and Giuliano . . . well . . ." She laughed. "Legend brings good and bad reports, truth and lies. You must learn not to worry over it, now that you are thus elevated."

"I am hardly elevated."

"Oh my, that modesty of yours is so endearing, Ginevra. Not elevated? You have had a painting, a statue, and many poems commissioned about you from some of Florence's most gifted minds and hands. Lorenzo the Magnificent spends hours conversing with your ambassador about Plato's dialogues and Petrarch's sonnets and how they apply to you and Lucrezia Donati. It is quite the bond between them now. So much so that my dear Giuliano grows envious and feels displaced in his brother's affections."

She continued, lowering her voice. "Especially since Lorenzo has made large unsecured loans to your Bernardo Bembo, in part to pay for all the art and poems he is commissioning to celebrate you. Lorenzo listens less and less to Giuliano on matters of business. So yes"—she gave a gentle laugh and then a tiny cough—"you have been much elevated."

Bernardo's propensity for extravagance and now taking on further debt—because of me—was alarming. I started to ask Simonetta what she knew of the loans. I also longed to tell her about my last encounter with Bernardo. It had been so . . . well . . . there was nothing courtly or tender about that kiss in front of Leonardo. It had frightened me. But Simonetta interrupted me by putting her arm through mine and laying her head on my shoulder. "I am so weary," she said. "May I rest here a moment on your soft shoulder?"

Closing her eyes, she shuddered with a suppressed cough. "Tell me of your artist, Ginevra. I only sat for Leonardo da Vinci a few times, but I found him so intriguing. Full of ideas."

I felt a sharp stab of jealousy as I wondered if Leonardo had shared his inner thoughts and dreams with her as freely and eloquently as he had with me. If he had stared at her face and the coloring of her cheek, hung on her stories. Simonetta was far superior in her beauty, her feminine decorum, and her gentleness. He might decide I was a lesser subject. "Did . . .

did he talk a great deal?" I asked.

"Oh, no, my dear, hardly at all."

I sighed with relief, even as I felt an idiot for doing so.

"But when he did open his mouth to speak," Simonetta continued, "I found myself questioning all sorts of things."

At that I laughed. "Indeed, I have had the same experience." I paused. "He has opened my eyes to so many things. Wondrous things. You know, he has such insight into women and our possibilities. It has been quite . . . liberating."

Simonetta tilted her head back a bit to gaze up at me. "Oh my, Ginevra. You must hide that."

"What?"

"That affection."

"But you say it is the talk of the city already."

"Not for the ambassador. I am not talking of that." Simonetta sat up and took my face in her two fragile hands. "For your painter."

I pulled back and frowned. "I have no affection for . . ." But at that moment I realized—with some dismay—that Simonetta might be right.

She nodded sympathetically. "I understand." She nestled back against me. "Despite my love for Giuliano, I have similar feelings for Sandro Botticelli. It is the deepest of romance to have someone study you so closely for hours to find what is noblest in you and then capture it in paint. There is nothing else like it. And yet, my dear, there is nothing to be done beyond that." She sighed. "But that is enough. Enough to cradle to your heart for life."

I was reeling with conflicting thoughts and the recognition of a dangerous, muddying undercurrent in my emotions when one of Verrocchio's apprentices ran into the studio, shouting for him. "Maestro!" The boy turned round in confusion, trying to locate his master. "Maestro, where are you?"

Simonetta sat up, and she and I both pointed within. The agitated apprentice darted inside. "Maestro! Maestro! The *tamburi*!"

I gasped, remembering Leonardo's anger at a man who'd dropped a letter into the box for denunciations, the box known as "the mouth of truth." His fury back then hinted that Leonardo was somehow familiar with the letter's accusations—or perhaps feared it was about him. A letter in that box was usually cause enough to haul a person in front of the dreaded Ufficiali di Notte—the tribunal in charge of purging Florence of what it claimed to be vice and sin.

There was a torrent of worried explanation of something that Simonetta and I could not make out. But then there was a large crashing within as someone threw and then kicked several objects. "God's blood!" Verrocchio shouted. "I warned him to be more careful. The fool!"

Verrocchio appeared looking red-faced and furious, and charged out of the studio without even glancing our way. His anxious apprentice dashed behind to keep pace. Then Giuliano appeared, worry marring his usual jovial handsomeness. "Come, my dear." He gently helped Simonetta to her feet. "I must take you home. And then tend to this trouble."

"What has happened?" she asked.

"It seems my cousin, Leonardo Tornabuoni, has been arrested on charges of sodomy along with three other men— all accused of being Florenzers and corrupting a young goldsmith apprentice. One of those denounced is Leonardo da Vinci."

21

"WHAT HAVE YOU FOUND OUT, SANCHA?" I GRABBED HER
hand to hurry her into the cellar, where we could whisper
without fear of being overheard.

I had been sitting by the window, watching for her
return from Florence's town hall, the Palazzo della Signoria,
where I had sent her to discover whatever she could about
Leonardo's arrest. I'd hidden myself behind a thick curtain,
knowing that exposing myself at a window might really
spark rumors of my heart wandering astray now that there
was gossip about Bernardo and me. Of course, anyone witnessing the mad flurry in which I hurtled down the stairs

once I spotted Sancha might have gossiped that I was a half-wit, possessed by the devil.

"Tell me!" I tugged on Sancha's hand.

"He is lucky, my lady. He will likely be released in a few days. It seems powerful arguments are being made for that. Someone important is pushing to get Leonardo and the other men out fast before too many questions can be put to the group."

I nodded. "That would probably be Lorenzo de' Medici. One of the men arrested includes a Tornabuoni, a cousin from his mother's family."

"Well then, my lady, you probably need not worry," Sancha said. "Unlike common folk, anyone connected to the Medici can usually evade any law."

But would that political favor extend to Leonardo?

"Because one of the group is a nobleman," Sancha continued, "they have all received food and a decent cell. No harsh inquisition." She paused a moment, thinking. "That painter of yours, he is very odd. The jailer told me he refused the meat given them—which no other prisoners are granted, believe me. They live on slop. Anyway, your painter said he ate nothing that had blood in it. Only vegetables and bread." She shook her head in bewilderment. "Imagine."

I frowned. "Tell me of the charges. I don't care about what he ate!"

Even in the gloom of the cellar, I could see Sancha scrutinize me. "I would not let him matter so much to me, if I were you, my lady. I thought him quite pleasing to the eye myself. But—"

"Go on, Sancha." I could tell she had learned something important.

"Well"—she chose her next words carefully—"I think there might be some truth to the charge. I think your painter may prefer the affections of men to women. And once the dye of love sets in the tapestry of a man's soul, it is rarely rewoven. I am sorry if that disappoints you."

I pulled away from her. "It's nothing like that. The man has painted my portrait. He is a very talented artist. I am concerned for his well-being, that he is not hurt or mistreated. That's all. And"—I fished for another plausible reason for my concern—"because he is painting my portrait, his reputation being sullied by an arrest, no matter what it is for, can affect this house's honor as well."

I don't think Sancha believed me for a minute. But she pretended she did and reported the facts she'd sweet-talked out of a guard. The name of the person making the denunciation was secret, of course, but it was likely someone in the neighborhood because of the letter's exact description of streets and houses. It accused Leonardo, the Tornabuoni cousin, a goldsmith, and a doublet maker of consorting with a seventeen-year-old boy named Jacopo Saltarelli. Jacopo lived in a goldsmith shop on the Vacchereccia, in the Santa Croce quarter. "Not far from here," Sancha pointed out.

I noted that it also was not far from Verrocchio's home, which Leonardo still shared with him and other apprentices.

Sancha continued. "Your painter may have used the boy, Jacopo, as a model for his art. My friend says there is a terra-cotta head of Christ as a youth that your painter created that looks very like this Jacopo. So they probably do know each other."

"That is not conclusive of anything, just because the apprentice modeled for Leonardo. I have sat for him myself, you know."

"The boy is reputed to solicit the affection of men, my lady, and to receive gifts and florins in appreciation of his . . . his beauty."

Nodding dumbly, I took it all in. What an idiot I had been to think there was a fledging attraction between Leonardo and me. Why should I care, anyway, when a hand-some ambassador loved me as his Platonic muse and I thrilled to his courtly attentions—it was the stuff of poetry. And yet, I had seen something in Leonardo's eyes the day I told him the Pygmalion story. Something. Our conversations felt as I had always imagined lovemaking would be—moments of delight and surprise, self-affirmation as well as generosity to the other person, an exciting, all-encompassing mutual dance of discovery, an intimacy of the souls.

I tried to shake off my hurt—it was silly, wounded conceitedness on my part. And greed. Yes, greediness that I wanted Leonardo's affections, too. My real worry should be Bernardo, I reprimanded myself, and if Leonardo's arrest would affect his wanting or paying for the portrait. Yes, Leonardo needed that commission, but I also wanted the statement about me, about women, that Leonardo was capturing in my gaze to be completed.

"Thank you, Sancha. I appreciate your finding out those things for me."

She caught my hand as I started back up the stairs to sunlight. "What I am about to warn you of is unlikely, my lady—most charges like this are dismissed with only a small fine of ten florins—but sometimes the punishment for vice is worse. Sometimes homosexual men are burned at the stake, like women are when accused of being witches. Or men are exiled. Or castrated. Or branded to humiliate them."

During dinner, I found it difficult to engage in idle conversation. Luigi wolfed his dinner, as was his wont. He had put on weight since our marriage. I pushed my tench fish round with my knife.

"Are you not going to eat that, wife?" he asked.

Shaking my head, I handed my plate to him. He quickly devoured my portion as I watched silently. When finished, Luigi leaned back in his chair and wiped his face with his napkin, eyeing me. "Today, I was called to the office of the Night Watch."

I looked up at him with surprise. But I had the sense to stay mute to see what he would say.

"A number of us were asked to . . . hmm . . . influence the tribunal on several matters." He stopped. "I have you to thank for that, you know."

My heart pounded. Was he being sarcastic? Was he in

some kind of trouble that was my fault? "How so, husband? For what were you called in?"

"For my opinion and my voice. I was asked for by the Medici family," he said quietly, "in a time they are in . . . need." He chose the last word carefully.

Should I pretend not to know what he was talking about? No. That seemed so false and insulting to him. I waited.

"I have an old friend who serves as one of its officers. So the tribunal heard me out. That will be a favor the Medici will need to return to me someday," he said. "Thank you. Your virtues, which are being so celebrated by the Medici circle, are what made them think to ask me."

I nodded. "Was your opinion . . . helpful?"

"I think so." Luigi clearly saw that I knew precisely what he was referring to. "The denunciation had no signature. Such accusations can be secret but not anonymous. A legal fact the magistrates often ignore, but cannot in the case of a powerful family. So it is likely the charges will be dismissed with the stipulation that they all will be watched in the coming months." He leaned forward and added in a low voice, "The Night Office hires spies and informants. Tell your painter."

I nodded again, grateful for the warning.

Luigi sighed. "The Night Office served a real purpose once. It was started to safeguard the convents, to prevent carousing men from climbing the walls to harass the sisters, or do worse. But then it expanded to all sorts of . . . all sorts of nonsense—like forbidding civic musicians who spread the Signoria's decrees by using herald trumpets from playing within fifty yards of a convent for fear the secular music might corrupt the sisters inside." He rubbed his forehead as if the thought gave him a headache. "Then it built the *tamburi* to encourage citizens to report acts of debauchery. All that's done is to promote slander and eavesdropping. Neighborhood gossip can totally ruin a man, so we must hide—" He stopped short. "Some things should be prosecuted and stopped, but some not. I don't know why private affections should matter to others."

He kept talking, sipping his wine, more in thought than conversation. "Dante's description of the seventh circle of hell in his *Inferno* makes clear what he believes awaits men who act on their love for each other. They are condemned to circle in a burning desert for eternity." He swallowed a large gulp from his cup. "But it is interesting, don't you think, that ancient Greek art and literature praise appreciation of the male figure and the closeness of male friendship?"

I was stunned, not by the Greek philosophy but that Luigi knew of it. I had never seen him pick up a book. "I did not know you read such things."

He smiled wanly. "Oh yes." He looked up at me then. "I suspect there are a great many things we do not yet know of each other, my dear."

I caught my breath. Now I knew. My husband's words told me that he might fit into the category of man Scolastica said used women to hide something, something Luigi could be condemned for by the city's moralizing gossipmongers.

Our cook bustled in to clear the table of dinner. Amid her clattering interruption, Luigi leaned across the table and quietly repeated, "Tell your painter."

Then he clapped his hands and rubbed them together. "What have you for me now, Maria?"

"A fine hazelnut pudding and sugared figs, signor."

"My favorite!" he exclaimed.

I felt my convent school naïveté wiped away just as surely as the cook cleared our table of dishes. But I also recognized in Luigi a new possible category of man to add to Scolastica's list: friend.

22

A WEEK LATER, SANCHA'S INFORMANTS TOLD HER LEONARDO would be released that afternoon. She and I walked to Verrocchio's studio so I could share Luigi's warning of future spying on him. Once we reached its courtyard entrance, I sent Sancha on to the market for vegetables so that I could talk with Leonardo alone, knowing it would be an awkward conversation at best, worsened if Sancha hovered nearby. But he was not there yet.

I was startled to see the studio's bustle had not slowed in Leonardo's absence, and it bothered me that I sensed no anxiety about his situation from his fellow artists. Apprentices still darted about; the walls continued to reverberate with pounding and chipping and shouts. Verrocchio's greeting was merry as ever. "Donna Ginevra! Have you come to see how your beauteous face is emerging from stone?"

I hadn't, but I smiled and said I could hardly wait to see his work. Following him inside, I did marvel at how much progress he had made within a fortnight. Emerging from the marble was a face, still scratched and scarred and not polished smooth, but lovely, its head tilted slightly, the hint of a smile, the hair exactly the way I wore mine. "Oh my, maestro. You have accomplished so much since last I was here."

Verrocchio beamed. "I threw myself into your portrait, my lady. Sometimes when I see a figure emerging under my hand, I cannot stop. I work night and day with the urgency of creating."

He went on, as if speaking to himself. "Work has always been to me what a good sermon is to the faithful. It is my solace, my bread. It is especially true when I am worrying about something. Something I cannot control or change." He paused and shook his head.

Ah, so he was concerned about Leonardo. I put my hand on his arm and smiled.

He patted my hand. "You know, my dear, I cast a statue of David for the Medici. It stands in their Careggi villa. Young Leonardo was its model. Oh, what a beautiful youth he was, graceful limbs, sweet smile. He was so excited to have come to Florence and to be working in this studio. I could barely keep up with his questions." Verrocchio paused. "Have you seen the statue?"

I shook my head. Although my relationship with Bernardo and his with the Medici had taken me to the palazzo several times over recent months, I had not been invited to that inner sanctum, the country villa where the Medici's Platonic Academy gathered to read aloud and discuss literature.

"No? A pity." He looked back to his growing portrait of me. "I must start to tap in the flowers you held." He trailed off. "You know my David does not hold a stone. Nor a slingshot. Try as I might, I just could not put them into that innocent David's hand, despite the biblical story. Of course, my David does grasp a small sword he used to sever the giant's head. And I laid the huge head of Goliath at his feet."

Depicting the youth who saved his people by felling a giant with one rock from his slingshot and not including any stone in his hand was certainly unusual. "Why did you choose to do that, maestro?"

Tears welled up in Verrocchio's eyes. "When I was a youth, I accidently killed a boy with a rock. The incident has been much on my mind the past few days, with Leonardo in prison. Being in prison, even for just a few days, changes a man forever. Especially a young man." He paused before continuing his story. "I have not been able to shake my memory of it. It was so long ago, happening in the heat of a moment. I just wasn't thinking. We were arguing, well, fighting. Young men's passions run too hot for them to control sometimes. But oh, what horrible results can come of them. The incident haunts me still. That boy died in terrible pain. I thought he would duck when I hurled that stone at him. Well . . . perhaps I thought that." He closed his eyes as if recalling the scene.

I had no idea what to say to such a confession. Brawls were commonplace on the streets of Florence. But I had never stood next to someone who had actually taken a life, whether intentionally or by accident. An awkward silence hung between us for several moments before Verrocchio spoke again.

"Ahhh, well. I hope you see my David someday. I would like to hear your opinion. The Magnifico was very taken with the tender youthfulness I was able to capture. But that was easy. It emanated from Leonardo as he posed. Sometimes the dialogue between an artist and his model is so complete, so intense and unfettered a connection, that the artist cannot help but fall in love with his model in some ways. And his model with the artist. We see into each other's hearts. Does that make sense?"

"Yes."

"It is almost a sacred bond, impossible for outsiders to really comprehend or accept." Verrocchio sighed.

"Oh, maestro, I know exactly what you speak of."

"Then you should write a poem about it, signora. Put words to the experience so others can feel it and understand." He pulled himself together abruptly and joked in a blustery manner, "No matter what Leonardo says of poetry being inferior, verse can explain things and inspire readers very well indeed."

Verrocchio waved his hand in the air as if ridding himself

of a fly. "Bah, that Leonardo. What trouble he is. And that Jacopo—*pppffffff*. Certainly not worth the stain an arrest leaves on a man, or his studio. I warned Leonardo to be careful of who his friends are. But he doesn't listen to me. He hung on my every word once, but now?" Verrocchio shrugged. "It is the way of apprentices once they become adults—so full of themselves. Of course, Leonardo is especially so." Even though he frowned as he spoke, concern and affection still laced his words.

"He is to be released today, yes?" I asked.

"Yes, yes. What is the time, my lady?" Verrocchio was suddenly energized. "He is to be released to me, since he still belongs to this studio."

"I heard the noon bell chime on my way here."

"I should go." He held his arm out to escort me to the door.

"Ahhh," I said, stalling, "my servant is not yet returned." I wanted to see Leonardo myself. "May I wait here until she comes back? I am forbidden to walk through the streets on my own."

"Of course, signora, of course!" He led me to a chair. "I hope to be back shortly with our Leonardo. If you are still here at that time, he can show you his portrait. It is nearly complete, just a few last strokes to be done." Verrocchio gestured to a stand that was draped. "Not as good as my sculpture will be, of course." He winked, his jocular humor reclaiming him. He left. Instantly, his apprentices scattered, too, for a bit of adventure during their master's absence.

All alone in the deserted studio, I stared at the covered painting. What temptation! I knew I should wait for Leonardo to
unveil his work, so I forced myself to sit, my foot tapping like
a drummer's baton. But I managed to remain so for only a
minute, if that, before I tiptoed over to the stand. Verrocchio
might be carving a marble image of me, but I was certainly
not made of stone. I could not wait a second longer.

I pulled up the tarp and was peeking underneath when I
heard, "How do you look, *carissima*?"

"Your Excellency!" I dropped the cloth and whirled
around. "What are you doing here?"

Bernardo chuckled. "Come to speak of the commission with the maestro." He approached and took my hand,
bowed, and kissed it.

His touch always sent a shiver through me. "Master Verrocchio is not here right now," I said nervously.

"Fortune smiles on me then." Bernardo stepped closer so
that his booted toes disappeared under my dress's hem. He
drew my hand to his chest, covering his heart with it.

I looked up into his face. So close. He smelled of leather
and cinnamon and jasmine mixed with musk—little of the
garlic and sweat stench that tended to ring other men. His
cheeks carried a few brown spots of age and sun scorching,
but his skin was still drawn taut over fine, prominent bones.
The wrinkles around his sea-blue eyes seemed appealing
brushstrokes of experience, not age, like he had spent many
journeys on the prow of a ship directing its course through

winds and waves. He was the age my father would have been if he were still alive, yet Bernardo's strength and vitality were as palpable and unnerving as a younger man's.

"Ah, that gaze of yours, La Bencina. So steady, so penetrating, so inquisitive. You look right into my soul."

Nervous, I pulled my hand away to clasp both of mine behind my back where he could not reach them. Bernardo might call my gaze steady, but his was making me feel disrobed. "Well, I hope you feel elevated then, my lord," I said, keeping to the Platonic concept that my role was to uplift and inspire his soul to look heavenward.

Bernardo looked surprised and then grinned. Seeing his reaction, I realized how my words could be misinterpreted. "Oh, my lord, I did not mean . . . ," I began. But then I blushed even more because my recognizing the potentially bawdy undertone in my statement indicated I might not be so innocent after all.

I backed up. He stepped forward. I backed again. He followed. Thus, as if in a pavane dance, we circled the painting.

Bernardo laughed. "Ahh, my dear, you do amuse me. You are as skittish as an unbroken horse before being bridled and ridden."

I gasped. Once more, I kicked myself for showing I understood the off-color wordplay. Trapped behind the painting, I took a deep breath and pulled the remaining shreds of my ladylike deportment back around me. "Shall we look at the painting, my lord?"

He hesitated a moment, still smiling, clearly regretting

my return to safe conversation. "Allow me." He lifted the cloth away.

We both caught our breath then. Leonardo had created an image so luminous, so lifelike, it was as if the painted Ginevra could blush and smile. But what really shocked me was the tinge of sadness, the yearning, the questioning, and the defiant invitation in my eyes to return my gaze and step into my mind, my very soul. *God help me,* I thought. How would Florentines react to such a bold female image?

I dared a glance at Bernardo to see his reaction. His jaw was clenched, his eyes slightly narrowed. "You are exquisite, *carissima.*" Bernardo's voice was deep and quiet, and I could not read its emotion. "Let us see the back." He took the portrait in both hands to carefully turn it round.

The verso was executed as we had designed—a subdued image of a laurel and palm wreath laced with a ribbon carrying the motto *Virtus et Honor.* Bernardo nodded, pleased. "I have begun identifying the manuscripts in my collection with our emblem."

He turned the portrait back so my painted face appeared again. "Lovely. Your fine countenance will keep me company in Venice, *carissima.* I will introduce you to my fellows in that city, and they will admire you and want to hear all about you and about us. I will look at this painting nightly and talk to it as if you were standing in front of me. Having this portrait with me will make my departure a little easier."

"You are leaving Florence?" I asked with alarm.

"Will you be disappointed to see me go, my dear Bencina?"

"Y–y–yes," I stammered. I was stunned. Bernardo had been in Florence for only sixteen months—sixteen exhilarating, confusing, life–altering months. I shook my head, looking down to the floor, trying to absorb the news. My heart ached. Was that love? Or was it just fear of drabness enveloping me again? No more portraits, no more philosophical debates, no more invitations to the Medici palazzo. No matter which was the real underlying reason, my answer was an honest one. "Yes," I whispered, "I will be terribly disappointed."

Bernardo cupped my face in his hands. "Then kiss me, *carissima*. Kiss me good-bye."

This time I did not pull back aflutter or afraid as he bent his head down and held his lips close to mine, his breath warm, willing my breathing to echo his, just as music can beckon the listener's heart to match its beat. He held himself close like that for a long, tantalizing moment, his eyes on mine, looking for agreement. When I did not blink, he smiled. Then his lips pressed my mouth, soft, a brush as pleasing as a spring breeze, a beguiling taste of sweetness, of new hopes. And then again, lingering, relishing, as one does the first juice of a plum after a long, cold, frugal winter.

So this was a kiss, a real kiss. Now I knew where love poetry came from. I returned it with the same kind of hunger I had first devoured verse.

23

OUR EMBRACE TIGHTENED. BERNARDO'S LIPS TRAVELED FROM my mouth, slowly, kiss by kiss by kiss to my eyes, to my temple, to my hair, to my ear. I felt him nip at my earlobe, and then a mesmerizing whisper blew into my ear. "I have never known a woman like you, Ginevra, my life . . . my love . . . my soul." Each word burned.

His thumb traced my jawline to come to rest under my chin. He pushed and tilted it up, my head fell back, and now his mouth wandered bit by bit down my throat. His other hand slid around my waist and gathered me to him. Our clothes crushed, rustled, wrinkling. His lips reached my shoulder, as his other hand traveled downward. I felt his fingers tug at the lacing of my bodice.

I caught my breath. Without realizing it, I had longed for such an embrace, for someone to cherish me this way. But this was anything but Platonic.

I pulled away. "No, my lord. I beg your pardon. I . . . I cannot do this. My honor. My husband."

He laughed, but it was hoarse with desire, not the warm, amused chortle I knew so well. "Come, come, Ginevra. That is no real marriage. It was arranged, a calculated merger of families, one of convenience only." He paused. "You and I, on the other hand, share true, heartfelt affection, our love of literature and art, great passions of the soul. Come, my dear, this is an expression of love. I promise." He reached for me.

I evaded him, retreating deeper into a corner behind the portrait.

"Where is that poet who captivated me with her sonnet about the unrepentant, fiery horse pulling the chariot of her soul?" He caught me and bent me backward, his mouth against my hair as he crooned, "Let go the reins. Let that dark horse lead you."

The arm encircling me tightened so that I was totally enveloped. He curled my body up into his, and only my tiptoes touched the floor. If Bernardo let go, I would have fallen to the ground, but instead, given his strength, we were fused as surely as two figures in a statue. Again he kissed me, tender but insistent. I was having a hard time knowing which limbs were mine in that embrace, an even harder time making myself want to break it.

But I wriggled free, prattling, "That poem was about my finding the wisdom to keep the two horses—one chaste, one not—working together . . . to keep me on my chosen path of virtue." I took a deep breath to steel myself. "This is not what we agreed, my lord, or what is heralded by Plato or Ficino or . . . or . . . Lorenzo de' Medici."

"Lorenzo?" Bernardo guffawed. "Do you realize how many illegitimate children he has probably sired?"

I tried to not show my shock. "Nevertheless, Your Excellency, I know what you value in me is my loyal, virtuous heart. You had the poet Landino compare those qualities of me to Petrarch's Laura, the most lauded lady in literature!" I quoted the last poem he had sent me, having memorized every word of it. "'For she surpasses Laura in chastity, beauty, elegance, and even her pious character.'" I looked at Bernardo defiantly now. "Landino also wrote, 'Mortals, learn that the beauty of the soul, not of the body, must be desired, and learn to love true grace.' It was your commission, so surely those are your beliefs. I trust you to hold to them."

Bernardo considered that a moment. And then he tried another tack, ever the persuasive, clever diplomat. "Come now, Ginevra, this is not the sweet young lady I beheld at the joust, the obedient niece Bartolomeo introduced me to, the inquisitive mind I saw looking so rapturously at Donatello's statue, the avid scholar who yearns to know the truth of life and its art." Those blue eyes twinkled mischievously as he added, "Nor is it the woman who looked without flinching at the bronze *David*'s manhood."

Oh sweet Mother Mary, he'd seen me. Sister Margaret had always said my brazen curiosity would be the hook on which the devil would catch me.

"Take pity on me, *carissima,* I have longed for you for months, commissioned poems and artwork from Florence's most renowned studio." He held out his arms, gesturing to Leonardo's painting and toward the corner where Verrocchio's sculpture stood.

Bernardo had indeed done all that. I felt my resolve weaken, wondering how I could be so ungrateful. Certainly I'd just felt great longing as he kissed me. It was a sweet ache. Lord knows many a soul succumbed to desire and transgressed, and then afterward begged forgiveness and received absolution in the confessional. It was done all the time in Florence.

"Yes, you see?" Bernardo seemed to read my mind and stepped toward me slowly, carefully, to not spook me as he continued his plea. "Was there ever as devoted a lover as I have been? A better champion? All Christendom will now know of you, La Bencina. You will not die, but live forever in art. Because of me."

It was true. "Why must you leave Florence, my lord? Why must things change?"

Bernardo stopped. His face clouded. "I have been called back."

"But why? Do they need you for another ambassadorship?"

"I am called back by the Council of Ten."

"The Council of Ten?" I knew nothing of Venice's politics. They were completely different from Florence's. Each Italian city—Florence, Venice, Milan, Naples, Ferrara—had their own government, their own armies, their own rulers. It was why they bickered endlessly and why treaties among them were so critically important.

"I am to answer ethical questions."

"My lord?"

"It seems they are not happy that I asked Lorenzo de' Medici for loans. The question I must answer is if I compromised Venice somehow in doing so, if I neglected my city's needs to advance my personal friendship with Lorenzo in order to obtain monies for my own household. And"— he paused for emphasis and swept his hand to point at the studio—"for these commissions."

And for how many gambling debts? I wondered.

"What some of the council members fail to understand— several of them never having been diplomats themselves—is that these commissions ultimately glorify our realm, not just me personally." He spoke with growing agitation. "My joining Lorenzo's philosophical circle, my Platonic romance with you, brought me and therefore Venice closer to the Medici."

I stiffened. So Scolastica had been right. Bernardo might indeed be taken with me, want me, but clearly he recognized the political advantage of our romance as well.

And what about me? If I was honest about my feelings? I certainly had gained social prominence through his attentions. My life had brightened, like a rosy dawn following a thick fog. But was that love? Or just infatuation?

Bernardo scowled and spoke with sudden fury. "My honor has become suspect! Life without honor is a living death. If I ever catch the bastard who twisted and used my private affairs to poison the council against me, I'll pay him back with my sword." He caught me by the elbow. "And it is all your doing, La Bencina." The term he had always used lightly, flirtatiously, he now drew out with sarcasm. "I did it for you. That gaze of yours goaded me into it."

"Me? What gaze?"

"What gaze?" he repeated. "That one!" He pointed to Leonardo's portrait. "Come, Ginevra, a truly modest woman would not look out at a man so unrelentingly—right into his soul, as well as revealing her own if the man braves entering that stare. You're like a siren, singing a song that Odysseus couldn't resist. Your painting betrays you. The painting I commissioned. The painting I will pay for—in more ways than one."

Having me by the elbow, Bernardo pulled us down to sit on a bench, crowded with drawings and small clay figures. He yanked me to him and kissed me again. But I did not feel love, or even passion, in it this time. This kiss tasted of resentment, of entitlement. Bernardo thrust his tongue hard past my lips and jammed his hand down the neckline of my bodice to grope my breasts.

"NO!" I squirmed and tried to push him away. This was

no expression of love. "Not . . . not like this."

He did not let go, and his mouth continued its voyage over me.

Panicked, I squirmed backward along the bench, bumping into some of the apprentices' little statue studies of draped clothing that had been drying on it. I reached down and grabbed one. Before Bernardo realized what I was doing, I brought it crashing down on his skull.

"God's wounds!" he cried, releasing me. His hand went to his head, but the figure had done little damage other than leaving a powder of crumbled plaster in his hair and a little trickle of blood along his forehead from a scratch.

I scrambled to my feet, my hands clenched in fists. "I will not yield to you this way, signor," I cried. "No matter how much you track me around this room. No matter how many arguments you make to convince me it is my obligation to reward you with my body. No matter what promises of fame you dangle before me."

He looked at me, amazed. But that quickly changed. For a few tense moments, his face darkened with wrath, his body coiled dangerously. I planted my feet firmly, anticipating his lunging at me. I glared back, my heart pounding.

Then, remarkably, Bernardo's expression lightened. He began to laugh—a deep, rumbling chortle. Dusting himself off, he stood. "You are a magnificent creature, Ginevra de' Benci. You are . . ."

"A mountain tiger," I finished for him.

He cocked his head, thinking for a moment, and then nodded, smiling with that warmth that had first charmed me. "Yes, just so. Just so. Caged, perhaps, but untamed. Just like the sultan's pet. I understand. It is in that gaze. And"—he rubbed his head—"in those claws." He laughed again. Then he grew serious. "You know, my dear, I would not wish, nor do I need, to force myself on an unwilling woman. There are plenty who ask to undress for me."

There was nothing malicious in his tone, just a matter-of-fact braggadocio with a tinge of teasing that now fell flat with me. But it was also an unspoken capitulation that allowed me to speak honestly. "I was not trying to provoke anything with my gaze and this painting. I was trying to do the exact opposite. To look out so the viewer could see that I am not just what men define me as—a saint, a bargaining chip, a mark of my family's fortunes, a political pawn, or . . . or a trophy. My own being, with my own thoughts, my own poetry, if you but look."

Bernardo held his hand out toward me and waited for me to take it. Gingerly, I did. "You overwhelm me, Ginevra." He paused. "When I speak of us, I will celebrate your virtue and your great spirit. I will talk of how you guided me to my best self, my *summum bonum*. Surely, we are owed heaven having denied ourselves it here on earth in this moment of passion. I hope you will remember all that came before this afternoon when you speak of me."

"Yes," I agreed, still not letting down my guard, but in

a treaty of mutual respect, mutual debt, and a fondness that once was.

Bernardo lifted my hand and kissed it lightly as he would do in court when introduced to a woman for the first time. "My lady," he said, and bowed. Then Ambassador Bembo walked out of Verrocchio's studio and out of my life.

Or so I thought.

24

After Bernardo left, I collapsed onto the bench, all the fierce energy that had emboldened me now drained away. I decided not to wait for Verrocchio's return. I brushed myself off, straightened my dress, smoothed my hair, took several deep breaths, and went to look for Sancha. I found Leonardo in the work yard instead.

He was sitting on a bench, leaning over clasped hands, looking at the ground. His great curly mane of hair, typically so carefully combed, was matted and tangled. His clothes were covered with grime.

"Maestro!"

Leonardo looked up, unsurprised, as if he had been waiting there for me.

"Where is Master Verrocchio?"

"Still talking with the magistrates."

I sat down beside him and put my hand on his arm. He looked horrible. "Are you all right?"

He shook his head. "Are you all right?" he countered.

I was startled by his question and the pointed way he asked it. Then I realized. "How . . . how long have you been here?"

"A while," he said. "Long enough."

I chewed on my lower lip. "So you heard?"

"Yes. Forgive me for not helping you. I . . . I was uncertain what to do. How you might feel about his advances."

I withdrew my hand from his arm in embarrassment.

"But you, Donna Ginevra, you were so resolute."

I sighed, relieved that Leonardo did not think I had somehow provoked Bernardo. Even though I had not done so, certainly the convent, Florence's society, books like Alberti's treatise on family, and priests in the pulpit said that if men acted inappropriately, a woman had incited it. I also knew that I had been lucky. Bernardo had not been drunk or egged on by other less honorable men. He had been willing to concede to my refusal. Many other men would not have.

"We cannot tell our hearts who to love or what to feel," I said quietly. "But we can decide whether to act on those emotions."

Leonardo nudged a pebble with the toe of his boot. "I know better than most how much courage and control that took."

I waited, wondering if he was thinking about some of his own recent choices. But if he was, he never shared that with me. Instead he talked of his mother. "I am the issue of such a moment, you know. As a servant brought from Constantinople, my mother had no choice but to concede to my father's desires. He did free her after I was born—I give him that. And he let me have five precious years with her before taking me to his parents' house. My mother is a good woman, devoted and generous. She always told me I could do anything, learn anything. I remember. But she made no argument when my father took me away from her."

I chafed at the comparison. I was neither slave nor servant. But Bernardo had certainly acted as if he had rights to me. Indeed, Florence considered all women property in some regard—belonging to our fathers, our husbands, our family. "I am so sorry she had to give you up, maestro, but it sounds like there was little she could have done. Such is the lot of women. Our fates are negotiated by men. I hope someday that will change. Perhaps our painting will help a little in that, yes?"

He nodded but remained unmoved.

"I am sure your mother's heart broke at your separation. But I am also sure she hoped it would mean a better life for you—that is a mother's dearest desire, after all. Certainly Florence has provided you that?"

"Perhaps. It is difficult to see that from a prison cell." Leonardo drew himself up. "Even so, I will not forget this strength of yours, Donna Ginevra. I will keep it in my heart as I paint other women. I will look for it in them."

"Oh, maestro, what a compliment. Thank you." I took a deep breath. "Now we must make sure you receive your commission for your portrait."

"He will not pay, signora." Leonardo's voice was contemptuous.

"What do you mean? The ambassador and I parted with respect. Our Platonic affections hold."

Leonardo raised an eyebrow. "We'll see."

I was able to share Luigi's warning to Leonardo before Sancha and Verrocchio returned. We did not discuss why Leonardo had been arrested. Just that he had been and that Luigi had passed along that the Officers of the Night sometimes employed spies to substantiate accusations that might otherwise not carry enough evidence to convict.

Leonardo was grim. "Nothing is so much to be feared as evil report."

I nodded. "So be careful."

"You, too, signora," he said. "Gossip will hound both of us for a while. But I have been thinking that patience protects against insults as clothes do against winter winds."

"Then we must learn to wear many layers," I said with a smile.

I walked home with Sancha along the Arno. I wanted

to breathe a while before buttoning on the role of wife. The evening light was soft, the Arno placid. The late April warmth turned the water blue again, after months of the river's currents running gray and winter-dull. White herons waded along the marshy edge. Swifts skimmed the air just above the mirrorlike waters, darting under bridges and then soaring up to take another dive and run. In the pink glow of twilight, Florence's tightly packed tan- and mustard-colored houses brightened to a rich, warm gold. Long reflections of them and their bright terra-cotta roofs shivered in the river.

I stopped to take it all in and raised my eyes over the city's fortified walls and watchtowers to the hills and mountains beyond. There, clouds lay flattened out on the peaks and slopes like cats stretching themselves out along the tops of garden walls to sleep. Beyond that, the heavens. *"I will lift up mine eyes unto the hills, from whence cometh my help."* Yes, I thought, exactly. A mountain tiger. Even if only in my heart, in my inner world. Nothing could change that. I smiled and felt a bit taller.

That was when an ungodly wail seemed to rise up out of the inner city. A rider thundered past us on his way to the Ponte Vecchio and out to the countryside. Down the street several men clustered, talking excitedly. One of them fell to his knees.

"What is happening?" I turned to Sancha.

More people gathered in knots of worried conversation. A bell began to toll.

"Hey, you there, fellow!" Sancha reached out and grabbed the arm of a liveried servant darting past us, clutching a message. "What is wrong? Why are people spreading an alarm? Are we attacked?"

"No! Worse!" he cried. "La Bella Simonetta is dead!"

✧ ✧ ✧

The hysteria lasted for days. Italians came from all over to mourn the beautiful Simonetta's untimely death from consumption. They jammed themselves through the city gates and clogged the taverns. Rumor spread that a new star was shining in the skies above Florence, and surely it was Simonetta's spirit. Each night, dozens of people stood along the city's walls past midnight, pointing and marveling that this beloved and beauteous young woman had climbed into the heavens alongside constellations of Orion and Hercules. The Night Watch gave up trying to enforce the city's curfew.

On the day of her funeral, thousands packed the streets. Simonetta's coffin was open as it was carried to the Church of Ognissanti, so the throng could see how exquisite she remained. Some even claimed she was more beautiful in death than in life. Poet Bernardo Pulchi, brother to Lorenzo's friend and poet Luigi, wrote a moving elegy.

He read it out loud, shouting the words so those within earshot could hear. Simonetta, he wrote, was on her way to the firmament to join Petrarch's Laura and Dante's Beatrice "like a new Phoenix." Such loud weeping followed that if Simonetta was not already there, the floor of heaven would have been rattled enough by Florence's sobbing that angels would have thrown open the pearly gates to see what the cacophony below was about.

Only then did the slow, sad procession start. The entourage following her casket was enormous, led by Giuliano and her husband, Marco, his parents, Lorenzo and the Medici clan, and their inner circle. I was surprised not to see Bernardo among them. Perhaps he had already left the city for Venice, his departure lost in the commotion over Simonetta.

My family was included directly behind the Medici. Luigi was among the city's officials, so I walked on my brother's arm instead, clinging to him as a shield against my own grief. I would sorely miss Simonetta, her quick affection and her good-natured advice. She felt more like a sister than my younger blood siblings did. Who would I confide in now? Who could understand the complications of my life, my affections?

Uncle Bartolomeo's young wife, Lisabetta, walked alongside me, too. She was as nervous and mousy as ever. Normally that would not have bothered me, but realizing this was the type of woman I was left with now that Simonetta was gone, I had to fight the urge to slap Lisabetta's simpering face.

Halfway to the church, Lisabetta slipped her hand in mine. "It is all so tragic," she said. "I am sorry for you, Ginevra. I know you two had become . . . well . . . very close."

I swallowed to suppress my sorrow. "Yes, she was a lovely woman. So unselfish, which was extraordinary given her beauty and all this adoration. We can learn from her example of modesty and kindness."

Lisabetta looked at me with some surprise. "Oh yes, of course, Simonetta Vespucci was an inspiration to us all. But I was talking about"—she didn't bother to lower her voice—"about you and the ambassador."

"What?" I stopped in my tracks, creating a little avalanche of people bumping into one another's backsides.

Giovanni apologized for us and then gently dragged me forward. "No matter what nonsense comes out of her mouth next," he whispered to me, "keep walking. Uncle Bartolomeo did not wed her for her wit."

"Oh, well," Lisabetta blithered on, oblivious to my growing discomfort. "Of course you will be upset—you and the ambassador were such a romance. All of Florence knows about your sad farewell. How your heart broke when he told you he had to depart for his beloved Venice. How you sobbed like Dido when Aeneas left her shores."

"What?" I stopped again, my voice raised this time.

Again, that ripple of people crashing into one another behind me. Again, Giovanni apologized, before urging me onward. "Keep moving, sister."

"Cristoforo Landino has written a lovely poem about your sorrow, commissioned by His Excellency Ambassador Bembo. My husband carries it for you. I know you will just love the verse."

I fought the urge to strangle her and squelched my fury at

241

the obvious fact that she had already read something that was addressed to me. I had to wait through Simonetta's funeral and an hour of tearful eulogies before I was able to ask my uncle for my poem as we left the church.

He, of course, took the opportunity to lecture me. "You are very lucky to have the affections of such an esteemed man." He refused to continue or to hand me the verse until I nodded obediently. "The fact that the Venetian ambassador, who has traveled the world, chose a Florentine lady to be his Platonic muse does our great city of Florence honor as well. And raises our family to fame, alongside the Medici, the Donati, and the Vespucci. Only a foolish girl would not see that blessing and act accordingly."

Again, Uncle Bartolomeo waited. I nodded dutifully, despite the fact that at this point, my face was burning with anger and embarrassment.

"Only an ungrateful wretch would cause such a great man—who has lavished such gifts upon her—embarrassment. Or stupidly fuel false accusations again him. If Bernardo Bembo's star sinks, niece, with the implication that he and Lorenzo de' Medici were too close in their personal friend-ship, it makes it much harder for Florence to navigate the waters with Venice, which is a critically important ally of ours against the Papal States."

I felt chilled all over. Was my uncle implying that by protecting my virtue and refusing to yield up my body or to be used by a self-aggrandizing man that I had somehow endangered Florence's foreign policy?

"This poem will help make it clear that his Platonic courtship of you was as much for state purposes as personal philosophic discourse," he pronounced, "if you behave accordingly."

Good God, I thought, what had my uncle done now? How had he misused me this time?

Uncle Bartolomeo smirked as he handed me the parchment, the seal broken. Clearly, he had already read and shared the contents with Lisabetta and probably a great many more.

I waited until I was safely home in my bedroom with the door locked before I opened the verse. I could see my uncle's handiwork immediately. I just couldn't believe Bernardo would be that cruel, that he would hide behind my skirts this way. The poem made it seem that Bernardo had had to refuse my over-ardent hopes and desires rather than the other way around, that I had misinterpreted what had been purely a courtly intent on his part:

Moreover, Bembo, Ginevra weeps at your departure,
and she protests that the gods are deaf to her prayers.
Alas, Bencia weeps that the deaf gods despise her pleas,
and that she is deprived of her chaste pleasures.

Therefore you will go, happy to see your beloved relatives
and your sweet children and your pious wife;
for finally, now that your great service has been performed,
your lustrum completed, you may rest at your ancestral home.

. . . the Venetian Senate will learn
of their citizen's great gifts,
what his envoy to different cities will have given to his
country. . . .

I did not read the rest. I crumpled the verse and threw it
into the piss pot.

25

HUMILIATED AND FURIOUS, I PUT ON MY BROWN DRESS AND my scapula and marched to Le Murate. I pounded on the outer door. Of course, Sister Margaret would have to be the one to answer. "It is close to Vespers, you may not enter now."

"Vespers? Wondrous. The perfect time for me to say my prayers in the chapel my grandfather built for you." I felt no shame or hesitation in throwing my weight about that evening. I wanted sanctuary, a place I could think through what I would do next, without men telling me what it should be.

Sister Margaret pursed her lips but grudgingly stepped out of the way.

"And after Vespers, sister, I will be spending the night,

perhaps the week, in the Benci cell that my grandfather also paid for and Abbess Scolastica promised would always be open to me and my kin."

Sister Margaret's face darkened like a squall line, but there was no arguing with that either.

I ended up staying for weeks. Juliet and I fell back into our schoolgirl friendship, a lovely balm to the wound of losing Simonetta as my confidante. Juliet and I talked of Ovid, Virgil, even the playful Boccaccio. I could only wonder where she had procured copies of his stories, as the bawdy romances must surely be forbidden to nuns.

I prayed. I read. I thought. I wrote—which I had failed to do when distracted by the intrigue of Bernardo's courtship and the excitement of the studio and conversation with Leonardo. The poems that came out of me in those first weeks were often angry, yet were still filled with a certainty about the majesty of the human soul.

I think that was Scolastica speaking to me. It was some of the best verse I'd ever written. I sent them to no one, other than one daring sonnet—about a mountain tiger—to a court musician who had been a dear friend since childhood. He was in Rome. I asked him if he could get a rosary blessed by the Pope for me. I thanked him by sending him the verse. He had been bragging to the ladies of that court of the witty banter and literary abilities of Florentine women and needed something to prove it. I hope the sonnet did so.

As more and more poems spilled out of me, I realized the outside world—especially while gossip swirled about

Bernardo and me—did not offer me the quietude or freedom that allowed my heart to sing out clearly, unaffected by others and their opinions or desires. So I found myself lingering in Le Murate.

I sent word to Luigi that I was not well and that rest and prayer seemed to be helping. His reply was polite and concerned, supportive of my staying. After our conversation about Leonardo, I assumed Luigi would be fine with my being away for a while. Perhaps he might fill the time with other company now that our marriage offered him a protective screen. He certainly took advantage of my absence to argue that his taxes be lowered, noting in a letter to the revenue collectors that his wife had been very ill for a long time.

I wrote to Leonardo, explaining my sequestering myself and expressing my gratitude for his painting and dialogue and all that both had inspired in me. I missed him. Enormously so.

Did I miss Bernardo? The affection I'd once had for him had been sullied by our last encounter and his—or my uncle's—public manipulation of our farewell to suit Florence's and Bernardo's political needs. Certainly Landino's verse guaranteed that Bernardo would be saved the embarrassment of people knowing I had spurned his advances. Who would believe me now after that poem had made the rounds of Florence's elite? If I stayed in the silence of the convent, I did not have to hear the speculation or pontificating about us. I could remember the self-confidence Bernardo had helped engender in me, the enlightening conversation and delightful banter around the Medici table. All that had been so gratifying, so expanding.

I certainly had not intended it to have this effect, but my cloistering played well in the court society surrounding the Medici. Lorenzo wrote me two sonnets, calling me a "devout, gentle spirit," "a lambkin," and praising my turning my back on a city "aflame with every vice." He alluded to "suspicion, disdain, envy, and anger" and told me to "let them talk. Sit and listen to Jesus."

I wrote back to thank him, never mentioning the rumored affair Florence gossiped he had just begun with my young aunt, wife to my uncle Donato. I couldn't help but wonder if Lorenzo's poetic praise of me was a way of trying to insure my favorable opinion, or loyal silence, regarding that dalliance. I had come a long way in my understanding of the secular world since my first sojourn at Le Murate. I decided to remain there indefinitely.

As a *conversa* laysister, I was free to come and go from the convent. The person I visited most was my brother. One afternoon, he led me to a small chamber off his bedroom. "I have something to show you in private, sister."

There was my portrait.

"But why did Bernardo not take it with him to Venice? Did he not want it?" His leaving it behind bruised my ego.

"I don't know," Giovanni said. "But Leonardo insisted you be sure to view the back of the portrait. He was adamant about it." Giovanni turned the panel so its reverse showed.

"Curiosity is killing me, sister. What is so special about the back side?"

I smiled. Oh, what a clever stroke for my honor Leonardo had parried. He had changed the motto on the ribbon from *Virtus et Honor*—a saying Bernardo claimed as an emblem for himself—to *Virtutem Forma Decorat*. That line could be translated two ways: "Beauty adorns virtue," or the one I preferred, "She adorns her virtue with beauty."

The motto now was entirely about me and my choices, the focus on my character and my mind, with physical beauty being almost an afterthought, a casual adornment, like a necklace I might don at the last minute to complement my natural appearance. Leonardo had used the word *forma*, which implies intellect as well as beauty, instead of the more typical Latin word used to describe a woman's prettiness, *pulchritudo*. It was an even sweeter shade of difference, because I knew Leonardo was struggling to teach himself Latin and such nuance bespoke careful thought, a true insight to me.

And I could guess that the change of the motto might have so annoyed Bernardo that he wanted nothing more to do with my painting.

I went back to the convent that evening, happy, and knowing exactly which man I truly missed, whose company I ached for and why.

26

Spring 1478

CLAIMING I NEEDED SOLITUDE TO RECOVER, I REMAINED AT
Le Murate for almost two years. I alternated between
sequestering myself to write, reminiscing about my time in
Verrocchio's studio and the Medici circle, and visiting home.
Mostly when I left the convent, I attended Florence's special holidays and masses or went to see my brother. During
this time, political alliances within and without the city were
shifting. Often my conversations with Giovanni were full of
gossip about Lorenzo's troubles with the Pope—troubles that
the Pazzi family stirred and kept simmering.

"So, what news is there, brother?" I asked one day, as I settled down into his rooms for a dinner of sea bass, potatoes, and mussels in piecrust. I have to admit such splendid food was another reason I liked to visit him. The convent's fare of broth and bread grew tiresome.

Giovanni leaned back in his chair and clasped his hands behind his head. "Well . . ." He paused and grinned at me. "Are you sure your feminine sensibilities are strong enough for men's politics?"

I bit into a dried fig and made a face at him.

"I do miss teasing you, sister." He laughed, and then grew serious. "Politics and diplomacy have become far more complicated and fraught with dangerous personal vendettas. I told you that Lorenzo refused to let his bank loan the Pope the monies he wanted to purchase the town of Imola for one of his nephews. The nephew is a cardinal, and the purchase was clearly part of Pope Sixtus's plan to expand the Vatican's powers geographically as well as spiritually. Honestly, the man acts more like a duke than a pontiff. So Lorenzo asked all Florentine banks, including the Pazzi's, to deny the Pope's request—for the sake of Florence's sovereignty in Tuscany, to prevent the Pope garnering too much political influence in our region."

I reached for some sweetmeats. "And? Lorenzo pressuring others to his will within Florence's governance is nothing new."

"And," Giovanni spoke emphatically, "the Pazzi seized upon Lorenzo's refusal as a way to weaken and wound the

Medici. The Pazzi went straight to the Pope and gave him the florins he needed. They also informed His Holiness that Lorenzo had tried to collude with other moneylenders to thwart the Pope's desires. The Pope was furious. He has removed the Vatican accounts from the Medici branch bank in Rome and deposited them with the Pazzi."

Now that was potentially devastating to the Medici fortune. I knew that much from growing up listening to my father. Rome was the mainstay of the Medici banking empire.

"The Pope also retaliated by appointing an archbishop for our region who is decidedly anti–Medici, ignoring all the candidates Florence suggested. It's a particular insult because the Pope has ignored Lorenzo's campaign for Giuliano to become a cardinal. Lorenzo and the Signoria struck back by refusing to recognize Francesco Salviati as archbishop."

"Ahhh." I began to see the trickling effect of all this into the lives of ordinary Florentines. "So that is why Florence was threatened with excommunication by the Pope. All the sisters in Le Murate were terrified about not being able to receive communion and being damned eternally."

"Indeed." Giovanni sat up and took his goblet of wine. "Lorenzo has finally acknowledged the archbishop, and things seem to have settled down. But you know how these things fester in Florence. Lorenzo has made new enemies for himself, and the Pazzi have grown stronger and bolder."

I thought of Simonetta's concerns for Giuliano's honor and safety, her hatred of the Pazzi. "But isn't Lorenzo's sister married to a Pazzi man?" I asked. "Surely that built a healing bridge between the two families and will keep them from open conflict?"

Giovanni smiled at me. "Ah, sister, you of all people should know that marriages aren't always the answers we think they will be." He patted my hand. "Now, enough of that. Tell me what you are writing. What poems do you have to share with me?"

I did not think much about our conversation again, and my next forays outside Le Murate's gates were uneventful. Until the fifth Sunday after Easter, April 26, 1478.

That day happened to be the second anniversary of Simonetta's death. I wanted to attend mass in the Duomo and be among her family and friends. Le Murate was also atwitter with the news that the newest cardinal, a beautiful seventeen-year-old nephew of the Pope, was attending the service at Lorenzo's special invitation—which I assumed was part of the Medici's resumed courtship of the Vatican to heal the rift Giovanni had told me of. Amid blushes and giggles, the young penitents and convent-school boarders begged me to go see and return to tell them what the youth really looked like.

The Duomo was packed. The April weather was beautiful and balmy, allowing many people to travel in from the countryside in anticipation of the coming week's Feast of the Ascension. As the Medici family waded through the thick crowd toward the front of the nave, stopping to greet friends and dignitaries, Lorenzo's mother spotted me where I stood with Giovanni. Luigi, as usual, was with his guildsmen. Lucrezia de' Medici reached out to take my arm. "My dear, it is so good to see you. I understand you have been ill. You are better, I hope?"

. I thanked her and said I was.

"I also have heard you have been writing a great deal. I would love to see your verses, child. We never really had the chance to share our poetry, did we?"

I was too pleased at the invitation to wonder what spies in the convent might have passed along that information. When invited to the Medici palazzo during Bernardo's and my Platonic courtship, my hope had been to share my poetry, but I had been too impressed and intimidated by the art contained in the household and the debate among the men surrounding the Magnifico to do so. Now I would far prefer to chat privately with this aged Medici matron, poet to poet, even though our writing was sure to be different. Despite my hours in Le Murate, my poems were not exactly devotional in nature.

The choirs began to sing. The Medici moved on. Lorenzo went to stand just to the right of the high altar.

Out of the corner of my eye I caught a patch of a salmon-colored tunic and a gold-brown mane of curls. I caught my breath. It was Leonardo. We had seen each other a few times because Giovanni was lending space within his rooms to Leonardo to paint. But there was bashful awkwardness between us then. Leonardo had left Verrocchio's studio and lived and worked on his own now. Oh, if only somehow I could happen upon him after the service. I stood on my tip-toes to watch where he ended up. But he was already lost in the wake of other bodies.

The throng was settling down and quieting in antici-pation of the service, when suddenly there was a rippling of elbows and loud shuffling as people moved aside to let Giuliano de' Medici pass. He was late for church, but no one seemed to begrudge him his tardiness. I watched him sail through the sea of vividly colored clothing toward the high altar. Still beautiful, still the embodiment of youth and its promise. His bearing was so graceful it was natural to note the two men who followed him, arm in arm, because they were such a contrast in roughness.

One was a Pazzi. Odd, I thought, given what Giovanni had told me about friction between the families. But I knew the man's brother was married to Giuliano and Lorenzo's sister, Bianca. No matter what intrigues were going on in back rooms, Florence's leading families were well practiced in presenting an air of unity and regal harmony to the public.

I and the multitude of other worshippers turned to the high altar and silenced as the service began. The liturgy washed over me, incense drifted like a thin fog up to the stained-glass windows, the voice of the priest lifted reso-nantly, and the congregation's answering "Amens" rumbled like distant thunder along the marble floors and walls.

The service came to the blessing of the communion bread. A cherubic-looking altar boy rang a small, high-pitched bell to announce the Elevation of the Host. We all lowered our heads and eyes in reverence as the priest began. "He took bread into his holy hands . . ."

"Take that, traitor!"

A thousand heads snapped up at once to the sight of two daggers raised above head level and brought crashing down to guttural shrieks of pain. There was another glint of blades, bloodied now, brought down again. More gurgling shrieks. People in front near the altar lunged back and pushed in fear, sending a swell of bodies knocking into one another. I fell to the ground, my skirts twisted and caught underfoot. Another woman washed over on top of me.

As I struggled to get out from under her and to my feet, I saw Lorenzo whip his cape around his arm in a makeshift shield of cloth and draw his sword to beat back two attackers, before leaping over the altar and away.

"Murder!" someone shouted.

"The dome is collapsing!" cried another voice farther back in the crowd, unable to see what was causing the furor near the altar.

"Run for your lives!" screamed many.

"Ginevra!" Giovanni grabbed my arm. "Get up! Hurry!" He yanked me and the other woman to our feet. Her husband caught her up and Giovanni clutched my hand, pulling out his sword to protect us both. "Come with me."

"What is it?" I gasped. "What is happening?"

"Assassins," he said. "Come, we will be trampled if we don't move." He half dragged me toward the doorway, dodging men rushing toward the high altar, shouting about protecting the Magnifico and Giuliano.

The rest of the cathedral was in chaos. The confused shouts about murder and catastrophe created a typhoon of panic.

Murder! The dome is collapsing! Run for your lives!

We popped out of the arched doorways, pushed through them by a storm surge of other terrified bodies. Giovanni pulled us into a curve in the cathedral walls and flattened us to the stone like flounder fish, then shielded my body against the scraping flood of frantic runners.

Murder! The dome is collapsing! Run for your lives!

The mob gushed down the streets, still howling.

"Fools!" Giovanni muttered. We almost had to peel ourselves off the stone, we had been pushed so hard up against it.

As we did so, a flotilla of men emerged from the cathedral, swords drawn, looking back and forth, scanning their surroundings. Buoyed and protected inside them was Lorenzo, holding a blood-soaked cloth to his neck.

"Giuliano," he cried. "What of Giuliano?"

Their silence told the tragedy.

Giuliano, Florence's beloved Prince of Youth, lay dead in a lake of his own blood in front of the high altar. He'd been stabbed nineteen times by the men who had accompanied him into the cathedral—Francesco de' Pazzi, who long ago claimed he'd unjustly lost a jousting championship to Lorenzo, and Bernardo Bandini. The Pazzi family and their allies had grown impatient with their less violent methods of insurrection—assassination through gossip, criticisms, and innuendos, and luring away banking clients in a calculated campaign to drain Medici coffers. They'd decided instead to grab power through murder.

Simonetta's fear that Giuliano's blithe, generous nature might keep him from recognizing the jealousy and hatred of other men had come true.

27

SUCKED INTO THE URGENT TIDE OF THE CROWD, GIOVANNI and I followed Lorenzo and his protectors as the great bell in the Signoria tower began to toll. Only in the direst trouble was La Vacca, "the cow," sounded. Its resonant lowing pulled cascades of citizens rushing out their doors, armed with swords and shields, hurriedly fastening on breastplates yanked from the home arsenal all Florentines seemed to have.

In the distance, we could hear shouts of "Vivano le Medici" and then a chant, growing in intensity and rage: *"Palle! Palle!"* The battle cry referred to the most recognizable element of the Medici crest—its cluster of golden, coin-like balls.

Enormous waves of people converged on via Larga as Lorenzo and his protectors disappeared behind the huge gates of the Medici palazzo. They shouted for Lorenzo to appear and tell them what to do.

"Palle! Palle!" The chant echoed along the streets. More men surged toward the Medici's fortress-palace from the direction of the Signoria.

Giovanni recognized a friend among them and called over the din, "Do you know what is happening?"

The man leaned in close to be heard. "While Lorenzo and Giuliano were attacked, Archbishop Salviati led a band of hired soldiers to the Signoria. He planned to capture the *priori* and take over our government."

"The archbishop? A man of God?" I couldn't help but gasp.

"Yes, my lady," the man said. "We think in revenge for Lorenzo refusing to recognize his appointment to the office."

Giovanni put his hand on my arm to quiet my questions so the man could talk. "What happened then?"

"Salviati demanded to be seen, saying the Pope had sent him on important business. But our *gonfaloniere* was suspicious and grabbed the archbishop by the hair and threw him to the ground and called the palace guard. Even his servants seized cooking-spits and impaled a few of Salviati's thugs themselves. Thank God they did, because within moments Jacopo de' Pazzi galloped in, leading an army of mercenaries that had been waiting just outside the city until the Medici brothers were killed. They are saying the Pope, maybe even the king of Naples and Giuliano's own godfather, the duke of Urbino, were part of the plot."

"God's blood!" Giovanni cursed. "Have the Pazzi and their army taken the Signoria?"

"No! Had the *priori* been prisoners of Salviati, they might have. But the Signoria servants, grown brave by their successful attack on Salviati's brigade, hurled stones over the battlements onto the soldiers below. That emboldened the crowd in the square. The people stood down Pazzi and his mercenaries, chanting *'Palle! Palle!'* The *priori* put nooses around the necks of the conspirators they held—including the archbishop—and hurled them out windows to swing and dangle until they choked. That's when the mercenaries scattered."

"What about Jacopo de' Pazzi?"

But before the man could answer, Lorenzo appeared at a second-story window. His luxurious tunic was covered in blood and his throat was bandaged, but he managed to call down to the crowd. "Citizens of Florence, please, control yourselves. My wound is not mortal. Let justice prevail. Save your energy to resist the enemies who engineered this conspiracy. They are likely to attack the city."

But somehow Lorenzo's self-effacing words seemed to make Florentines' blood boil. Their favorite son, Giuliano, lay dead, mutilated. Their trusted civic leader, the Magnifico, who had brought them honor and grand entertainments, was injured—at the hands of a haughty family that had never done anything to help the common Florentine. Every man in the city could sing at least one of the colorful songs Lorenzo had written for Carnival. He seemed one of them.

Like waters are sent roiling by the wind, a storm of fury broke lose, breaking the dikes of self-control. Cursing, waving swords or kitchen knives or pitchforks, the mob swept out into the city, seeking other conspirators.

Watching the madness take hold, Giovanni said, "Come, Ginevra, I need to get you home. Now! Hurry!"

We hastened through the streets, Giovanni clutching his sword with one hand, holding on to me with the other as men knocked into us in their hurry. We turned a corner too hastily and crashed headlong into a gang of drunkards, delighted to have a legitimate excuse for havoc. Before Giovanni could raise his sword, one of the reprobates swung a knife to my brother's throat. "What about this one?" the man asked his friends. "He seems in a hurry. Well-dressed. I bet he is a Pazzi. I say we gut him." The point of his knife drew a spot of blood.

"No, please, I implore you," I gasped. "We are Benci. Friends to the Medici."

Another man staggered toward my brother. He reeked of wine. "Wait. Maybe. No. I don't recognize him." He shrugged as if to tell his companion to go ahead.

"Hold, signori," I cried, and this time I put my hand on Giovanni's arm to stop him from speaking. I knew he would do so in anger and sensed that would further enrage this horde. I tried flattery instead. "You look like clever gambling men to me. Surely you recognize the Six Hundred. His horse Zephyrus won the *palio* two years back. Please tell me one of you won a good wager that day."

The men stuck out their lower lips and nodded. "I won fifteen florins on that horse," the main drunkard proclaimed. He stepped so close to Giovanni their boot toes touched. He eyed my brother up and down slowly, taking a pinch of Giovanni's ribboned azure-blue sleeve between his thumb and fingers to rub it. Such luxurious material in such dirty, bloodied hands was a startling image. "Hmmm. Good cloth. Yes. You could be the Six Hundred." He focused intensely on Giovanni's face, breathing heavily on it. Giovanni winced from the smell. "Yes," the man decided. "Yes, I think you are him."

Giovanni yanked away his arm and glared. My brother was no coward. But arguing the point with these ruffians could get us killed.

"Come, brother, please." I tugged on his hand. "Let us go."

Before we continued on our way, I turned to thank the man who'd identified Giovanni. I wished I hadn't. Beside him stood another man I hadn't focused on before. In one hand he held a jug of wine, in the other a severed arm, dripping gore.

He saw where I looked. "We're leaving this at the Magnifico's door," he said, bragging. "It's part of a priest who worked for the archbishop. Someone is carrying his head around the streets on a pike. I'm not sure where the rest of his body is."

Giovanni got me to the next street before I vomited.

❖ ❖ ❖

"Where is your master?" Giovanni shouted, when we'd pounded on my front door long enough that Sancha finally cracked it open, peeping around to make sure it really was us. Even Sancha, with her stout heart and no-nonsense bravery, was afraid that day.

"He's gone to the Signoria. That's where the guild leaders are gathering. In case war is declared."

Giovanni kissed me on the forehead. "Bolt the door behind you, sister. Luigi is well-known as a Medici follower. As long as you stay off the streets, you will be fine."

"But where are you going?"

"I want to make sure Mother and our sisters are all right. You know Uncle Bartolomeo will only be looking out for himself."

"But, brother!"

"I'll be all right." He smiled at me. "Just use that wit of yours to charm anyone who comes. The Six Hundred, indeed. Thanks a lot, sister!" He disappeared down the street.

"Come into the kitchen, my lady. I will get you something soothing. What a day, what a day," Sancha muttered as we walked down the hall to the back of the house. She warned me not to be startled when I saw the boy who slept in Luigi's store at night to watch its cloth. "He was bloodied by the mob."

Given what I had just seen, a few scratches would hardly affect me. But I asked how it happened. "That boy is young and sweet. Why in the world would anyone attack him?"

Sancha stopped and turned. "Because he is young and sweet and gentle . . . and pretty, my lady." She shook her head. "This vengeance against the Pazzi allows for all sorts of pent-up hatreds and stupidity to erupt to the surface. There are men out there using the conspiracy as an excuse to go after anyone they don't like, with the claim that the poor souls might be involved in the plot against the Medici."

I froze. I understood exactly what she was saying. "Leonardo!" I darted to the kitchen, scaring the poor battered houseboy, and grabbed a knife. I was out the door before Sancha could stop me.

"My lady!" I heard Sancha running after me. "This is madness."

"Go back to the house, Sancha!" I shouted.

"I will not." She caught up with me.

"Sancha, go home."

"No. Why are you doing this?" She put her hand on my arm. "This man is not for you."

I hesitated.

Sancha pressed her point. "This is a fool's errand, my lady. Look about you." She pointed up the street to the Piazza di Santa Croce, where men were cheering, shouting, and shoving one another.

A bloodthirsty rage had indeed taken over the city, but there was a wildness boiling up in me, too. I felt a certainty about what I needed to do, stronger than anything I had ever felt before. "Go home, Sancha. It may be a fool's errand, but it is my errand, not yours."

She crossed her arms. "No, my lady. If you are out and about in this lunacy, I am, too."

Another group of men rushed past us. *"Palle! Palle!"* they shouted, shaking their fists. One of them eyed Sancha appreciatively and slowed.

No turning back now. I was endangering her as well as myself by standing there. I grabbed her hand. "Come on then."

We hoisted our skirts and ran. Leonardo's rooms were just on the other side of Santa Croce. We had to get across the piazza, but it was writhing with groups of men bellowing and smashing things on the ground. I thought fleetingly of the joust that had been held in that square, of Giuliano's triumph that day, of Simonetta's beauty, of the beautiful banner Leonardo had helped paint. What a contrast this scene was to that glorious day of chivalry, the best of man's creativity, sense of honor, and agility. This was the worst of humankind.

Quickly, I realized why such violence raged in front of the steps of Santa Croce. The Pazzi had built an enormous, elaborate chapel adjacent to the church, commissioned of Brunelleschi himself, most likely to compete with the Medici's San Lorenzo church. The mob was looting it.

"Palle! Palle!"

"Come, Sancha, we must stay on this edge and try not to be noticed." We slid along the shops fronting the square, staying in the shadows as best we could.

We emerged onto an alley on the other side of the piazza.

"Just up this way a bit, my lady," Sancha said, trying to

catch her breath. We were winded. Ever my gatherer of gossip, Sancha had found out Leonardo's whereabouts many months before this.

The narrow street was filled with the stench of garbage and dye vats. It was hard to breathe in the foul-smelling air.

Abruptly, Sancha yanked me to a halt. "Look, my lady."

There was Leonardo, easily spotted in the distance because of that vibrant rose-colored tunic of his. He was backed against a wall, facing three men. One of them was jabbing Leonardo's chest with his finger. His companions leaned toward Leonardo threateningly as the man spoke.

"It's the man from the *tamburi*. Do you remember, my lady?"

I looked at Sancha and then back to Leonardo. Yes, now I did. The man Leonardo had argued with the day Sancha and I followed him to Verrocchio's studio. The man who had dropped an accusation in the "mouth of truth." Perhaps he had been Leonardo's accuser as well when Leonardo had been arrested for allegedly being a Florenzer.

"Leonardo!" I called, waving, and rushed toward them. "I have been looking for you everywhere." I threw myself past the men to Leonardo and wrapped my arms around his neck. Assuming the man threatening Leonardo might have been involved in his denunciation, I knew exactly how to discredit him. I clung to Leonardo, saying in his ear, but careful to be loud enough for them to hear, "Now's our chance, my love. My husband is away."

Leonardo's accuser was dumbfounded. His friends looked

at him like he was an idiot. I smiled at them in my most courtly manner, putting my arm through Leonardo's, and said, "Good sirs, thank you for protecting the maestro. I can see you escorted him in safety to his studio. He and his old master Verrocchio are great favorites of the Medici. Lorenzo will be so grateful for this service of yours. He has lost so much already this day with the death of his brother. In his current grief, he would punish severely anyone who might harm the painter Leonardo da Vinci."

One of his companions punched Leonardo's accuser in the chest, sending him staggering back a step. "You trying to get us drawn and quartered?"

"Come on," the other said. "We waste time here. I know where some of the Pazzi bank workers live."

They skulked away down the street.

I'm not sure how we made our way back to my house. Our escape was a blur of anxiety and hurry, as more and more men flooded the streets. *Palle! Palle!* The madness only seemed to grow.

Once safely behind our heavy wooden door, bolted shut, the noise of anger in the street muffled, my knees buckled. I collapsed to the floor.

"My lady!" Sancha cried.

"I have her," Leonardo said, lifting me gently.

"Take her to her chamber at the top of the stairs. I will fetch water."

Their voices sounded far away. I felt myself sway and dip

up and down as Leonardo climbed stairs and then the soft-
ness of my bed as he laid me down. I opened my eyes, but the
room seemed to spin.

"Here, my lady." Sancha pressed a cool, wet cloth to my
face.

"Let me." Leonardo took the cloth. "Get her some warm
wine. That will revive her."

But the sound of his voice did that well enough. My
vision cleared, the room stopped whirling. I focused on that
excellent face, so finely chiseled.

Leonardo pressed the cool cloth to my forehead, my face,
and my throat. "You are a madwoman."

"Probably so."

We laughed.

"Maestro," I began.

"For God's sake, call me Leonardo. You just risked your
life for me." He stopped moving the cloth along my neck and
stared in that intense, inquisitive way of his. "That gaze . . .
that gaze of yours . . . it . . ." He paused.

My heart began to skip.

Leonardo took a deep breath. "Your gaze captivates . . .
but . . ." He stopped again. "Do you understand?"

Slowly I nodded. "We cannot tell our hearts who to love
or what to feel."

"Ah. I recall your saying that before. You are indeed a
poet, wise and beautiful." He took my hand. "And what does
your heart feel, Ginevra de' Benci?"

Should I tell him? Should I tell him that in my hours at

269

the convent it was his face that sweetened my thoughts, our banter I remembered? That when I dreamed of love, it was his hand holding mine as it did now?

I studied his expression a moment longer. I had thought when Leonardo stood up for me with Bernardo in the studio that day, when he changed the motto on my portrait to make the painting such a celebration of my person, that he must feel a stirring for me as well. But I could see no heat, no longing in his face—although there was a true fondness for me clearly etched there. And admiration—perhaps for my mind, perhaps because I had fought being, in essence, owned by Bernardo. *Sweet Jesu*, love is a bittersweet fruit indeed. Bernardo had wanted me, I wanted Leonardo, and he . . . well, the crucible, the hell-hot test of love was to give it whether returned or not.

I smiled slightly. "What my heart feels is its own mystery."

He kept staring, as always. "I will remember that smile . . . for inspiration."

"Then I am to be your muse?"

"You already have been. Any woman I paint in my future will have a spark of you in my depiction of her. Or"—he paused—"at least I will be searching for it."

I thought of Simonetta, of her saying that the inherent romance between a painter and a subject as he searched to find the noblest in her to immortalize was almost a sacred bond. Of Verrocchio calling that dialogue so intense, so complete, that the artist and his subject saw straight into each other's hearts. It was a love few could understand and that could satisfy for a lifetime. They were right. How could I be disappointed in being a muse for Leonardo da Vinci? I had sung of the treasures in women's hearts and minds and made men listen as Abbess Scolastica had implored. Leonardo had helped me do so.

"Then it is well enough, maestro," I said.

"You overwhelm me, my lady." Leonardo leaned forward and kissed me gently on the lips. Once. I knew it was in good-bye. And that was enough, too.

EPILOGUE

I beg your pardon. I am a mountain tiger.

TIGERS ARE SOLITARY CREATURES. I KNOW SOME OF YOU might prefer to hear that Leonardo and I lived happily ever after, perhaps together. That was not our history. What mattered were our conversations as he painted me and what we created in my portrait. In it, he found his artistic voice, his vision. In it, I live on to speak to you, about myself, about the treasure inside women's hearts and minds.

Like the sultan who brought the Caspian mountain tiger to Venice and enchanted people of that city to look and wonder, write and sing, Leonardo and I made the people of our time realize there was much to be seen and learned about the person of a woman, behind her gaze—if you met and entered it. The outcome of such an exploration cannot be predefined or controlled. It is full of surprises, and yes, marvelous contradictions.

I beg your pardon. I am a mountain tiger.

Lorenzo de' Medici did survive the Pazzi revolt. After days of horrendous violence in which scores of people were butchered by the mob, Florence calmed and seemed even more devoted to the Medici rule. Lorenzo continued to be the great arbiter of taste and culture in Florence until his death in 1492, the patron who nurtured one of the greatest, most productive periods in the history of art. So many legendary artists blossomed during the Medici family reign— Donatello, Brunelleschi, Botticelli, Verrocchio, Ghiberti, Pollaiuolo, Ghirlandaio, and, of course, Leonardo da Vinci.

Sadly, though, Lorenzo's interest in Leonardo faded, especially after Giuliano's death. Other patrons employed him, but always distracted with a thousand new ideas all at the same time, Leonardo took too long to complete his paintings. Soon the commissions dried up like oil paint left out too long—there were so many other gifted artists in Florence willing to keep to a deadline and who were more, shall we say, agreeable to following directions.

His truest friend and ally, Verrocchio, left for Venice to create an equestrian monument to General Bartolomeo

Colleoni, thanks to Bernardo Bembo's influence with the committee choosing the artist. And a young Michelangelo became the talk of Florence.

Leonardo needed a new stage, a fresh start.

He moved to Milan, arriving as a musician, an emissary of goodwill from Lorenzo the Magnificent, carrying a horse-head lyre Leonardo had carved himself. There he served primarily as an engineer. After showing Duke Ludovico Sforza his designs for war machines and water hydraulics, Leonardo embarked on one of his other great loves—inventing.

From that his fame, and his artistic wings, grew.

Leonardo did not depart Florence without leaving behind precious reminders for me. He entrusted my brother with the safekeeping of an unfinished *Adoration of the Magi*, astounding in its composition—thick with men crowding forward in amazement, horses nervous and agitated. Mary sits in the absolute center, calm, smiling down on her baby boy, who reaches gleefully for a jeweled chalice a Magi holds up toward him.

"You know, sister," Giovanni said one day, "I swear I see some of you in that Madonna's face."

The loveliest part of the scene, however, was what I took to be Leonardo's self-portrait—a youthful shepherd in the bottom right corner, his gaze turned outward to the viewer, while his inside arm points to Mary as if to say, "Look! Look what I can paint."

I would stand in front of it and remember it all, including that kiss.

I continued to write and to come in and out of the sanctuary of Le Murate, relishing its quietude, which always seemed to open the floodgates of my verse, enjoying the conversation of women who did not hold back their opinions for fear of what men across the table might think. When I visited my brother and his children, I delighted in playing and reading with them, and encouraging their little souls to sing out—loudly.

So where are my poems? There, too, I followed my mentor, Abbess Scolastica. I took them with me, as a reminder of this good earth, this miraculous life of ours. Just as I had tucked her embroidery into Scolastica's coffin, Sancha, then old but still fiercely loyal, slipped them under my dress as I lay in state in my casket.

Besides, I prefer you come to know me as Leonardo wanted, through the gaze he inspired and captured. And the one line of verse that remains says enough.

I beg your pardon. I am a mountain tiger.

AFTERWORD

The good painter paints two principal things—man and the intention of his mind. The first is easy and the second difficult.

—LEONARDO DA VINCI

EACH DAY, A STEADY STREAM OF VISITORS SEEK OUT THE POR- trait of Ginevra de' Benci, hanging in Washington, DC's National Gallery of Art. Many, clutching brochures and art books, rush straight for her on a pilgrimage to see the only Leonardo on permanent display in America. Others notice her as they meander the museum's airy marble halls.

Inevitably, when they catch Ginevra's gaze, they stop. They approach the double-sided display almost on tiptoe, captured by that intent, intelligent, slightly defiant look in her eyes. They circle, taking in her image and the motto on the back. They linger. As they finally pull themselves away— perhaps to find Verrocchio's terra-cotta statue of Giuliano de' Medici, resplendent in his jousting breastplate, housed in an adjacent room—her viewers glance back once more, as if bidding a reluctant adieu. She is that luminous.

No, Ginevra de' Benci is not smiling or as polished and impressive as Leonardo's *Mona Lisa*. She is not as dramatic as his *Last Supper*, or as delighting as his *Virgin and Child with Saint Anne*. She is the astounding but still tentative work of a young artist, displaying a few technical immaturities, as Leonardo struggled to learn how to mix and apply oil paints and to perfect the proportion and perspective of the human face. Even so, Ginevra is haunting. In her portrait are glimmers of all that comes later in his masterworks. Some art historians even speculate that this small, intense poet-teenager sparked Leonardo's ability to recognize, respect, and then convey female promise. His commitment to portraying women as strong, thinking, capable beings was a stunning novelty and daring innovation in fifteenth-century Italy.

Da Vinci's Tiger is fiction, my interpretation and drama-tization of Ginevra de' Benci's life, rooted in fact, carefully researched. This is what historians know of her:

She was the granddaughter and daughter of affluent bankers with close personal and financial ties to the Medici. She was educated at Le Murate convent, which her father and grandfather generously supported, and which was run

by Abbess Scolastica Rondinelli. Possessing a worldly intellect and business acumen, Scolastica improved conditions at
the convent and played the politics of the city well. Her lay-
students not only "learned the virtues" but also how to read
Latin. Ginevra did come and go from the convent throughout her life. The black scarf she wears in her portrait looks to
be a scapular, a devotional ornament like a priest's vestment,
which would mark her as a *conversa*, a laysister of the order.

At sixteen, Ginevra was married to Luigi Niccolini, a
wool merchant twice her age and of lesser lineage, finances,
and social standing. Her dowry was a rather staggering 1,400
florins. Because her father had died, her uncle Bartolomeo
probably negotiated her betrothal. Given their ages, it's plausible he and Luigi were friends. At the time of the nuptials,
Luigi had not held significant office. But he was chosen to be
Florence's highest magistrate, the *gonfaloniere*, one month after
the Pazzi assassination, when Lorenzo de' Medici needed to
consolidate support following the murder of his brother.

When Venetian ambassador Bernardo Bembo came to
Florence in time for the joust of 1475, he was smitten. Taking
Ginevra as his Platonic love, he commissioned poems about
her, including those by Cristoforo Landino quoted in this
novel. By all accounts, Bembo was charismatic, handsome,
well-read, and extravagant, but perhaps of dubious ethics.
Clearly he was a nimble politician, serving the watery king-
dom of Venice in many posts and in many capacities despite
several controversies he stirred up.

It makes sense that Bembo would choose Ginevra.

Contemporaries praised her beauty, her virtue, the delicacy of her hands, her embroidery, plus her keen intellect and clever conversation. And her poems. Tragically, only one line of her poetry—about the mountain tiger—remains. But that was certainly enough to make me want to write about her! We know of the line because it is referenced in a letter from a court musician in Rome. He asks for a full copy of Ginevra's verse to prove to Roman society the wit and sophistication of Florentine ladies. (The Petrarch-styled sonnet Ginevra is too shy to read at the Medici banquet was imagined and written for this novel by researcher and theater artist Megan Behm.)

Exactly who commissioned Ginevra's portrait has been debated for decades. Because she is not bejeweled in the typical way of betrothal and wedding portraits of the time, it's unlikely that it was commissioned for either of those nuptial events. Most art historians now agree that Bernardo Bembo is its most logical patron, and, given Leonardo's career timeline, that the Venetian commissioned the portrait during his first ambassadorship to Florence (1475–1476). No one knows for sure when Ginevra's likeness was completed.

Her portrait was a turning point in Italian Renaissance painting, representing many firsts. In addition to being Leonardo's first portrait and probably his first solo commission, *Ginevra de' Benci* is the first Italian portrait to turn a woman from profile to a three-quarter, forward-facing pose, looking toward her viewer. It is the first "psychological" portrait designed to reveal the sitter's "motions of the mind," as Leonardo termed it; the first portrait to integrate the sitter into an uninterrupted natural landscape; and one of the first Florentine paintings to be done in oils rather than tempera, the egg-based paint favored by Italian artists.

The juniper, or *ginepro*, bush behind her was initially a vibrant, almost emerald green, providing a stunning color contrast and framing of Ginevra. But Leonardo was a novice in mixing colors with oil, and the evergreen bush has since faded to an olive-brown, clouding much of its original meticulous detail. Also, infrared study of the portrait revealed that Leonardo changed the verso's motto to *Virtutem Forma Decorat*, "She adorns her virtue with beauty," or "Beauty adorns virtue." The original *Virtus et Honor* that lies beneath lends credence to the belief the portrait was commissioned by Bembo, since he used the motto himself. But it appears Bembo did not take Ginevra's portrait with him when he returned to Venice. In fact, the location of her painted likeness was lost for centuries.

As to the other real-life people and characters in my interpretation of Ginevra's life? Her brother Giovanni and Leonardo da Vinci were obviously friends. The artist left several of his possessions with Giovanni when he departed for Milan, including his unfinished *Adoration of the Magi*. Giovanni was derided as "the Six Hundred" for the exorbitant price of his Barbary horse. (Footnotes are the best! They revealed "the Six Hundred" and the facts of Uncle Bartolomeo's *armeggeria* and flaming-heart float.)

Simonetta Vespucci was the Platonic idol of Giuliano

de' Medici—both of them much beloved by Florence. Art historians believe her face was Botticelli's model for Venus in his famous *Birth of Venus* and Flora in his *Primavera*. He did indeed paint a banner of her as Pallas for the joust where she was Queen of Beauty. The artist was so enamored of La Bella Simonetta that he begged to be buried at her feet thirty-five years after her untimely death from what was probably tuberculosis. Historians also speculate Simonetta was the inspiration for Leonardo's *Madonna of the Carnation*, mainly because of the Medici symbols included in the painting and the similarity of the Virgin Mary's face and hair to the idealized females Verrocchio painted. I do not know for certain that she and Ginevra were friends, but a footnote in material about Le Murate indicates that Ginevra's aunt was Simonetta's mother-in-law, so surely they knew each other. They certainly shared a kinship born of being lauded throughout Florence as Platonic muses. By all accounts, Simonetta was well-read like Ginevra, kind, and a particularly graceful dancer.

The basic details about the Medici are factual: Lorenzo's Platonic love, Lucrezia Donati; the joust's spectacular pomp; the urban legend of Lorenzo climbing convent walls; his horsemanship; the *palio*; his penning bawdy Carnival songs as well as the loftiest of sonnets; his circle of friends and their philosophies and sometimes controversial opinions regarding the church; the politics of Florence; the sumptuous pageantry of feast days and the Pazzi conspiracy's violence.

Fabric and clothing were critically important to Florentines, sometimes totaling 75 percent of their wealth.

Sancha is the only major character to be completely fictitious. But she is reflective of the era.

I have no direct information about the relationship between Leonardo da Vinci and Ginevra other than her portrait itself. Clearly there was enormous respect and insight into her soul in its making, just as Simonetta and Verrocchio describe the almost sacred romance between an artist and his subject, a poet and her muse.

After Bembo returned to Venice, Ginevra did live primarily at Le Murate. Some historians have seen that as sad. I like to believe it was a conscious, wise, and satisfying choice of self-definition on her part, in keeping with a number of other educated noblewomen and writers of Ginevra's time who dared to protest the restrictions on women. Several of them remained cloistered so they could pursue their intellectual curiosity and dreams.

Fifteenth-century Florence, under Cosimo and his grandson Lorenzo de' Medici, is unparalleled in its pageantry, passion, and percolating new ideas. It's hard to imagine one city producing so many artists within a few decades—Brunelleschi, Donatello, Luca della Robbia, Ghiberti, Botticelli, the Pollaiuolo brothers, Perugino, and Michelangelo, to name the most important. And of course, Andrea del Verrocchio and his apprentice, Leonardo da Vinci. Many of these artists were nurtured and employed by the Medici. A few even lived for a time at the Medici palazzo. With such fervent patronage from its political leaders, Florence became an artistic mecca that set in motion the Renaissance, liberating the hearts and creativity of an entire continent.

Over the years, Verrocchio's talents and accomplishments have been overshadowed by his most gifted student. But in the 1470s, Verrocchio was one of the most acclaimed and sought-after artists in the city, remarkable in his output and diversity, a goldsmith, engineer, sculptor, and painter. His influence on Leonardo was vast. Many scholars now speculate that several innovations once credited solely to Leonardo, such as the subtle blending of light and shade called sfumato, might actually have been Verrocchio's idea first, or a joint discovery between them. Verrocchio's sketch of a horse that included precise measurements of the steed's limbs in relation to one another may slightly predate Leonardo's famous *Vitruvian Man*—acclaimed for the figure's perfect proportions. Clearly Leonardo emulated the charming and lovingly animated female faces Verrocchio drew.

The men must have been close friends. The younger artist stayed with his master long beyond his apprenticeship. One leap of imagination I take is the competition between Verrocchio and Leonardo regarding Ginevra, but this invention is inspired by fact. Verrocchio did create a sculpture, *Lady with Primroses*, about the time Leonardo painted Ginevra's portrait. Just as Leonardo's portrait was groundbreaking, so too was this sculpture. It was the first Italian portrait sculpture to extend below the shoulders and to convey movement, the figure appearing to have just gathered up flowers in the way Verrocchio carved and turned her shoulders. The good-natured teasing between the two men in Chapter Fifteen is culled from Leonardo's notes about the superiority of painting over sculpture and poetry.

The face, dress, and hairstyles of the two art pieces are strikingly similar, and the figure in the statue cradles blossoms that may have been referenced in one of the poems written about Ginevra. Primroses were also part of Bembo's family crest. Strengthening the hypothesis that Ginevra was the model for both works is the fact that Leonardo's painted Ginevra appears to have originally held blossoms in a pose similar to Verrocchio's statue. At some point, the bottom third of Ginevra's portrait was cut off, probably because of damage. A study of hands with a sprig of flowers sketched by Leonardo is the basis for the assumption that the missing portion of the painting showed Ginevra holding a blossom.

Much of Leonardo's dialogue comes from his own writings, and my depiction of his appearance and personality are taken from contemporary descriptions of him. In April 1476, Leonardo was indeed arrested, accused by a letter dropped into a *tamburi*—the box Florentines used to charge neighbors of breaking the city's prejudicial "morality" laws. The term *homosexual* was not yet coined, so I use the words of Leonardo's Florence—*sodomy* and *Florenzer*.

The city was known for its celebration of Plato's ideals, including the Greek teacher's lauding of love between men. Neoplatonic philosopher Marsilio Ficino interpreted that affection and mentoring to be chaste, like Platonic love. The legal issue for Florence during Leonardo's time arose when men were believed to have physically acted on that love. Any intimacy that was not procreative—designed by nature to result in babies—was deemed taboo in the fifteenth century. Leonardo's arrest seemed to deeply affect him. He left Verrocchio's studio and home. His exact whereabouts in Florence after that remain cloudy. He became zealously protective of his ideas. Historians also speculate that the arrest may have dampened Lorenzo de' Medici's interest in Leonardo. The Magnifico did not lavish the same kind of patronage on Leonardo that he did on other artists. In 1482, Leonardo sought a new home and fresh start, moving to Milan, initially as court musician and engineer.

You will find images of all artwork mentioned in this novel in a visual companion on my webpage, www.lmelliott.com. If you travel to Florence, you can walk streets little changed since Ginevra's time and find her childhood palazzo. It still stands as a private home on what is now named via dei Benci, between the Ponte alle Grazie bridge and Santa Croce. Be sure to visit the Bargello museum to enjoy Verrocchio's *Lady with Primroses* statue. See if you agree that it is Ginevra.

Also in the Bargello stands Verrocchio's *David*, a beautiful, youthful depiction of the biblical hero. It is said a teenaged Leonardo was the model for the bronze statue. Its graceful figure and sweet-smiling face will give you an idea of the adult man Ginevra would have known.

Fewer than twenty paintings exist that Leonardo created either alone or with another artist like Verrocchio. We almost lost *Ginevra de' Benci*. She resurfaced in the possession of the royal family of Liechtenstein about three hundred years after Leonardo painted her. During World War II, the aristocrats protected her from Hitler's treasure hunters by hiding the portrait in a wine cellar in the family castle. In 1967, after much secret negotiation, the National Gallery of Art purchased Ginevra's portrait for five million dollars, the largest sum ever paid for a work of art at that time.

I hope you view Ginevra in person. Look into her eyes and interpret for yourself the "motions" Leonardo saw in that eloquent mind of hers. Some think her melancholy, imposing even. I found an exquisite self-possession, strength of character, and inquisitive nature implied in that composure and steady gaze, in the skeletal details of her life, and in that one incredibly bold line of verse. But see what you find and imagine about her—that's precisely what Leonardo wanted and Ginevra graciously and bravely granted us.

ACKNOWLEDGMENTS

THIS NOVEL WOULD NOT EXIST WITHOUT THE PATIENCE, faith, and adroit editing, both sweeping and fine-tuned, of my amazing editor, Katherine Tegen.

It also would not have the humanity or the thematic and historical depth I hope it does without the influence and help of my adult daughter and son, Megan and Peter, themselves now accomplished creative artists. Both traveled to Florence to research. Both read the manuscript multiple times at various stages, lending me their own imagination, artistic eye, and interpretive talents. Their insights bolstered characters, cut fat, pushed dramatic moments to their fullest import, and honed the issues raised by Ginevra's life and

Leonardo's portrait of her. They prodded me to be brave, to add bittersweet humor. Peter saved me from a tepid, unsatisfactory ending. Megan's ability to research and make sense of information, minute or large, added dimension and pith to Ginevra's personality. Her edits and comments kept the manuscript and its themes on track and a story about female choice and agency as well as art and love.

Zach Mott translated Landino's poems from Latin to English for me. I also must thank Professor Monique O'Connell of Wake Forest University for helping me refine my characterization of Venetian ambassador Bernardo Bembo and WFU Professor Bernadine Barnes for helping me interpret conflicting scholarship around *Ginevra de' Benci* and to highlight Verrocchio's talents. My love of Renaissance thinking began many decades ago as an undergraduate student at Wake Forest. It was a special pleasure to "return home" for encouragement and mentoring of what I believe to be a beautifully complex and inspiring life that demanded exploration.

BIBLIOGRAPHY

I USED ADDITIONAL RESOURCES TO GUIDE ME IN WRITING *Da Vinci's Tiger*, but these proved the most comprehensive and helpful, and are excellent sources for your own exploration of fifteenth-century Florence, Leonardo, his peers, Ginevra, and other women of the Renaissance.

LEONARDO, VERROCCHIO, AND GINEVRA:

Atalay, Bulent, and Wamsley, Keith, *Leonardo's Universe: The Renaissance World of Leonardo da Vinci,* National Geographic Books.

Bambach, Carmen C., editor, *Leonardo da Vinci, Master Draftsman*, The Metropolitan Museum of Art and Yale University Press.

Brown, David Alan, *Leonardo da Vinci: Origins of a Genius*, Yale University Press.

————, editor, *Virtue and Beauty: Leonardo's Ginevra de' Benci and Renaissance Portraits of Women*, National Gallery of Art and Princeton University Press.

Butterfield, Andrew, *The Sculptures of Andrea del Verrocchio*, Yale University Press.

Christiansen, Keith, and Weppelmann, Stefan, editors, *The Renaissance Portrait: From Donatello to Bellini*, The Metropolitan Museum of Art and Yale University Press.

Clark, Kenneth, *Leonardo Da Vinci, Revised Edition*, Penguin Books.

Kemp, Martin, *Leonardo da Vinci: The Marvellous Works of Nature and Man*, Oxford University Press.

————, editor, *Leonardo on Painting*, Yale University Press.

Klein, Stefan, *Leonardo's Legacy: How Da Vinci Reimagined the World*, Di Capo Press.

Nicholl, Charles, *Leonardo da Vinci: Flights of the Mind*, Viking Penguin.

Richter, Irma A., compiler, *Leonardo da Vinci: Notebooks*, Oxford World's Classics.

Vasari, Giorgio, *The Lives of the Artists*, Oxford World's Classics.

ARTICLES ON GINEVRA:

Bull, David, "Two Portraits by Leonardo: Ginevra de' Benci and the Lady with an Ermine," *Artibus et Historiae*, Vol. 13, No. 25.

Fletcher, Jennifer, "Bernardo Bembo and Leonardo's Portrait of Ginevra de' Benci," *The Burlington Magazine*, Vol. 131, No. 1041.

Garrard, Mary D., "Who was Ginevra de' Benci? Leonardo's Portrait and Its Sitter Recontextualized," *Artibus et Historiae*, Vol. 27, No. 53.

————, "Leonardo da Vinci: Female Portraits, Female Nature," adapted from *Brunelleschi's Egg: Nature, Art, and Gender in Renaissance Italy*.

Walker, John, "Ginevra de' Benci by Leonardo da Vinci," *Report and Studies in the History of Art, National Gallery of Art*, Vol. 1.

THE MEDICI:

Hibbert, Christopher, *The House of Medici: Its Rise and Fall*, William Morrow.

Martines, Lauro, *April Blood: Florence and the Plot Against the Medici*, Oxford University Press.

Unger, Miles J., *Magnifico: The Brilliant Life and Violent Times of Lorenzo de' Medici*, Simon & Schuster.

THE RENAISSANCE:

Aston, Margaret, editor, *The Renaissance Complete*, Thames & Hudson.

Brucker, Gene, *Florence: The Golden Age, 1138–1737*, University of California Press.

Cahill, Thomas, *Heretics and Heroes: How Renaissance Artists and Reformation Priests Created Our World*, Nan A. Talese, Doubleday.

FitzRoy, Charles, *Renaissance Florence on Five Florins a Day*, Thames & Hudson.

Frick, Carole Collier, *Dressing Renaissance Florence: Families, Fortunes and Fine Clothing*, Johns Hopkins University Press.

King, Ross, *Brunelleschi's Dome: How a Renaissance Genius Reinvented Architecture*, Penguin Books.

Randolph, Adrian W. B., *Engaging Symbols: Gender, Politics, and Public Art in Fifteenth-Century Florence*, Yale University Press.

Trexler, Richard C., *Public Life in Renaissance Florence*, Cornell University Press.

LE MURATE:

Ciapelli, Giovanni, and Rubin, Patricia Lee, editors, *Art, Memory, and Family in Renaissance Florence*, Cambridge University Press.

Strocchia, Sharon T., *Nuns and Nunneries in Renaissance Florence*, Johns Hopkins University Press.

Weddle, Saundra, editor, *The Chronicle of Le Murate*, by
    Sister Giustina Niccolini, Centre for Reformation and
    Renaissance Studies.

POEMS:

Chatfield, Mary P., translator, *Cristoforo Landino Poems*,
    Harvard University Press.
Thiem, Jon, editor, *Lorenzo de' Medici: Selected Poems and
    Prose*, Penn State University Press.

VIDEOS:

*Ginevra's Story: Solving the Mysteries of Leonardo da Vinci's
    First Known Portrait*, National Gallery of Art.
Medici: Godfathers of the Renaissance, PBS.

Turn the page for a sneak peek
at L. M. ELLIOTT's next novel,
Hamilton and Peggy!

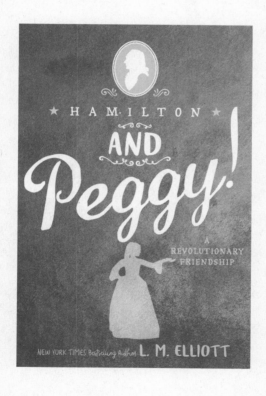

Though I have not had the happiness of a personal acquaintance with you, I have had the good fortune to see several very pretty pictures of your person and mind which have inspired me with a more than common partiality for both. Among others your sister carries a beautiful copy constantly about her, elegantly drawn by herself, of which she has two or three times favoured me with a sight . . .

You will no doubt admit it as a full proof of my frankness and good opinion of you, that I with so little ceremony introduce myself to your acquaintance and at the first step make you my confident.

*P*eggy Schuyler kicked out from under her heavy blankets, too preoccupied with a letter she had received to sleep. It came from an aide-de-camp to General Washington who proclaimed to be besotted with her sister Eliza—some silver-tongued man named Alexander Hamilton.

She shoved back the green toile bed curtains, gasping as frigid air pierced her linen chemise. "Good God! Can it possibly be this cold? Again?"

Teeth chattering, Peggy stirred the embers in the fireplace and dropped a split log from the basket onto them with as little noise as possible. It was still dark. She didn't want to disturb Moll, the enslaved woman who tended her fireplace and slept just above her bedroom in the attic.

Peggy definitely didn't want to wake her three younger brothers, slumbering next door. Endearing boys, but what a raucous rabble—especially the seven-year-old, Rensselaer, who had just gone through breeching and was racing around the house crowing about the fact he had finally graduated to wearing pants instead of dresses. For sure, he'd rouse little Cornelia, still in a trundle bed in her parents' room. And Peggy wanted to analyze Alexander Hamilton's words more closely, privately, without her mother insisting she read them aloud to the family.

The splintery wood sparked, sputtered, and caught flame as Peggy hurriedly bundled herself in shawls and slipped her feet into soft buckskin moccasins that the Oneida tribe once gave her father, General Philip Schuyler. They were artfully decorated with porcupine quills and blue-jay feathers.

Peggy never let her mother see that she had pilfered the colorful slippers from her father's closet. They were definitely not lady shoes. But her feet ached with a strange malady sometimes, especially on shivering days like this, and the moccasins were soft and forgiving. They also reminded Peggy of the vast New York wilderness just a few dozen miles north of their Albany mansion, and the elusive Iroquois who remained loyal to her father and the Patriot cause. Silently gliding through forests of towering oaks and chestnuts, they gathered information on Loyalist Tory rangers who could strike the city at any moment.

Quaking, Peggy toasted herself by the fire. "It's cold enough for Hell to freeze over," she muttered. "All right, Lord, maybe this is proverb. Are you sending us a sign that our improbable revolution may actually succeed? Please? If we just screw our courage to the sticking place?"

Peggy preferred quips to prayer, intelligent bargaining to pleading. Wit was her bayonet, her way of leading a charge. She detested the woman's role of patiently sitting, smiling like a painted fashion doll while men battled and argued philosophy that could end tyranny. But she knew talking out loud in this manner was ridiculous. Her imaginary conversations were a recent habit, born of being deserted by her two older sisters, with whom Peggy had shared her bed and her every thought for all twenty-one years of her life.

Born in less than three years from oldest to youngest, the Schuyler sisters had been a giggly triplet-like brood, tight-knit and entwined. As a trio, they complemented and balanced one another, each recognizing and coaxing out the best in the other two. Like pieces of those new jigsaw puzzles, only put together did the Schuyler sisters present a complete portrait, with the most beautiful and vibrant image of each clearer.

But Angelica had married, seduced by an ever-so-charming card gambler. And now Eliza, logically next in line to marry, was gone to Washington's winter headquarters at Morristown to visit their aunt and her husband, who was surgeon general to the Continental Army.

And Peggy? Here she remained in Albany, alone, feeling bereft not only of her big sisters' company but somehow of definition and purpose without her arms linked in theirs. She loved her little brothers and sister. But Peggy couldn't share her heart with them. They couldn't finish her sentences with her own thoughts the way Eliza and Angelica could.

Who was she without her big sisters? She had always been "and Peggy," introduced third whenever the Schuylers greeted guests to their family houses. Witty, elegant Angelica; kind, affable Eliza; *and* Peggy. Within the circle of family and friends she was always described according to her older sisters' attributes: "She's saucy like Angelica. She's artistic like Eliza."

As she stared at the flames, Peggy's hurt at being left behind turned to annoyance. It would be nice occasionally to be described purely as herself. In truth, with her sisters, Peggy was often reduced to confidante and accomplice. Rarely was she the center of anything. She was beginning to feel like Cinderella, always helping her sisters dress for balls she wasn't attending, relegated to chores. Peggy was forever helping their mama and watching after the increasing brood of younger siblings.

And here was this letter, from another male intruder into the Schuyler sisterhood who seemed to think Peggy would happily become handmaiden to a romance that would take away her middle sister, too. This poet-penned aide-de-camp, this Alexander Hamilton, who wrote to introduce himself and to make Peggy his ally in his courtship of Eliza. And the bait to lure her in was complimenting her person and mind as Eliza had depicted it in a pretty miniature painting? As if Peggy was so easily manipulated by flattery.

But the thought that had kept her tossing and turning? Eliza was obviously falling for this man. Normally her gentle sister would be far too modest to show her artwork to anyone. This was dangerous. Peggy must remain a watchful sentry to Eliza's enormous heart. She had learned the pitfalls of not being on guard for a sister the hard way with Angelica.

After lighting a candle, Peggy pulled Hamilton's letter out from its hiding spot behind the cushion of a wingback armchair next to the hearth. She tucked her feet up under her, huddled in her shawls, and began to read.

I venture to tell you in confidence, that by some odd contrivance or other, your sister has found out the secret of interesting me in every thing that concerns her.

Hmpf. As if the sweet Eliza was some calculating enchantress, fumed Peggy. She squinted at the parchment.

The handwriting was neat and elegant. One would never know Hamilton had written his appeal in the middle of a war. Or in a camp laid waste by four feet of snow that refused to melt—where stubborn, stoic Patriots slept crammed together in tiny log huts, lying side by side with their feet to a fire, to share body warmth and make it through the night without frostbite.

> *I have already confessed the influence your sister has gained over me; yet notwithstanding this, I have some things of a very serious and heinous nature to lay to her charge.*

Peggy fairly growled at that line. What could Eliza possibly be guilty of?

> *She is most unmercifully handsome and so perverse that she has none of those affectations which are the prerogatives of beauty. Her good sense is destitute of . . . vanity and ostentation. . . . She has good nature affability and vivacity unembellished with that charming frivolousness which is justly deemed one of the principal accomplishments of a* belle.

Hmpf again. Well, all right, he had that correct. Eliza was all earnestness. She did not play games. She did not pull on heartstrings for amusement. No, that was Angelica. The famed "thief of hearts," as one officer had called her.

Peggy dropped Hamilton's letter. Her room filled with the memory of her sisters' mingled chimes of laughter. Their reading poetry aloud to one another's sighs of romantic appreciation. Their harmless gossiping about the dashing soldiers surrounding their father, when he commanded the Northern Army.

That had all changed the summer of 1777. When New York was burning and Americans were dying in apocalyptic numbers. When Angelica made her own defiant claim for liberty and breathlessly whispered, "I have a secret. Tonight, my dearest sisters, I elope with John Carter! You must help me escape."